BECAUSE OF YOU

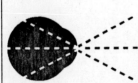

BECAUSE OF YOU

ROCHELLE ALERS

THORNDIKE PRESS

A part of Gale, Cengage Learning

GALE
CENGAGE Learning

Detroit • New York • San Francisco • New Haven, Conn • Waterville, Maine • London

GALE
CENGAGE Learning

Copyright © 2010 by Rochelle Alers.
The Wainwright Legacy Series #1
Thorndike Press, a part of Gale, Cengage Learning.

Thorndike Press® Large Print African-American.
The text of this Large Print edition is unabridged.
Other aspects of the book may vary from the original edition.
Set in 16 pt. Plantin.

LIBRARY OF CONGRESS CATALOGING-IN-PUBLICATION DATA

Alers, Rochelle.
    Because of you / by Rochelle Alers.
        p. cm. — (The Wainwright legacy series ; #1) (Thorndike Press large print African-American)
    ISBN-13: 978-1-4104-3591-0 (hardcover)
    ISBN-10: 1-4104-3591-1 (hardcover)
    1. African American lawyers—Fiction. 2. Man-woman relationships—Fiction. 3. Large type books. I. Title.
PS3551.L3477B43 2011
813'.54—dc22   2010051216

Published in 2011 by arrangement with Harlequin Books S.A.

Printed in Mexico
1 2 3 4 5 6 7 15 14 13 12 11

Dear Reader,

When readers are asked why they read romance, the reason I hear most often is the family-themed miniseries. I've created a few over the years: the Coles, the Blackstones, the Whitfields and the Eatons. But now there is a new family waiting to take center stage — the Wainwrights.

Romance readers first met Jordan Wainwright in *Man of Fate* from The Best Men series, and got another glimpse of him in the online read *Man of Fame.*

When I introduced Jordan Wainwright in *Man of Fate,* I wanted to know why a man born of privilege would walk away from his family's real estate empire and a prize position with a prestigious New York City law firm to champion the *little guy* in a community undergoing gentrification. These questions are answered in *Because of You,* when family secrets surface and rivals must face the truth before it destroys everything they have worked for.

In *Because of You* we see a very different Jordan, who works hard, plays hard and loves even harder. He is a man who is used to getting what he wants, and when he meets Aziza Fleming, he knows he must have her. Set against the backdrop of the fast-paced, glamorous and edgy chic of Manhattan, the sizzling passion between Jordan and Aziza promises forever.

Look for the Wainwright Legacy to continue with Super Bowl champion quarterback Brandt Wainwright in *Here I Am,* in early 2011.

Yours in romance,
Rochelle Alers

So she caught him, and kissed him, and with an impudent face said to him, I have peace offerings with me; this day have I paid my vows. Therefore I came forth to meet thee, diligently to seek thy face, and I have found thee.

— Proverbs 7:13–15

PROLOGUE

"Mr. Humphries?"

Raymond Humphries opened his eyes but didn't bother to turn around when he heard his personal secretary's voice. A hint of a smile tilted the corners of his mouth. Minerva Jackson, or Min, as he affectionately referred to her whenever they weren't in the presence of others, was the love of his life *and* the keeper of all his business and a few personal secrets.

"What is it, Minerva?"

"Mr. Ennis is here to see you."

Raymond swiveled in the leather executive chair. The same supple leather also covered the love seat, sofa and chairs next to the mahogany table in an alcove he used for small, intimate meetings. A larger conference room was set up on the first floor of the town house that housed the offices of RLH Realty, Ltd. The three-story structure was one of nearly a hundred buildings RLH owned and managed throughout Harlem. A reporter had dubbed him the "Emperor of Harlem Real Estate," a sobriquet Raymond modestly accepted.

His large, penetrating dark eyes met a light brown pair that changed color with her mercurial moods. And lately Min's moods had veered from syrupy sweet to unbridled rage. Maybe, Raymond thought, it was time he let her go — with a generous severance package of course. He would continue to spend time with her, but only away from the office.

"Send him in. And hold my calls."

Minerva's full lips parted when she stared at her boss. Raymond Humphries was only her boss at the office. In the bedroom she was boss. He was rapidly approaching his seventy-fifth birthday, yet he looked twenty years younger. His wasn't tall, only an inch above her five-eight height, but his slim physique and ramrod-straight posture gave him the appearance of being much taller. His personal barber cut his graying hair to camouflage the thinning strands on the crown, and Raymond had a standing weekly appointment for a full body massage and a monthly European facial; the features he'd inherited from his beautiful mother made him almost too pretty for a man. His skin, the color of polished rosewood, was clear and virtually wrinkle-free. The exception were the lines around his eyes when he smiled.

He was the only man she'd known who, once he had begun a regimen, he didn't vary from it. The year he'd celebrated his sixtieth birthday, he'd begun tennis lessons. Raymond had quickly become addicted to the game, installing an indoor court on the lower level of the brownstone. Minerva cursed the times when he left her bed before dawn to go into the office to practice with his coach.

"But Mrs. Humphries said she will call you back at ten."

"Tell her I'll call her back." That said, Raymond swiveled again, rudely and unceremoniously dismissing his secretary.

"If you say so," Minerva drawled sarcastically.

"Get out, Minerva!"

The fastidiously dressed middle-aged woman with a flawless café au lait complexion and stylishly coiffed, chemically straightened hair turned on her heels and stomped out of the office of the man who in the past month had changed in front of her eyes like a snake shedding its skin. Even after a snake shed his skin for a new one he'd still retain the behavior of a reptile. However, it wasn't the same with Raymond Humphries. He may have looked the same, but Raymond had changed. Most of the time he was curt to the point of rudeness, short-tempered and exceedingly condescending. Perhaps, she mused, it was time to move on — to get another job.

Affecting a professional smile, she walked into the reception area. "Mr. Ennis, please follow me." She escorted the man into her boss's office. The first time she'd met the man, she'd stood several feet away from him, fearing he would smell. Yet upon closer inspection she had discovered he was clean — it was just his scraggily beard, matted hair and rumpled clothes that reminded her of the homeless man who sat on a wooden box outside a corner store near her subway station.

Donald Ennis pulled back his shoulders in an attempt to appear taller than his five-six stature. "Thank you," he mumbled, giving the uptight, prissy woman a sidelong glance.

He knew she didn't like him, and the feeling was mutual. Each time he came to see Raymond Humphries she turned her nose up at him as if he were offal. What Minerva Jackson didn't know was his unkempt appearance was a foil, a carefully scripted persona for his profession. She didn't sign his checks, so he couldn't care less what she thought of him.

Raymond was up on his feet, hand extended, when Donald walked into his office, closing the door softly behind him. "Good morning, Ennis." He shook his hand, then indicated a chair at the conference table. "Please sit down."

Donald sat while Raymond stood close by, no doubt watching for his reaction when he stared at the half-dozen black-and-white photographs, some shot with a long-range lens. "What do you want?"

"Do you know who he is?" Raymond asked, answering the question with a question.

"Who doesn't?" It was another question. It was a game the two men played, matching wits. "Only someone dead or living under the proverbial rock wouldn't recognize Harlem's hottest slick-talking shyster lawyer."

Raymond sat, tapping one of the photographers with his finger. "Slick-talking — yes. Shyster — hell, no. This young boy knows his stuff."

Donald flashed a rare smile. "He's smart *and* ballsy. He proved that when he called

13

out his grandpappy for being a slumlord all the while television cameras were rolling."

Raymond nodded. "It was a risky move, but fortunately for him it worked. Next month my son-in-law will announce he's challenging Billy Edwards for his state assembly seat and I don't want anything to jeopardize that."

Robert Andrews, married to Raymond's daughter Diane, was CFO of RLH Realty.

"What does his election bid have to do with Jordan Wainwright?" Donald asked.

"There's more to Wainwright becoming partner in a Harlem law firm than his reputation for helping the so-called little guy. I believe he staged that televised press conference to embarrass his grandfather, because Wyatt Wainwright is using his grandson as a pawn." Raymond held up his hand. "And before you ask me for what, I'll tell you. It isn't enough that Wainwright Developers Group owns most of the prime real estate on the Upper East and West Side, SoHo, Chelsea and Tribeca. Now they've set their sights on Harlem. I don't know how they did it, but they've managed to buy the buildings on one-fourteen right from under our noses. I don't want Robert embroiled in a real estate war where the fallout could be his losing the election."

"So, you think the grandson is slumming in Harlem to identify potential parcels for his grandfather?"

"I know he is," Raymond confirmed. "I want you to use all your resources to keep tabs on Jordan Wainwright 24/7. I want you to report back to me where he goes and who he meets until after the election."

Donald nodded. "Does he live in Harlem?"

"No. He has a duplex on Fifth Avenue, facing Central Park."

A beat passed. "That means paying off the doormen. And that's —"

"Don't worry about the money," Raymond interrupted, visibly annoyed with the private investigator. "Just do what I pay you to do. If Robert is able to run a campaign free of scandal and goes on to win the election, then maybe you'll get that apartment in the building you so badly want as a bonus."

Donald schooled his expression to not reveal the rush of excitement that made him want to jump for joy. He'd made it known to Raymond that he was saving money in order to purchase an apartment in one of his renovated buildings overlooking the East River. The real estate mogul paid him well whenever he had him investigate something or someone, but the jobs had not come as frequently as they had in the past. He would give Raymond Humphries what he wanted, and then in turn Donald Ennis would give his oversexed, young girlfriend what she wanted: an apartment in Manhattan with a view of the river.

Raymond stood up, Donald rising with him. "Ms. Jackson will give you the envelope with all the data you'll need on Jordan Wainwright. Next year this time I intend to throw a blowout of a victory celebration for my daughter's husband. Please don't disappoint me, Ennis. Leave the photos," he said when Ennis gathered them off the table. "There's an extra set in the envelope." The P.I. knew whenever he picked up an envelope it was sealed with his illegible signature scrawled over the flap — a signature impossible to forge.

He was still standing, staring at the space where the P.I. had been, when Minerva entered his office closing the door and the distance between them. A sensual moue parted her lips. "What are you up to, Slick?"

Raymond froze. It'd been a long time since anyone had called him by his childhood nickname. All the kids from the neighborhood had called him Slick until he married Loretta Clarke. Then, he'd become

Mr. Humphries.

Running a finger under Min's jawbone, he gazed into her beautiful eyes. They were now a dark green. "Go home, put on something real sexy and we'll have lunch in bed."

"Are you trying to distract me, Ray?"

He frowned. "What are you talking about?"

"What's the connection between you, that nasty-looking little man and Jordan Wainwright?"

Raymond lowered his hand. "Some time when you cross the line I usually let it go. This time I'm not. Don't ever mention Jordan Wainwright's name to me again."

"Or you'll what?" Minerva crooned, her mouth inches from her boss's.

"I'll step on you like a bug."

It took a full minute before she realized the man she'd loved without question was serious. She took a backward step, swallowed the acerbic words burning her tongue and turned on her heels. "I think I'm going to work through lunch and then go home — *alone*."

"I really don't care, *Miss Jackson*," he flung at her retreating back. "You can stay, or go home for good. Frankly, I don't give a damn one way or the other. And if you slam the door you're fired!" The door closed with a barely perceptible click.

When he'd begun sleeping with Minerva Jackson, Raymond knew he had to be careful not to divulge too much during pillow talk. He'd never mentioned Jordan Wainwright to Min and had no intention of ever discussing him with her. There were some topics that were taboo, and Wyatt Wainwright's grandson was categorically off-limits when it came to his mistress.

Jordan Wainwright was his *and* his wife's business.

CHAPTER 1

Jordan Wainwright turned the collar to his ski jacket up around his neck and ears as sleet pelted his face and exposed head. He chided himself for not accepting the doorman's offer to hail a taxi to drive him sixteen blocks to where his parents lived in a Fifth Avenue beaux arts mansion overlooking Central Park.

It was Christmas Eve, and he'd promised his mother he would spend the upcoming week with her, while reconnecting with his sister and brothers. Since joining Chatham and Wainwright, PC, Attorneys at Law, he hadn't had time to do much socializing. The exception was business-related luncheons or dinner meetings with his partner, Kyle Chatham.

Jordan had hit the snooze button on his love life after a whirlwind summer romance ended. Natasha Parker had returned to culinary school *and* her estranged husband, whose existence the very talented aspiring chef had neglected to disclose. He'd made it a practice *not* to date married women *and* those who were on the rebound. And, whenever Jordan ended a romantic liaison, he was usually reluctant to start up a new one, unlike some men who jumped right back into the hunt.

He'd recently celebrated his thirty-third birthday. And although he hadn't ruled out any plans to settle down, he wasn't actively looking for someone with whom he could spend the rest of his life. This didn't mean he hadn't kept his options open for a casual relationship.

The cell phone attached to his waistband vibrated. Taking a hand from his jacket pocket, he plucked the phone off his belt, punched a button without looking at the display and announced his standard greeting. "This is Jordan."

"Where are you, darling?"

"I'm on my way, Mother."

"Don't tell me you're walking."

Jordan smiled. "Okay, I won't tell you that I'm walking."

"Why didn't you have your doorman hail a taxi?"

"Because I could be at your place by the time he flagged down an empty taxi. Remember, Mother, this is New York and whenever it rains or snows a yellow cab without an off-duty sign becomes as scarce as hen's teeth."

"If you hadn't wanted to take your car out of the garage, then you could've called me and I would've sent Henry to pick you up."

"Hang up, Mother, because I'm on your block."

"You must be chilled to the bone," Christiane Wainwright cooed.

"A little," he half lied. "Goodbye, Mother." Jordan ended the call, mounting the steps to the magnificent building, spanning half a city block, where he'd grown up and still maintained an apartment.

He'd placed his booted foot on the first step to the four-story gray-stone when the massive oak doors festooned with large pine wreaths and red velvet bows opened. "Thank you, Walter." The formally dressed butler who also doubled as his grandfather's valet had come to work for the Wainwrights the year Jordan was born. Walter Fagin was one of six full-time, live-in household staff that included a chef, driver, housekeepers and a laundress.

"It's quite nasty out there, Master Jordan."

Jordan slipped out of his jacket, handing

it to Walter. "If it gets any colder, then we're definitely going to have a white Christmas."

The lines around bright blue eyes deepened when the older man smiled. "It's been a while since New York City has had a white Christmas."

Sitting in an armchair in the expansive entrance hall, Jordan unlaced his boots, leaving them on a thick rush mat, because he didn't want to track dirt onto the priceless Persian and Aubusson rugs scattered about the gleaming marble floors. Lifelong habits weren't easy to forget.

The mansion was decorated for the season: live pine boughs lined the fireplace mantel, as a fire blazed behind a decorative screen. Lighted electric candles were in every window, and the gaily decorated eight-foot Norwegian spruce towered under the brightly lit chandelier that hung from a twenty-foot ceiling. Some of the more fragile glass ornaments on the tree were at least two hundred years old.

He always remembered the lengthy lecture from Christiane Wainwright about rugs and furnishings that had been passed down through generations of Johnstons who'd made their fortunes in shipbuilding, the fur trade and maritime insurance. With the advent of train and air travel, the family had shifted its focus to banking.

When Christiane Renata Johnston had married Edward Lincoln Wainwright at twenty, her net worth was estimated to be close to twelve million dollars. However, Edward was purported to be worth twice that amount when he came into his trust at twenty-five. With the Johnstons and the Wainwrights, it wasn't who had amassed the most money, but rather whether it was old or new money.

The Johnstons were old money, and the Wainwrights were new money — a fact that Wyatt, the Wainwright patriarch, was never allowed to forget whenever he was with his daughter-in-law's family.

"Master Jordan, Madame Wainwright has held off serving dinner until you arrive," the butler announced as Jordan stood up and walked toward the wing of the mansion where the apartments were located.

"Please tell my mother to begin serving without me. I want to get out of these wet clothes," Jordan said, not breaking stride.

He made his way across the expansive space his parents used as a reception hall whenever they hosted a gathering of less than fifty to an alcove where an elevator would take him to the private apartments.

His grandfather had claimed the entire

first floor, Jordan and his brothers Noah and Rhett had bedroom suites on the second floor, his father, mother and sister Chanel had the third floor, and the three suites on the top floor were set aside for houseguests.

It took Jordan less than ten minutes to change out of his slacks and into a pair of charcoal-gray flannel with a black cashmere mock turtleneck sweater and imported slip-ons. Although he'd told Walter to instruct Christiane to begin dinner without him, he knew she would wait for him to put in an appearance. Her mantra was never begin a meal unless everyone was seated at the table. The exception was whenever Edward called to inform her that he would be working late.

He took the staircase instead of the elevator, and, after walking through a narrow hallway to the opposite wing of the house, he entered the brightly lit dining room. It was the smaller of two dining rooms in the mansion. Christiane held family dinners in this room because she claimed it was less formal and more intimate. Who was his mother kidding? A table for sixteen wasn't what Jordan thought of as intimate. After all, there were six people who lived at the house: his parents, his grandfather, his two brothers and his sister.

Everyone was seated, awaiting his arrival: his mother, father, grandfather, sister, her friend Paige Anderson and his brothers Noah and Rhett. A pretty dark-haired woman with sparkling light brown eyes clung to Rhett as if she feared he would disappear. It was only the second time Jordan could recall Rhett bringing a woman to a family get-together.

Rounding the table, he leaned over, kissing his mother softly on her cheek. "Sorry I'm late."

Christiane reached up and patted his arm. "That's okay, darling." Her shimmering emerald-green eyes met her eldest son's. There was a hint of laughter in his hazel orbs. "Did you change out of your wet clothes?"

Jordan winked at her. "I changed upstairs."

He wanted to tell his mother that she had to stop treating him as if he were six years old, but knew it was futile. Christiane said "once a mother, always a mother," regardless of how old her children were. She was the mother of four and still without grandchildren — something that had become a bane of her existence. Many of the women in her social circle were grandmothers or had married children. Although three of her four children were in their twenties and thirties, none seemed remotely interested in exchanging vows.

"Grandpa," he said, acknowledging Wyatt Wainwright sitting at the head as the family's patriarch.

"We're so glad you decided to drag yourself away from Harlem to visit with your family," Wyatt drawled facetiously.

"Grandpa, why do you always have to start with Jordan?" Noah Wainwright asked.

"Watch your mouth, son." Edward Wainwright glared at his middle son, who was his spitting image in every way except temperament. Noah's mood swings kept everyone off balance *and* on guard because of his sharp tongue. "After all, we have guests present."

A pale eyebrow lifted a fraction when twenty-three-year-old Noah leaned back from the table. Shaggy ash-blond hair framed a deeply tanned face. He'd cut short his stay in the Caribbean to return to the States to share Christmas with his family. His blue eyes changed color depending on his mood. Noah was very angry because he'd been coerced into joining the family's real estate firm after Jordan had refused to take over the reins from their father.

"That has never stopped Grandpa from saying what he had to say."

Jordan gave Noah a look that he had no trouble interpreting. He wanted his brother to drop it. A barely discernible smile parted Noah's lips as he nodded. Shifting his gaze, he glared at the elderly man with a shock of thick white hair and sharp, piercing sky-blue orbs that hadn't faded despite having lived seven decades. The coal-black eyebrows of his youth remained. The less he said to Wyatt the better it was for grandfather and grandson. He nodded to the young woman sitting beside his youngest brother. Rhett would celebrate his twenty-first birthday in another month, and he was just beginning to assert himself.

Taking his seat, he leaned to his right and pressed a kiss to his sister's hair. "What's up, Charlie?"

Chanel Wainwright flushed a bright pink. Jordan had promised never to call her Charlie within earshot of their mother. "Don't call me *that* around Mother," she whispered with clenched teeth.

Jordan wanted to tell his sister that if their mother hadn't named her children after a character from *Gone with the Wind* and her favorite fragrance, she wouldn't have a problem explaining her name.

"Hi, Jordan," said a soft girlish voice.

He leaned forward, smiling at Paige. "Hello, Paige. Where are your parents?"

"It's all right, Jordan," Christiane said, as she signaled for the first course to be served. "Paige's folks went to Monte Carlo for the holiday and I told them Paige could stay with us rather than with a sitter."

Jordan resisted the urge to roll his eyes. He couldn't and would never understand why people had children only to hand them over to a nanny or sitter, while they continued to live their lives as if by their leave. Only parents without a conscience would leave their only child — a sixteen-year-old girl — with the family of her friend to fly across an ocean to gamble and party on the French Riviera.

When — no, if — he married and had a family, he would make certain to play an active role in the lives of his children. That was where Christiane differed from her peers; she hadn't left child-rearing to nannies, housekeepers or au pairs. Her face was the first one Jordan had seen when he woke up and the last one before he'd closed his eyes at night. Even Edward had become a more involved parent. Jordan didn't agree with everything his parents said or did, but there was never a question as to their unwavering support when it concerned their children.

The mood lightened considerably after several glasses of wine accompanied by asparagus soup, a radicchio, fennel and walnut salad, rib eye roast with a mustard and black peppercorn sauce, winter greens with pancetta and potatoes au gratin. Chanel and Paige asked to be excused before dessert was served. The chef had outdone himself when he'd prepared Apple Charlotte with whipped cream.

Jordan was amused when Rhett, who was not yet legal, refilled his wineglass. He knew his brother had begun drinking before he'd celebrated his twenty-first birthday, but usually not in front of their parents. He, on the other hand, had raided the liquor cabinet at fourteen and had drunk so much that he had been sick for more than a week. It was another ten years before he took another drink.

"Jordan, are you currently dating anyone?" Christiane asked, breaking into his thoughts.

Tracing the rim of the wineglass with a forefinger, he stared at the prisms of color on the glass reflected from the chandelier. "No, Mother."

"Didn't you tell me you were seeing a girl?" Edward said, accepting a cigar from the engraved silver case Wyatt had handed him. "Thanks, Dad."

"I was," Jordan said truthfully, "but it was nothing more than a summer fling."

Christiane sat up straighter. "Who was she, darling? Do I know her family?"

A pregnant pause ensued before he said, "Her name is Natasha Parker, and I doubt whether you'd know her family."

All traces of color disappeared from his mother's face, leaving it frighteningly pale. "Not that girl who worked with Jean-Paul for a few days." Her words were a breathless whisper.

"She's a woman, not a girl, Mother."

Wyatt did something he rarely did in the dining room. He lit his cigar, inhaled deeply and blew out a perfect smoke ring. A gray haze obscured the sneer around his mouth. "It didn't take long, did it, Jordan? I had no idea you liked dark meat. But then I really shouldn't be surprised, because what else is there in Harlem."

Noah flashed a white-tooth smile. "Does she have a sister?"

"Don't you mean a *brother?*" Wyatt drawled.

Touching the corners of his mouth with a damask napkin, Noah pushed back his chair and stood up. He pointed to his parents.

"Now you see why I don't bring a woman into this." He shifted his angry gaze to Rhett. "Get your girlfriend out of here before she finds herself with a bull's-eye on her back."

The young woman whom Rhett had introduced as Amelia pressed a hand to her chest. "Please don't mind me. I grew up with my folks going at each other like cats and dogs. After a while, I learned to tune them out."

Jordan joined Noah when he, too, stood up. "Excuse me."

Turning on his heels, he walked out of the dining room, his brother following in his footsteps. He knew if he'd stayed what would've ensued would have been an argument that would have been certain to pit him and Noah against their parents *and* grandfather. Edward was fifty-five, yet he still hadn't been able to stand up to his tyrannical, controlling father. Wyatt had clawed his way out of poverty on New York City's Lower East Side to create a real estate dynasty second only to Douglas Elliman in New York City, and now at seventy-eight, he was tough as steel and wasn't above using his fists when necessary to prove a point.

"When are you going to learn not to

entertain Grandfather's taunting?" he asked Noah.

"I just can't stand it when he comes off so condescending. And just because I won't subject a woman to his holier-than-thou attitude he thinks I'm gay."

"He is who he is," Jordan said, taking the spiral staircase instead of the elevator to the second floor and their suites. "After I had that dust-up with him last year I made myself a promise never to let him see me that angry again."

"How do you hold your temper?"

Jordan pushed open the door to his apartment that included an en suite bath, dressing room, living/dining room area and a utility kitchen. He probably would've lived in the mansion until he married if he hadn't had such an angry confrontation with his grandfather. The apartment suite afforded him complete privacy, and a fulltime household staff was on hand to provide him with whatever he needed regardless of the day or the hour. However, purchasing the maisonette less than a mile away gave him something he hadn't been able to achieve living under the same roof as his family — independence. Noah preceded him, flopping down on a club chair with a matching footstool, while he draped his long frame over a sofa.

"Remember, Noah, I've got ten years and a lot more experience, and with that comes maturity. I learned more working as a litigator protecting the interest of well-heeled clients than I had in three years of law school. And now working in Harlem with clients whose needs are as great or even greater than those at Trilling, Carlyle and Browne has forced me to examine who I am and what I want for my future."

"What *do* you want, Jordan?"

"I want the best for the clients of Chatham and Wainwright."

Noah gave him a long, penetrating stare. Ten years his senior, Jordan was considered tall, dark and handsome. His black hair and olive coloring was a dramatic contrast in a family where everyone was blond. However, whenever he saw photographs of their grandfather in his youth, the resemblance between Wyatt and Jordan was uncanny. Wyatt Wainwright had been quite the rake with his raven hair and penetrating blue eyes.

"What about your personal life?" he questioned again.

"What about it, Noah?"

"Don't you want to get married? Start a family?"

Jordan rested his head on folded arms as he lay across the sofa. "I suppose I do one of these days."

"Why are you so ambivalent?"

"I'm not ambivalent. It's just that I haven't met the right woman."

"You haven't met the right woman and I have."

Sitting up as if he were pulled by a taut wire, Jordan planted his feet on the carpet. "Who is she?"

"You'll meet her if you come down to the Bahamas with me."

"When are you leaving?"

"Tomorrow night. I'm not coming back until January the third."

Jordan shook his head. "I wish I could. I promised Brandt I would attend his New Year's Eve party." Their professional football player cousin hosted a New Year's Eve bash at his penthouse every two years.

"Damn! I forgot about that," Noah said under his breath. "Well, maybe you'll meet her another time. Now, tell me about your summer *liaison*."

Leaning back, Jordan stared at objects in the room that were as familiar as the back of his hand: the suede and leather seating grouping, the marble fireplace with the mantelpiece lined with family photographs, the floor-to-ceiling windows with glorious views of Central Park. As a child he'd spent countless hours sitting on the padded window seats watching the change of seasons.

The park had become his personal playground when he'd ice skated at Wollman Rink and walked the 86th Street transverse road to the West Side to visit the American Museum of National History several times a month.

It was at the Museum of the City of New York, the Metropolitan Museum of Art and Natural History, where he'd lost himself in art and history, where he'd escaped the orderly life his mother had created to mold him into someone he hadn't wanted to be. Christiane Wainwright had wanted him to attend the boarding school where countless Johnston men had received an exemplary education. But it was Jordan's first memory of his father asserting his authority when he told his wife that he refused to warehouse his son in a drafty New England school where he would act and react like a robot instead of a six-year-old boy. He'd been quick to remind her that their son was a Wainwright, not a Johnston. His parents had finally reached a compromise, and he had been enrolled in a prestigious Upper East

Side preparatory school, where all of the students arrived and were picked up in chauffeur-driven limousines.

Life as Jordan knew it changed the year he'd celebrated his tenth birthday. With Noah's birth he was no longer an only child. Rhett was born less than two years later, and Chanel five years later. He was seventeen when his sister was born, and her birth was a mixture of delight and sadness for Jordan. The joy of having a baby sister had softened him. But because he'd left for college, then enrolled in law school he'd missed seeing her first steps, hearing her talk in sentences and other important milestones during the first seven years of her life.

"Jordan!"

He jumped as if coming out a trance. "What's up?"

A frown marred Noah's handsome features. "I asked you about Natasha Parker."

Jordan closed his eyes. "There's not much to tell. She needed money for tuition for her last year in culinary school, so I hired her to teach me to cook —"

"Did you learn how to cook?" Noah interrupted, smiling.

He nodded. "I can put together a nice breakfast and grill steaks and fish. We got close, real close, but we both knew it was going to end once she returned to school."

"Where's she in school?"

"Rhode Island."

"Come on, Jordan. It's not as if Rhode Island is halfway across the country. You could still see her."

Jordan shook his head. "No, I can't. She's married. I didn't know it at the time, but she and her husband were separated."

"When did you find out?"

"He was involved in an accident, and that's when she told me."

"Were you in love with her?"

The sweep hand on the clock on the mantelpiece made a full revolution before Jordan spoke again. "No. If I was, I would've fought to keep her. What's up with you asking if she had a sister?"

Noah closed his eyes for several seconds, long pale lashes brushing the top of his cheekbones. "I don't have a particular type when it comes to women."

Attractive lines fanned out around Jordan's eyes when he smiled. "I take it you like a little diversity."

"It's more than a little, big brother."

Jordan sat up, leaned over and bumped fists with his brother. He knew instinctually when Noah did decide to marry, the woman he would choose was certain to change the *complexion* of the family in more ways than one.

The brothers talked for hours about the women they'd dated and those they wished they hadn't. It was close to ten when Noah retreated to his own apartment and Jordan went into the bathroom to shower before climbing into bed. He was asleep within minutes of his head touching the pillow. He'd promised his mother he would spend the week with her, but chided himself for giving into her plea that she didn't see him enough. He loved Christiane, but could only take his grandfather in small doses. Hopefully the week would go quickly, and after the first of the year he wouldn't be obligated to hang out with his family again until the Easter break.

CHAPTER 2

Aziza Fleming pulled the cashmere shawl tighter around her shoulders before settling back against the Town Car's leather seat. It was New Year's Eve and she was on her way to a party when she wanted nothing more than to be at home, in front of the television watching the ball drop, while toasting the new year with a glass of champagne.

Instead of stockings, a pair of designer stilettos, a dress that revealed more than it concealed, she would've preferred a pair of lounging pajamas and thick cotton socks. However, she'd caved when her brother threatened to come to Westchester and forcibly drag her out of the house to attend a party hosted by his pro ball teammate on New Year's Eve at an Upper East Side penthouse.

Her brother Alexander Fleming claimed she worked too hard and was alone much too much. But what her football player brother failed to realize or understand was that she was content being alone. It wasn't as if she couldn't find a date — if she needed one. It was that she didn't want to date anyone. She had a career she loved, owned a house in a community she liked and enjoyed decorating it, and most of all she'd learned to love herself.

At thirty-one she was five years older than Al, as most people called him, but he'd appointed himself her protector. Aziza constantly reminded him that she could take care of herself; however, as the only girl with two older brothers and one younger she had grown up very much the tomboy. She could fend for herself, whether it was with words or, on rare occasions, with fists. Her father had insisted she take martial arts training along with his rough-and-tumble sons.

She still fought, but now it was for her clients: women contemplating divorce, seeking custody of their children or pursuing delinquent child support or alimony payments. All of her clients were women, but there was one exception: Brandt Wainwright. The high-profile superstar NFL quarterback, who roomed with her brother whenever they played away games, had hired her to handle his legal affairs. If it had been anyone other than Brandt hosting the

New Year's Eve gathering, she would still be sitting in her family room staring at a wall-mounted flat-screen television — her Christmas present to herself — rather than in the back of a limo.

Aziza closed her eyes, sinking deeper into the supple leather seat. It was minutes after ten, and in less than two hours it would be a new year. She rarely made New Year's resolutions, and this year was the same. The first and only time she had, it was to marry her high school sweetheart. The man she'd loved had turned into someone *and* something else within minutes of their exchanging vows.

Lamar Powers believed that wearing his ring and taking his name was a symbol of ownership. What he'd failed to realize was that growing up with three brothers, Aziza had been forced to assert herself. Unfortunately their fairy-tale romance had ended before it had a chance to begin. She'd tried to make a go of her marriage, but it ended after a year.

The smooth motion of the wheels suddenly stopped, and she opened her eyes. The drive from Bronxville to Manhattan had ended much more quickly than she'd anticipated. The driver had pulled up in front of a towering high-rise in the fifties between First and Second avenues. The glowing numbers on the vehicle's dashboard showed the time. It was 11:16 p.m.

The rear door opened and she placed her hand on the driver's outstretched palm, as he gently pulled her to her feet. Aziza flashed a warm smile. "Thank you."

The driver's dark eyes lingered briefly on the long shapely legs in sheer black hose and the stilettos that made her legs look even longer than they were under the fitted black wool gabardine dress with a generous front slit. "Just call me when you're ready to leave."

Aziza smiled. "I will."

Alexander had arranged for the driver to pick her up and take her back home once she was ready. She'd told him that she hadn't wanted to come into Manhattan, yet her protests had fallen on deaf ears. Once her brother set his mind to something, it would take a minor miracle for him to change it. Rather than engage in a verbal exchange with Alexander, she'd given in. Besides, what did she have to lose by leaving the house for a couple of hours? Partying with jocks wasn't something she liked or looked forward to, yet she'd always enjoyed Brandt Wainwright's company.

■ ■ ■ ■

The elevator doors opened and Aziza walked into the penthouse with its panoramic views of the East River and bridges linking the island of Manhattan with the other boroughs. A slight smile parted her lips. Everyone was wearing the ubiquitous black. Dimmed recessed lights and dozens of candles provided a sensual backdrop to music coming from concealed speakers. She guessed there had to be at least sixty people milling around the expansive entryway and great room, but then a roar of laughter went up from another area beyond where she stood. Although Brandt had invited her to his home in the past, she'd always declined, deciding it was better not to mix business with pleasure. She walked into the space that took up two top floors of the opulent high-rise.

Removing her shawl, she folded it and draped the cashmere wrap over her left arm. She spied Alexander as he leaned down to hear what an attractive woman with a profusion of braided hair brushing her bare shoulders was saying to him. Whatever it was must have been funny, because he threw back his head and laughed loudly.

Aziza smiled, although she couldn't over-hear what they were saying. Her brother, who was chocolate eye candy, and could lay claim to above-average intelligence and a quick wit, never failed to attract the opposite sex.

"How long have you been here?"

Turning, she glanced over her shoulder and smiled up at Brandt Wainwright. The quarterback had become the NFL's latest heartthrob, appearing on the covers of most men's and sports magazines. Nicknamed the "Viking," because of his long ash-blond hair and piercing sky-blue eyes, Brandt garnered attention from legions of women wherever he went. He loved women and they loved him back. Dressed in street clothes, he appeared taller and larger than he did in uniform. Standing six-five and weighing in at two hundred fifty-five pounds, Brandt Wainwright was an imposing figure of rock-hard muscle. Even the black pullover and slacks failed to mask the power in his athletic physique.

"I just walked in."

Brandt angled his head and kissed her cheek. "That's good, because I threatened to fire anyone on staff if I didn't see every guest with a glass or a plate of food." Raising his hand, he beckoned a young woman

44

balancing a tray with glasses filled with colorful concoctions. Taking a glass, he handed it to Aziza. "I know you like amaretto sours."

She shifted the tiny silk evening purse to her left hand, their fingers brushing when she accepted the glass. "Thank you." Aziza took a sip of the cocktail, smiling at her host over the rim of the glass. "It's perfect."

Reaching out, Brandt took her upper arm and steered her out of the living room and down a wide hallway to another wing of the penthouse. "Come with me. I want to introduce you to my cousin. I told him about you and your sexual harassment case."

Aziza stopped. "How did you know about that?" Only Alexander knew about her plan to sue a former employer for sexual harassment.

"Al told me when I asked why you didn't work for some firm in the city. But, don't worry about my cousin. He's one of the best litigators in the city," he explained quickly. "And, there is no doubt he will be able to help you win your suit."

"My case aside, if your cousin is an attorney, why did you ask me to represent you?" she asked.

She practically had to shout to be heard

45

over the sound of voices raised in laughter when they entered a room that was as large as some multiplex movie theater. Reclining black leather chairs were lined up theater-style in front of a high-definition wall-mounted screen that was as least seventy inches. A powerful sound system blared music from one of the channels with images of partygoers gyrating to a popular dance tune filling the screen.

Brandt's expression changed, becoming impassive. "I try not to involve family in my personal business. The attorney I had on retainer before I hired you, who happens to be a *very* distant cousin, had a habit of talking to the press. I had to remind him that he was my lawyer, not my publicist. But I suppose his obsession for fifteen minutes of fame cost him a client and my friendship. Even though I can't change the fact that we're related, I do have the option of not having to deal with him." He rested a hand on the back of a man in a black mohair jacket, interrupting the conversation between his cousin and one of his teammates. "Excuse me, Donnie, but I need to talk to Jordan for a few minutes."

It wasn't until the tall, slender man with short-cropped black hair turned around that Aziza was able to connect the name Wainwright with the man who'd become something of a local celebrity around Harlem.

Smiling, she said, "I never thought I would have the pleasure of meeting the 'Sheriff of Harlem.' "

A rush of color darkened Jordan Wainwright's face. He didn't think he would ever get used to the sobriquet after he'd won a landlord-tenant case that had garnered national attention.

Jordan hesitated for several seconds as the beautiful woman standing less than a foot away shifted her cocktail to her left hand before he extended his. She was so breathtakingly beautiful that he'd found himself at a loss for words. Recovering quickly, a smile parted his lips.

"Jordan Wainwright."

Aziza grasped the long slender hand that tightened slightly around her fingers before Jordan eased the slight pressure. Her gaze was drawn to his firm mouth when he smiled. His teeth were white and perfectly aligned. She knew people who paid orthodontists thousands of dollars to have teeth like his.

His face was as perfect as his teeth. A lean jaw, strong chin, high cheekbones, sweeping, arching eyebrows and large jewel-like hazel eyes that seemingly didn't look at her, but through her. She was mesmerized.

"Aziza Fleming."

His eyebrows lifted slightly. "So, you're Al Fleming's sister."

She nodded. "That I am."

Brandt slapped Jordan's back again. "I'll leave you two to talk. Jordan, if Aziza needs anything, please make certain she gets it."

Jordan nodded as he tucked the slender hand into the bend of his elbow. Not only did Aziza Fleming look good, but she also smelled delicious. If he were given three guesses as to what she did for a living, he would've struck out. He never would've thought she was an attorney.

She was tall, even without the stilettos. He was six-two in bare feet and Jordan estimated Aziza had to be at least five-eight or nine without the sexy heels. Her hair was dark, thick and brushed off her face and secured into a loose ponytail behind her left ear. He moved closer and went completely still. The asymmetrical neckline of her dress hadn't prepared him for the wide bands crisscrossing her back to reveal an expanse of flawless brown skin from nape to waist. Aziza Fleming's round, doll-like face with a hint of a dimpled chin, large round eyes that tilted at the corners and a full, lush mouth had him completely enthralled.

48

"I see that you have a drink, but have you eaten?" he asked her.

Aziza knew not to drink anything alcoholic without eating, or she would find herself slightly tipsy. "No, I haven't. And I make it a habit never to drink on an empty stomach."

"Well, if that's the case, then I'll make certain you get something to eat before we talk."

She walked alongside Jordan as they made their way down another wide hallway. "What did Brandt tell you about me?"

"All he said was that you handled his legal affairs, but it was Al who mentioned that you had a pending lawsuit against a former employer for sexual harassment."

Aziza groaned inwardly. "I wish he hadn't said anything." Her voice was barely a whisper.

Jordan released her hand, placing his at the small of her back. She stiffened against his splayed fingers for several seconds before relaxing. "Why didn't you want him to say anything? Whatever you tell me will be confidential."

Aziza gave Jordan a sidelong glance, silently admiring his patrician features. It had been a long time, much too long, since she'd found herself attracted to a man.

There was something about his striking looks that radiated sensuality, recklessness *and* danger. He had proven that when he'd stood in front of television cameras to enumerate the building violations in his family-owned properties.

"That would apply *if* I were your client and you were my attorney."

Jordan smiled. "You're right about that. But try to think of this as an unofficial consultation. I've handled several harassment cases and, fortunately, won them, so maybe I can give you a few pointers to help you out."

"If it's all right with you I'd rather not discuss my business here," Aziza said softly. It wasn't that she was paranoid, but she couldn't run the risk that someone would overhear their conversation. After all, there were a lot people in the penthouse, and there was a saying about the walls having ears.

Jordan led Aziza into a room that Brandt had set up as his library and home office. After he touched a dimmer switch on the wall, the space was flooded with light. His gaze lingered on the skin on her back when she walked into the library. Whatever she'd used on her body had left a sprinkling of shiny particles that shimmered like gold dust.

Al Fleming had mentioned his sister had been sexually harassed, and Jordan believed that any man who forced his attention on a woman was in the same category as deviant sexual predators.

But he could easily see why a man would come onto Aziza Fleming. The woman was sexy without even trying. Her face, slender, curvy body and shapely legs that seemed to go on forever were enough to elicit dreams that were unabashedly erotic in nature.

"We'll talk, but not about your case. Please make yourself comfortable and I'll bring you something to eat."

"Thank you."

Aziza felt a sense of relief. Jordan hadn't tried to pressure her into divulging the details of her impending lawsuit. And although Jordan Wainwright looked nothing like the men to whom she usually found herself attracted, there was something about his understated sophistication that she was drawn to.

Setting the glass down on a side table, Aziza strolled around the room that was lined with floor-to-ceiling built-in book-shelves on opposite walls. The instant she'd met Brandt Wainwright, she'd realized he was what she called the trifecta: face, body and brains. He'd graduated with degrees in business and economics, but it was professional football that had become his calling and passion. The former Stanford University star and Heisman Trophy runner-up had been drafted by the NFL and had signed to a three-year contract for an unheard-of amount for a rookie quarterback.

The library furnishings were not what one would expect of a professional athlete. There were no trophies or pictures with celebs, framed newspaper stories or magazine covers. It appeared lived in, a place where Brandt came to read and relax. Dark brown leather chairs and a love seat, a massive mahogany antique desk, a leather desk chair, neutral colored walls and a sisal rug seemed better suited for a businessman. Brandt had once said that if he hadn't become a professional athlete, he would've gone to work in his family's real estate firm.

Aziza crossed the room and stood at the window, staring down at the traffic and pedestrians who looked like miniature toys. It was a mild New York City New Year's Eve with temperatures in the mid-forties, and that made for larger-than-usual crowds of partygoers.

Her gaze lingered on the dark surface of

the East River before shifting to the rooftops of buildings with water towers and heating and cooling units. There had been a time when Aziza loved commuting into the city from her Westchester home. It was during the half-hour train ride and the ten-minute walk from Grand Central station to the Park Avenue office building on Thirty-Second Street that she'd mentally reviewed the cases she was working on or planned her day.

As a thirty-one-year-old, childless divorcée, her only responsibility and focus was her career. She'd lived and breathed the law, and her ex had accused her of loving her work more than she'd loved him. No matter what she'd said or did, it hadn't been enough to change Lamar's mind, and in the end she'd stopped trying.

His attempt to control her life, while quietly sabotaging her career, had left her with no choice but to break off the relationship. It hadn't been easy. Not when they'd been together since grammar school, throughout high school, college and then law school. Once she'd left Lamar, Aziza felt as if she'd lost a limb — a diseased limb that had to be amputated, or the poison would kill her spirit.

Don't let anyone kill your spirit, or take your

53

joy. She'd grown up with her grandmother's wisdom. And when she'd told her Nana that Lamar was killing her spirit, Emma Fleming's advice had been to walk away and not look back, and that was what she'd done.

Aziza shook her head. She wished she could erase the memory of Lamar as easily as hitting the delete key. She didn't know why, but she hadn't thought of him in more than a year.

Why now? she mused.

Why now when she finally had a successful law practice?

Why now when she'd completed renovating her home to suit her personal taste and lifestyle?

"What are you doing hiding out here?"

Aziza turned to find the broad shoulders belonging to her brother Alexander Fleming filling out the doorway. "Hey, you," she crooned, approaching him, arms outstretched. "I saw you when I came in, but you were busy with a very pretty sister with braided hair."

Alexander flashed a slow smile, his dimples dotting his lean face like thumbprints. He hugged Aziza, while pressing a kiss to her cheek. "Don't get any ideas, Zee. She's Damien Harvey's girlfriend." He kissed her again, this time on the forehead.

"Thanks for coming."

"Did I have a choice? You'd threatened me with bodily harm."

Alexander laughed. "The only harm would've been the way you'd look if I had to go into Neanderthal mode and carry you over my back to bring you here." He winked at his sister. "I must say you clean up very nicely."

She returned his wink. "Thank you."

Standing back, Aziza studied her brother's face. He had classic good looks with strong masculine features and large eyes that were an odd shade of gray — eyes he'd inherited from their paternal grandmother, Emma Fleming.

Resting her hands on the lapels of his black wool jacket, she angled her head. "Where's *your* woman?"

Alexander's expression changed as if he was trying to conceal his innermost feelings. "I've decided to start the year solo."

"What about Cynthia? I thought the two of you were getting serious."

Shoving his hands in his pants pockets, the MVP defensive end stared at the lights on the bridges spanning the river. "We split up. Unfortunately, Cynthia is drama personified. Things would've been okay if she didn't have to run everything we said or did

55

past her girlfriends." His eyes met his sister's. "What's up with women spilling their guts about what goes on between them and their man?"

Aziza held up her hands. "Please, don't lump me in that category. I only have two girlfriends, and we never discuss our men or lack thereof."

"I know you told me you're not interested in getting married again, but what about dating?"

"What about it, Al?" She'd answered his question with a question.

"One of the guys on the team told me that he'd like to take you out once the season is over, but I told him I can't speak for my sister."

"You approve?"

"He's all right."

Aziza pondered her brother's response. If she was going to date someone, he had to be better than *all right.* "Don't tell me he's coming out of a bad relationship, because if he is then I'm not the one."

Alexander exhaled an audible sigh. "Other than an occasional baby mama drama, he's a good guy."

"No, Al. Forget it. I'm not getting involved with some man with a psycho ex-girlfriend. Call me selfish, but if I'm not a baby mama, then I'm not going to put up with it. Why don't you guys marry these women when you get them pregnant? It would prevent a lot of problems."

"Back it up, Zee. I'm not a baby daddy."

"I'm not talking about you, Al. How many guys on your team are paying out huge chunks of money for child support? Probably too many to count," she said, answering her own questions. "Wouldn't it be easier to get married and take care of their wives and children without all the drama?"

Alexander recognized the look in Aziza's eyes. He'd seen it enough to know that she was ready to go off on a rant about how a lot of men couldn't be trusted. He knew she'd soured on marriage because the man she'd believed she knew had turned into someone she didn't really know, and her mistrust in men was exacerbated whenever female clients came to her with their custody or child support or sexual harassment problems. He'd been shocked when she'd agreed to become Brandt Wainwright's legal counsel. Brandt was her only male client.

"What do you want me to tell him?" Alexander asked.

"Is he here tonight?"

Her brother nodded.

"If that's the case then I'll tell him myself."

"No, Zee. I don't need you to get in his face and lecture him about his responsibilities. I'll tell him you're currently seeing someone."

"Whatever," she drawled. "You know I'm not into stroking the egos of overgrown . . ." Her words trailed off when she detected movement behind her.

"I'm sorry. I'll come back." Jordan Wainwright had walked into the library holding a bottle of champagne and two flutes, as a waiter stood behind him with a tray balanced on one shoulder.

Alexander beckoned. "Come on in, Jordan. I was just leaving." He turned back to Aziza, kissing her cheek. "Don't forget to save me a dance."

She smiled. "Okay."

Alexander had told her there would be dancing in the penthouse atrium, and she'd promised to dance with him at least once before leaving. Ever since he'd been a contestant on *Dancing with the Stars,* Alexander had become a dancing dynamo. During the off-season, he'd taken up ballroom dancing. It had been hard to imagine her six-four, two-hundred-twenty-pound brother tiptoeing across a dance floor until the show had aired. Not only was he light on his feet, but also graceful.

He'd also gotten her to take dancing lessons while she was going through her
divorce. Spending hours on the dance floor
was the perfect antidote to her pity party,
and like her brother, she'd discovered she
was hooked. She still took lessons at a local
dance studio several days a week. The dance
workout was a substitute for jogging during
the winter months and had helped tone her
body.

Alexander approached Jordan. "Thanks
for agreeing to help Zee out," he said.

"I'll do what I can," Jordan replied in a
low voice.

Aziza stood off to the side, watching as
the waiter set up a table, covered it with a
tablecloth and a platter filled with an as-
sortment of crudités and hot and cold hors
d'oeuvres. She hadn't meant to go off on
her brother, but she'd grown tired of the
behavior exhibited by so many professional
athletes. Most of the time they were let off
with a slap on the wrist because they were
star athletes.

"That's a lot of food," she said to Jordan
when he took her hand and led her to the
love seat.

Jordan sat down beside Aziza. "It just
looks like a lot. Besides, I haven't eaten all
day, so I doubt if any of it will go to waste."

59

She leaned to her right, and her bare shoulder brushed against his jacket. Aziza stared at Jordan, noticing for the first time the length of his lashes. *It's not fair,* she thought. Women spent a lot of money for false eyelashes while Jordan Wainwright was born with lashes that were not only thick but long.

"How did you get special service?" she whispered as the waiter uncorked the champagne with barely an audible pop.

Tilting his head at an angle, Jordan gave her a wink. "It helps when you have the same last name as the man hosting tonight's fête."

Aziza couldn't help but smile. "So, are you saying being a Wainwright has its privileges?"

"It does," he admitted modestly. "But so does being a Fleming."

She sobered quickly. "Al's the celebrity in the family, not me."

"I could say the same about Brandt."

Aziza shook her head. "You can't be that self-effacing, Jordan. Not after that stunt you pulled on TV."

She couldn't believe that Jordan, who'd represented a Harlem tenant's committee, had announced at a news conference that the owner of several buildings with numerous housing violations was his grandfather. Headlines referred to him as the Sheriff of Harlem. When he'd become a partner at Chatham Legal Services, most of the local politicos turned out to welcome him to the neighborhood as one of their own.

Jordan stared at his highly polished shoes. "I did what I had to do for my clients." His head came up and he gave Aziza a direct stare. "I'm certain you do the same for your clients."

The seconds ticked as she met his penetrating stare. "Of course I do."

A hint of a smile softened his firm mouth. "Good. That's one thing we can agree on."

Green-flecked irises moved slowly from Aziza's delicate face to her bare shoulders. He didn't know why, but he wanted to press his mouth to her skin to see if she tasted as good as she looked.

Jordan knew it wasn't going to be easy to remain unaffected around Aziza Fleming. Her beautiful face, gorgeous body and intelligence would certainly test his professional integrity. What he had to do was think of her as his client. Not only couldn't he cross the line, but he was determined *not* to cross the line.

"What does Aziza mean?" He had to say something — anything except stare at her as if she were something to be devoured.

Aziza lowered her gaze, her eyes fixed on Jordan's strong neck. He'd worn a mock turtleneck under his jacket. He was the epitome of casual sophistication.

"It's Swahili for *precious.*"

"The name is perfect." His words sounded neutral in tone.

"Mr. Wainwright, do you want me to pour the champagne?"

The waiter's question shattered Jordan's fantasy. "Yes, please," he said, as he continued to stare at Aziza's lush lips.

He took a flute of pale bubbly wine from the waiter, handed it to Aziza, then took the remaining one, holding it aloft. He waited until the waiter left the library, closing the door behind him. Jordan touched his glass to hers. "Here's to a successful working relationship."

Aziza lowered her lashes, unaware of the seductiveness of the gesture. She felt as if she was being sucked into a vortex from which there was no escape. Jordan Wainwright looked nothing like the men to whom she found herself attracted. Yet there was something about him that was so masculine, so sensual that she found it almost impossible to control the butterflies in her stomach. Raising the flute, she took a sip of champagne. It was an excellent vintage.

"Would you mind if I serve you?" Jordan asked after he'd taken a sip from his flute.

She swallowed, nodding. "Yes, please."

Reaching over, he picked up a cocktail napkin and then a toast point covered with Almas pearly white beluga caviar. Holding the napkin under her chin, Jordan watched as she took a bite. "How is it?"

With wide eyes Aziza savored the lingering taste on her tongue. "It's incredible." She opened her mouth and then closed it when Jordan popped the remaining piece into his mouth.

"It is delicious," he agreed, chewing slowly.

"Hey! That was mine."

Leaning closer, he pressed a kiss to her ear. "There's plenty more where that came from." Jordan went completely still when he heard cheers coupled with the distinctive sound of exploding fireworks. He'd become so engrossed with Aziza that he'd lost track of time. He angled his head and slanted his mouth over Aziza's slightly parted lips. "Happy New Year."

CHAPTER 3

Aziza felt the soft brush of Jordan's mouth on hers. It was more a mingling of champagne and caviar-scented breaths than an actual kiss.

"Happy New Year, Jordan," she whispered, praying he wouldn't feel the runaway beating of her heart slamming against her ribs.

There was a tradition that said the person you find yourself with on New Year's Eve when the clock strikes midnight will be the one you would spend the year with. She didn't know Jordan Wainwright. And she hadn't wanted to get to know him *that* well and didn't want to know if or whether he was involved with a woman. And even if he wasn't, she didn't have time for a man — not when she'd just gotten her life back on track.

Sitting up straight, Jordan smiled, recognizing the expression of surprise freezing Aziza's features. "Are you all right?"

She blinked. "I'm good. Really."

Jordan drained his flute. "We should've been with the others counting down the seconds."

"It's okay. If I hadn't been here I would've been home dressed in my most comfortable jammies watching the ball drop."

Jordan's expressive eyebrows lifted a fraction. "Alone?"

A smile crinkled the skin around Aziza's eyes. "Is that a subtle way of asking me whether I'm involved with someone?"

"I'd like to believe I was being direct," he countered.

"Well, counselor, the answer to your *very direct* question is no." She shifted slightly on the love seat until they were facing each other. "What about you? If you weren't here, where would you be?"

"Probably in the Caribbean with my brother and his girlfriend."

It was Aziza's turn to lift her eyebrows. "What about your girlfriend?"

"My, my, my, counselor. Aren't you direct."

"That's the only way I know how to be, counselor," Aziza countered with a grin.

"The answer is I don't have a girlfriend."

"Why not, Jordan? You seem like a nice guy."

Jordan was hard-pressed not to laugh at Aziza's crestfallen expression. Did she really feel sorry for him? "Thank you. But it's been said that nice guys usually finish last."

There he was again, Aziza mused. She didn't understand Jordan's self-deprecation. "I don't believe that. Nice guys may not choose wisely at times, but that doesn't mean they always wind up on the losing end."

"So you say there's hope for me?"

Picking up her flute, she sipped her champagne, staring at Jordan over the rim. The illumination from the lamp on a side table slanted over his lean face, and in that moment she sucked in her breath. His eyes were now a rich mossy green.

"You don't need hope, Jordan. You're the total package." A rush of color darkened his face with her compliment. "Are you blushing?"

Jordan glanced away. "Men don't blush." Reaching for the bottle, he refilled his glass. "What else would you like?" he asked, gesturing to the tray with prosciutto-wrapped breadsticks, stone wheat crackers, oysters, quail eggs, tiger shrimp, sushi, lobster and crabmeat and a variety of cheeses.

Aziza wanted to tell Jordan he *was* blushing but didn't want to make him feel more embarrassed than she assumed he was. "It's my turn to serve you." She knew she shocked him when she picked up a pair of chopsticks and clamped the sushi and fed it to him. They alternated feeding each other the gourmet treats while drinking champagne to cleanse their palates.

The rich food and three glasses of champagne left Aziza full and languid. Kicking off her heels, she tucked her feet up under her body and closed her eyes. "I think I'm a little tipsy."

Jordan stood up, removed his jacket, then sat again, cradling her stocking-covered feet between his hands. "You only had three glasses to my five."

"Only three. Two is usually my limit," she said without opening her eyes.

"Are you driving?"

"No. I have a driver."

"Where do you live?" he asked.

"Bronxville." Aziza opened her eyes. Jordan's jacket had concealed a rock-hard upper body. His neck wasn't as large as her football player brother's, or his teammates, but it was obvious he worked out regularly.

"Where do you live?" Her voice was soft, the timbre low, sultry.

"Manhattan."

"Where in Manhattan?"

"The Upper East Side. My apartment building faces Central Park."

"Why didn't you just say that you live on Fifth Avenue?" she asked. A beat passed. "What are you hiding, Jordan?"

His fingers tightened on her instep. "Nothing. What makes you think I'm hiding something?"

"I don't know. Call it a hunch, woman's intuition."

He massaged her instep before moving up to her ankles. "What else does your woman's intuition tell you about me?"

Aziza tried to will her mind not to think rather than enjoy the sensual fog of premium French champagne and the sexy man rubbing her legs and feet. "I think you're uncomfortable being a Wainwright. It's probably why you decided to expose your grandfather as a slumlord and why you decided to work for a small Harlem law firm rather than your family's real estate company or a prestigious Wall Street firm."

Jordan's expression remained impassive. He hadn't known Aziza Fleming an hour, and she didn't realize how close she'd come to the truth. "You're wrong about one thing."

"What's that?"

"I'm proud to be a Wainwright. The name gives me entrée to places open to a privileged few, while it also allows me to do things for other people with less."

"Tell me about your family."

Jordan shook his head. "I'll leave that for another time."

"Why?"

"I can't tell you about the Wainwrights without revealing my mother's side of the family. Have you ever heard the Cher classic hit 'Gypsies, Tramps and Thieves'?" Aziza nodded. "If she'd been singing about the Wainwrights and Johnstons, then it would've been miscreants, pimps and thieves."

"You're kidding."

"I wish I was, Zee," he said, shortening her name.

"Where did you go to college?" Aziza asked.

"Harvard, undergraduate and law. After law school I went to work for my father, but after a few years I was bored. I quit and worked as a litigator for Trilling, Carlyle and Browne."

She whistled softly. "They're one of the top firms in the city."

Jordan nodded. "My salary topped out at high six figures, including bonuses, but the trade-off was working an average of sixty to seventy hours a week. That left very little time for socializing. Whenever I was able to take a vacation I was too tired to do anything more than sleep, get up and shower, eat and then sleep some more. I knew I couldn't continue at that pace, so I walked into the office of one of the senior partners and handed in my resignation.

"My grandfather wanted me to come back to Wainwright Developers Group to head the legal department and set my own hours, but that would be like taking a step backward."

"What did you finally decide to do?"

Jordan's hands moved up and over her calves. "I moved out of my parents' house, bought a condo and spent the next four months relaxing in a villa in Costa Rica while it was renovated and decorated."

Aziza stared at the long fingers gently massaging her legs and feet, wondering if Jordan knew how much his light touch had aroused her. The area at the apex of her thighs pulsed with sensations she hadn't felt in a while. She wanted to tell him to stop, but didn't because the seemingly innocent stroking was so pleasurable that she wanted it to go on — forever.

"How could you go away and not monitor

what was being done?"

"The architect and interior designer emailed me weekly updates."

She smiled. "Clever."

"The internet ranks right up there with the finest French champagne and Persian beluga caviar."

Aziza wrinkled her nose. "I wouldn't know about that because someone ate mine."

Jordan rolled his eyes. "Okay, I'm sorry I ate your caviar. I'll make it up to you."

"How?" she asked, pouting as she'd done when her older brothers wouldn't let her tag along with them whenever they'd wanted to hang out with their friends.

"I'll buy you a tin."

She shook her head. "I don't need a tin. One toast point or a tiny spoonful will do."

Jordan released her legs and got up from the love seat. "I'll go and see if there's any left."

Aziza watched him leave, silently admiring the way his trousers fit his waist and hips. It was obvious Jordan didn't buy his clothes off the rack. She unfolded her legs, slipping her feet into her shoes, and stood up. Walking across the room, she opened the door and plowed into her brother.

"I was just coming to get you. You did promise to dance with me," Alexander said when she gave him a blank stare.

She held back when he grasped her hand. "I need to wait for Jordan to get back."

"Jordan will know where to find you."

Aziza knew physically she was no match for Al, so she followed his lead where revelers had crowded into the atrium that was designed to resemble an indoor rainforest. A DJ was busying spinning tunes, while couples were on their feet dancing to an infectious Black Eyed Peas song.

"Now, isn't this better than sitting home alone?" Alexander said in her ear as he swung her around and around in an intricate dance step.

"It's all right," she admitted.

"Liar!"

"Okay. I'm having a good time."

The truth was Aziza was really enjoying herself, and she knew Jordan was responsible for keeping her entertained. She'd felt comfortable talking to him, and he exhibited none of the brashness she'd seen during the televised news conference. Perhaps that was what he'd wanted the audience to see. After all, she'd performed more times than she could count in the courtroom. Some judges didn't care for theatrics, so Aziza knew to keep it to a minimum.

Alexander tightened his grip on his sister's

waist. "Does Jordan Wainwright have anything to do with you having a good time?"

Aziza missed a step, then caught herself. "Why would you ask me that?"

"Do you realize the two of you have been behind a closed door for more than an hour?"

"Hel-lo, Al. Weren't you the one who wanted me to talk to Jordan?" Eyes narrowing, Aziza stopped midstep. "I hope you're not thinking I would . . ." Her words trailed off.

Alexander pulled Aziza closer. "Don't turn around, but Jordan's standing there staring at you like a lovesick adolescent. I told you not to turn around!" he said when his sister ignored his warning.

Jordan held up a piece of toast with caviar, put it into his mouth, chewing it as if in slow motion, then made a big show of wiping his hands. "No, he didn't," she whispered.

"What the hell is going on, Zee?"

"He ate my caviar." Aziza managed to free her right hand, made a fist and pretended to blacken both his eyes.

This was an Aziza Alexander hadn't seen in a very long time. She'd always been a practical joker and had the most carefree and spontaneous laugh of any woman he'd known. She was as tough as she could be feminine, and he'd believed growing up with three brothers had prepared her to navigate the male-dominated law profession. What she hadn't been prepared for was being sexually harassed, or her husband not having her back. The result was she'd lost her husband *and* her job with the law firm that had recruited her even before she'd passed the bar.

That spark and zeal for life she'd always exhibited hadn't burned as brightly as it had before she'd married Lamar, but tonight it was back. And he felt sorry for Jordan Wainwright, because there was one thing Alexander knew about his sister, and that was she was a scrapper — in and out of the courtroom. If the high-profile attorney wanted to play with fire, then he'd better be prepared to be singed.

He smiled. "Maybe I should rephrase my question."

"And what's that?"

"Do you like Jordan?"

Aziza's brow furrowed. "Like him how? The way a woman likes a man?" Alexander nodded. "No, Al. It's nothing like that. He's nice and he makes me laugh." *And he's very easy on the eyes,* she added silently.

"Would you ever consider dating him?"

"I doubt it," she said quickly.

"Why?" Alexander questioned.

"He's a lawyer, and you know that we don't mix."

"Just because Lamar was a horse's ass doesn't mean you have to lump all attorneys in that category."

"Don't forget about the one who sexually harassed me, then got his buddies to cover his ass. So, right about now I'm not feeling the male species."

The song ended, and Alexander led Aziza over to a corner of the atrium where they were partially concealed by the leaves of a banana tree. "You can't blame all men for a few idiots. Remember what you told me about women when Nikki cheated on me, then posted it on her Facebook."

Aziza lifted a glass of water off the tray of a passing waiter and took a deep swallow. "Maybe we're the Flemings who're destined to be unlucky in love. Nana and Grandpa were together more than fifty years before he passed away. Mom and Dad will celebrate their fortieth anniversary this year and Danny and Omar have passed the seven-year-itch mark. It's just you and I who seem to keep blowing it."

Pausing, she took another sip of water. "You're only twenty-six, so you have plenty of time to date before deciding to settle down. Fortunately, you don't have to concern yourself with a biological clock." She had another four years before she was considered high risk.

Alexander stared at his sister, wondering if she was aware of what a gift she would be to a man. She was pretty, smart and would enhance his image — but only if he wasn't intimidated by her intelligence. It'd happened with his ex-brother-in-law, and no doubt it would happen again with other men with whom Aziza found herself involved.

"Here comes your admirer," he whispered when he spied the teammate, who was interested in Aziza.

Aziza's senses were on full alert when she saw him approach. He was at least six-foot-eight and as wide as a French-door refrigerator. His bright red hair and beard reminded her of the disgraced ex-baseball great Mark McGwire, but the resemblance ended with hair color. The behemoth heading toward her was a full head taller and outweighed her by at least two hundred pounds.

He dipped his head and planted a noisy kiss on her cheek. "I've been waiting a long time to meet you."

Aziza went completely still, wondering what Alexander had told him about her. She wasn't aware that she was staring, her mouth gaping. "It's . . . it's nice meeting you, too," she gasped breathlessly when she'd recovered her voice. She offered her hand. His smile was so wide she could see his molars. "I'm Aziza."

A large hamlike hand rubbed his thigh before he extended his. "Trevor Butler."

She shook his hand. "It's nice meeting you, Trevor." Aziza knew it was time to end something before it even began. "Al mentioned that you wanted to take me out, but what he didn't know is that I'm seeing someone."

Trevor's face seemed to crumple like an accordion. "Is he here?"

Aziza felt a wave of panic when she realized she had to back up her lie. *If* she was involved with someone, then it would make sense that they would spend New Year's Eve together.

"Yes, he is." She took several steps from behind the large plant, her eyes scanning the crowd for Jordan. She spotted him standing off to the side, arms crossed over his chest. Raising her hand, she beckoned for him to come, sighing inwardly when he wove his way through swaying couples to

77

close the distance between them.

Looping her arm over the fabric of his sweater, she leaned in close to Jordan. "Baby, I don't know if you know your cousin's teammate, but this is Trevor Butler." The two men exchanged handshakes.

Jordan, who'd quickly picked up on Aziza calling him *baby,* followed her cue when he saw lust in the linebacker's eyes. It was obvious he'd been coming onto her, and a quick glance at Alexander Fleming validated his suspicions. Wrapping his arm around Aziza's waist, he pulled her close.

"I didn't get the chance to talk to you at the last party," he admitted to Trevor, "but I want to congratulate you, because without your defense, you guys never would've made it to the Super Bowl."

Trevor's expression brightened. "Thanks, man." He nodded to Aziza. "Your lady is gorgeous."

"I think so, too," Jordan countered without a bit of modesty. His fingers tightened on Aziza's waist. "Come, *baby.* You did promise me one dance before we leave." The tempo of the music had changed from upbeat to a slower rhythm.

"Don't you dare say anything," Aziza cautioned quietly when Jordan pulled her close to his body.

He pressed his mouth to her ear. "You owe me, baby."

"No, I don't. You didn't have to play along if you didn't want to."

"I can always go back and tell Trevor that we just broke up."

"You wouldn't dare."

Jordan smiled. "I dare, because I just saved your gorgeous behind from a man who was literally devouring you with his eyes."

"I don't know why my brother didn't tell him that I don't date."

"Have you ever dated?"

Aziza gave Jordan an incredulous stare. "Of course I've dated." She and Lamar had dated each other.

He stared back under lowered lids. "Why is it that you don't date now?"

"I have a problem with trust."

"You don't trust men?"

She nodded.

"Does it have anything to do with your suit?"

A beat passed before Aziza said, "It goes deeper than that."

Jordan's expressive eyebrows lifted a fraction. "A bad relationship?"

Aziza's eyelids fluttered. "How about a bad marriage?"

Her revelation that she'd been married rendered Jordan silent, and for the first time in a very long time he was at a loss for words. He, who'd earned his living debating and negotiating, was suddenly speechless.

"I'm sorry, Zee."

"I'm not, Jordan. I'm just glad I got out of it before it was too late."

"You're going to have to trust me if you want my help with your case."

"A professional relationship is very different from a personal one. What we'll have is the former."

"I promise not to cross the line," Jordan said, when it was the opposite of what he wanted to do.

He liked Aziza because she was easy to talk to, straightforward, feisty and funny — a winning combination. She hadn't freaked out or gone ballistic when he'd kissed her, and although she'd used him to parry Trevor Butler's romantic notions, she'd managed to let the man down while not destroying his pride. Aziza had admitted she didn't trust men, but it was obvious she didn't hate them either.

He'd met women who'd complained about dating men who were misogynists, but he could say the same thing about women who were man-haters.

"Your promises aren't worth the breath it takes to make them. What about my caviar? You weren't very nice when you made a big show of eating it in my face."

Jordan buried his face in her fragrant hair. "I told you that I'll buy you a tin."

"And I told you I don't need a tin of caviar, Jordan. I don't eat it that often or give dinner parties where I can serve it to *my* guests."

"I'll eat it."

Aziza missed a step but Jordan tightening his hold around her waist kept her from losing her balance. "You're going to eat *my* caviar?"

"Yep. You can serve it whenever we get together to go over your case. We're going to have to meet at your office, because if you come to mine then you'll become a client of Chatham and Wainwright."

"I work out of my home."

Jordan's smile was dazzling. "Then I'll come to your home. Unless . . ."

"Unless what?" she asked when he didn't finish his statement.

"Unless you'd prefer to come to mine."

"It's all right, Jordan. We can meet at my place, because I need to give you tapes."

Jordan stopped, his hand gripping her upper arm as he led Aziza out of the atrium.

Skirting a couple locked in a passionate embrace, he pulled her into an alcove between the living room and formal dining room.

"You have tapes?"

A sensual smile parted Aziza's lips, bringing his gaze to linger there. "Yes." The word was barely off her tongue when she found herself lifted off her feet and Jordan's mouth on hers.

"Get a room, cousin," Brandt drawled, grinning from ear to ear as he strolled by with a buxom brunette clinging to his arm.

If the floor had opened up under her, Aziza would've easily crawled in and disappeared. If it had been anyone but Brandt, her client, she wouldn't have been so embarrassed. And it wasn't as if she could play it off that she and Jordan were exchanging the obligatory New Year's kiss.

Brandt winked at her before she cast her eyes downward. "Don't worry, counselor. When it comes to Wainwrights, Jordan happens to be the best in the bunch."

"That's nice," Aziza mumbled under her breath. "Please put me down," she ordered Jordan between clenched teeth. Her feet touched the floor and she turned and walked in the direction of the library to retrieve her wrap and purse, Jordan following.

He caught up with her. "Where are you going?"

"Home," she flung over her shoulder.

She wasn't as upset with Jordan as she was with herself. Her image had to be impeccable if she was going to go public with a lawsuit charging a prominent attorney with sexually harassing his female employee; if anyone saw her locking lips with Jordan Wainwright at a party hosted by Super Bowl MVP quarterback Brandt Wainwright, then her display of affection could be called into question. Most cell phones came with cameras.

"I hope you're not going home because Brandt saw us kissing."

"Don't flatter yourself, Jordan. It's time that I head home." Aziza entered the library, retrieving her shawl and purse, while Jordan picked up his jacket. She opened her purse, took out her cell phone and called the driver.

"I'll ride with you downstairs."

"I'll be all right."

Jordan reached for her elbow. "I said I'll ride downstairs with you."

Their eyes met and held for a full minute in what had become a stare-down. Aziza knew she couldn't afford to alienate Jordan because she needed his legal help. Not only was he a more experienced attorney, but he also had the name.

She needed Jordan when he didn't need her. "Okay. You can ride with me down to the lobby."

Jordan bowed low as if she were royalty. "Thank you."

Aziza rolled her eyes at him. "I still owe you a knuckle sandwich for eating my caviar."

"I thought we settled that. When do you want to meet?" he said, deftly changing the subject.

"Whatever's convenient."

They arrived at the elevator. He punched the button and the doors opened. "What are you doing Sunday afternoon?"

"Watching the play-offs."

"What if I come over after the game?"

Aziza shook her head. "That'll be too late. If you can get to my place by one, you can work in my office while I fix Sunday dinner."

The doors opened and Jordan let Aziza precede before he walked in behind her. "You cook?" he teased, pushing the button for the lobby.

"I try. What I can promise is that you

won't get ptomaine poisoning."

"If that's the case, then I'll come early. Don't you think you should give me your address and phone number?"

Smoothing her shawl, Aziza wrapped it around her upper body with a dramatic flourish. Smiling, she peered over her shoulder. "Ask your cousin."

If Jordan was serious about helping her build her case, then he would follow through and contact her. If not, then she would have the memory of spending two hours with a man who'd unknowingly reminded her that she was a woman — a woman who'd denied her femininity for much too long.

"Tease," Jordan whispered close to her ear as the car reached the lobby.

He followed Aziza through the lobby, nodding to the doorman on duty, and out to the street where a Town Car idled at the curb. The driver got out and came around to open the passenger door, but Jordan preempted him and helped Aziza as she slid onto the leather seat.

Leaning in, he stared at her face in the soft glow of the high-intensity lamp behind the rear seats. "I'll see you Sunday around one."

Aziza smiled, her gaze moving slowly over the lean face with the dramatic hazel eyes.

"Happy New Year, Jordan." Placing two fingers to her mouth, she touched her fingertips to his slightly parted lips. They stared at each other, the silence swelling to deafening proportions. "Close the door, Jordan."

Blinking as if coming out of a trance, Jordan stepped back and closed the door with a solid thud. He stood at the curb a long time, long after the taillights from the limo disappeared into the blackness of the night.

Then he returned to the building, when the doorman opened the door for him. Shoving his hands in the pockets of his trousers, he waited for the elevator, his mind awash with the time he'd spent with Aziza Fleming. He was able to recall her every expression, the sound of her sexy voice, the color of her face that was an exact match to the exposed skin on her bare back.

However, what he didn't want to remember was how she'd tasted, because the sexy lawyer was forbidden fruit.

He could look, but not taste.

Looking was safe.

Tasting was too much of a risk, and he didn't want to do anything that would risk or jeopardize their very fragile professional relationship.

CHAPTER 4

Bracing his back against the tiles in the shower stall, Jordan closed his eyes as lukewarm water beat down on his head. He had a headache, his mouth felt as if it'd been filled with cotton and his stomach was doing flip-flops. It wasn't how he'd wanted to start the new year.

After watching the car with Aziza drive away, he'd returned to the penthouse and had tried to get into the mood of the festive holiday, failing miserably. He'd switched from drinking champagne to downing shots. It had all ended when some woman tried putting her tongue into his mouth. He'd gagged and forcibly pushed her away. He did remember finding his way to the bathroom in one of Brandt's guest bedrooms where he'd brushed his teeth and rinsed his mouth before falling across the bed, fully clothed. The sun was high in the sky, the penthouse silent as a tomb when he'd ridden the elevator to the lobby where the doorman had hailed a taxi to take him uptown.

Groaning, he opened his eyes and pushed the button on the dispenser filled with shampoo. He went through the motions of washing his hair, then his body with a shower gel that complemented his specially blended cologne. It took two cups of strong black coffee and a slice of dry toast for him to settle his queasy stomach.

He felt like a caged cat, pacing the length of his home office until he called the garage where he stored his car and requested that it be parked in front. The temperature had dropped more than twenty degrees in twenty-four hours, and with the steel-gray sky and the forecast of rain mixed with sleet, he slipped into a ski jacket over a rugby shirt and jeans. Instead of running shoes, he'd selected a pair of rugged Doc Martens.

Jordan wasn't certain what had triggered his state of agitation but knew it wouldn't be assuaged if he remained indoors. Instead of leaving his apartment through the high-rise lobby where the doorman monitored everyone coming and going, he left through the side door that led directly from the apartment to a side street.

He hadn't realized until after he'd purchased the maisonette how much he'd come to value his privacy. Although he had an apartment suite in the Wainwright mansion, Jordan had never invited a woman to spend the night there. If they did sleep together it was either at her place or in a hotel. Never one to kiss and tell, he also did not advertise or flaunt his affairs, which was why it had surprised him when he'd kissed Aziza where anyone could see them. He knew he'd shocked his parents when he'd revealed that he'd been seeing Natasha Parker, but whom he'd dated or slept with was not their business.

He walked out to find Fifth Avenue a bustle of activity with post-holiday shoppers and out-of-towners crowding buses that ran along Central Park. Pedestrians with cameras stopped to photograph one another, using the park as the backdrop. Jordan turned down a side street to the east side rather than attempt to navigate the crowds strolling Museum Mile. The first day of the year had fallen on a Friday, which left Saturday and Sunday for everyone to recover from their revelry before beginning a new week.

It wasn't until he was seated behind the wheel of the black-on-black two-seater BMW roadster that he abandoned his initial intent to drive down I-95 to hang out in D.C. until Sunday, and he decided to go to his office in the brownstone in Harlem's Mount Morris Historic District.

Donald Ennis waited for Raymond Humphries to return to the phone. He'd heard Minerva Jackson's voice in the background, so he assumed Raymond was at her place. He would've thought the real estate mogul would've been at home with his wife instead of with his secretary, who obviously was his mistress.

Donald had spent the past two weeks shadowing Jordan Wainwright. There was nothing the young lawyer had done that had set off alarm bells, but that was only his opinion, and Raymond Humphries did not want or pay him for his opinion. He'd agreed to contact Humphries every other Friday. If something out of the ordinary happened, then he was to contact him immediately.

"Sorry about that, Ennis. I had to tell Minerva something. What do you have for me?"

"Not much. Wainwright went to his grandfather's place Christmas Eve and hung out there for a couple of days. When he did leave it was with his sister and another kid about

90

his sister's age. They walked to the Met, stayed about three hours and then walked to 72nd and Third Avenue. He only interacted with the girls."

"He had to do more than hang out with a couple of teenage girls for the past week."

"You didn't let me finish," Donald snapped.

"Watch your tone, Ennis."

The P.I. counted slowly to ten in an attempt to bring his temper under control. When he'd first done investigative work for Raymond Humphries, he'd had to remind the man that he wasn't one of his employees who relied on him for a paycheck. Donald Michael Ennis was a highly regarded intelligence operative whose career had ended when he'd been diagnosed and had failed to seek treatment for Ménière's syndrome. The recurring dizziness, tinnitus and slight loss of hearing in his left ear had led to early retirement. He'd allowed six months of feeling sorry for himself before deciding to set up a private investigation agency. He'd hired a streetwise friend and a cousin, both of whom had one foot in the criminal world.

"You pay me, Humphries. Not own me."

"Point taken," Raymond drawled.

"My man told me Wainwright returned to his place New Year's Eve, then left again later that night. He went into a building where Brandt Wainwright owns a penthouse. He was seen again sometime after one when he was talking to a woman before she got into a limo."

"Do you know who she is?"

"Not yet. But I have the limo's license plate number. As soon as we track down the driver, we'll know who she is and where she was going."

"Where's Wainwright now?"

Donald shifted on the park bench across the street from Jordan Wainwright's apartment building, stretching out his legs and staring at the scuff marks on his boots. He pressed the cell phone closer to his ear for warmth. He'd spent the better part of an hour sitting on the bench after his friends reported that Jordan Wainwright had returned home earlier that afternoon. It wasn't easy casing out a building facing the park because of ongoing police patrols. He didn't want to be questioned about watching residents who paid seven figures for their condos and co-ops. Doormen were very protective of their tenants, but there were always a few who were willing to provide a *little information* on the comings and goings, if the price was right.

"My man just sent me a text that he's

heading uptown. If he goes anywhere other than his office, then I'll get back to you with his whereabouts."

"Who the hell works on New Year's?"

"Doctors, cops, bus drivers —"

"Yeah, yeah, yeah," Raymond intoned, cutting him off. "Just keep watching him. Let me know if you need more *resources.*"

"I'm good for now," Donald replied.

He ended the call, pushing the cell phone into the pocket of his down-filled jacket. Blowing on his hands, he rubbed them together to generate heat. He'd forgotten his gloves — again. Standing and pushing his stiff fingers into the pockets of the baggy wide wale corduroy, he waited for the traffic light to change before crossing the street to wait for the bus to take him back uptown.

Jordan drove along Adam Clayton Powell Jr Boulevard, then turned on 121st Street. If he hadn't called the garage to have his car ready, he would've either walked or taken a taxi to the office. Walking from 98th and Fifth to 121st Street was a workout.

Three boyhood friends who'd pooled their resources to purchase the three-story brownstone had set up their practices on each floor. Kyle Chatham, his former mentor and senior law partner, occupied the second floor. Financial planner Duncan Gilmore's offices spanned the first floor, and psychotherapist Dr. Ivan Campbell counseled patients on the third floor of the nineteenth-century landmark structure that had been renovated for business use.

Miraculously, he found a parking space, maneuvering up to the tree-lined curb. He got out, locked the door and bounded up the staircase to the front door. Brass plates affixed to the side of the building indicated the location of each business.

Jordan unlocked the front door and punched in the code to disarm the security system. He reset it and walked past the elevator in the entryway and into the reception area furnished with comfortable leather seating, a wall-mounted flat-screen television and potted plants. Whenever the office was open during the winter months, a fire roared in the huge fireplace.

The soles of his shoes made soft squishing sounds on the marble floor when he made his way to the staircase. It wasn't until he'd exited the last stair that he was aware he wasn't the only one in the building. The sound of music floated down the hallway from the conference room.

Walking past his office, he stopped at the open door. Kyle Chatham sat at the conference table amid stacks of law books and legal pads. A pullover sweater, jeans and boots replaced his tailored suits.

"Happy New Year, Chat."

Kyle's head popped up, his eyes growing wider when he saw Jordan standing in the doorway. "Happy New Year to you, too. What the hell are you doing here?" It wasn't often that he saw Jordan unshaven. "You look a little green around the gills."

"Champagne and shots are a lethal combination."

"What's up with the frat boy antics?"

Jordan shook his head. "Don't ask."

"But I am asking, partner. I don't remember ever seeing you overindulge."

Crossing his arms over his chest, Jordan angled his head. His partner and former mentor was quintessentially tall, dark and handsome. Women were drawn to his angular face with chiseled cheekbones, deep-set, slanting, catlike, warm brown eyes and close-cropped black hair with a sprinkling of gray. He and his fiancée, Ava Warrick, were to be married in Puerto Rico the next month.

"Brandt and some of his boys started challenging one another, so I had to get my cousin's back."

"That's when you should've bailed, Jordan. You know you can't hang with those guys. They're twice your size and have hollow legs."

"I discovered that when I woke up this morning."

"Why, then, are you here instead of sleeping it off?" Kyle asked.

"I came to look up some decisions on workplace harassment for a friend." His cousin had given him Aziza's address and phone number. He planned to call her later that evening and confirm a time for his arrival. "Why are you here instead of home with your beautiful fiancée?"

Kyle massaged his forehead with his fingers as he stared at his junior partner. He and Jordan had worked together at Trilling, Carlyle and Browne where he'd become the younger man's mentor.

"I wanted to go over some details on this attempted rape case that has been literally kicking my behind. I should've passed on this one, but I couldn't leave this kid's fate in the hands of a public defender who will probably get him to take a plea where he will spend the next eight to ten years of his life behind bars."

Slipping out of his jacket, Jordan entered the room and draped it over the back of a chair and sat down. "You took on the case because the kid is innocent."

Kyle ran a hand over his face. "But it all comes down to 'he said, she said.' "

Kyle leaned forward. "If he puts her on the stand and she breaks down, then our client's fate is sealed and he's going to go away for a long time. His mother didn't sacrifice working two jobs to send her son to college to have him become a felon."

Jordan continued to peruse the file. When Kyle had set up K.E. Chatham Legal Services, he'd established a routine of Monday-morning staff meetings where open cases were reviewed and updated. But since he'd made partner, Jordan and Kyle alternated chairing the meetings.

"This case is not about rape, Chat."

Slumping back in his chair, Kyle stared across the table at his partner. "You tell me what it's about."

Nothing on Kyle Chatham moved, not his eyes, not his chest when he held his breath. He'd questioned himself when Jordan had come to him asking to join his firm. What he couldn't fathom was why a Harvard-educated lawyer from one of New York City's wealthiest families had resigned positions with his family real estate empire and a Park Avenue law firm to work in Harlem. Their clients weren't remotely close to the well-heeled corporations they'd represented in the past.

"Talk to me, Wainwright."

Jordan smiled for the first time since he'd woken up earlier that morning with a pounding headache. "They're together as long as they're students, but after graduation she expected to become Mrs. Robinson Fields. The script is flipped when he tells her that he's moving on and dating someone else."

Pushing back his chair, Jordan stood. "On that note I think I'd better leave."

"How long are you going to hang out here?"

Jordan shrugged broad shoulders. "I don't know. Why?"

"Just asking."

"If I don't see you before you leave, then I'll see you Monday morning."

He hadn't lied to Kyle. He didn't know how long he would be at the office when it came to researching cases. When he'd worked for Trilling, Carlyle and Browne, he had been second chair with two harassment cases, while workplace harassment at Wainwright Developers hadn't been an issue. Wyatt Wainwright may have ruled his company with an iron fist, but he'd always generously compensated his employees for their hard work.

Jordan walked into his office, touching the wall switch and flooding the space with light. Tossing his jacket on a leather chair, he rounded his desk and sat down. His personal secretary had stacked files on a side table for the Monday-morning staff meeting.

Picking up a remote device, he pressed a button and music flowed from the speakers of a stereo unit concealed behind the doors in the mahogany armoire that matched the desk and tables. The melodious strains of a violin filled the office.

Jordan switched on his computer, and while waiting for it to boot, his cell phone rang. He answered it without looking at the display. "This is Jordan."

"Jordan, Aziza."

His heartbeat kicked into a higher gear when her sultry voice came through the earpiece. He knew the only way she could've gotten his cell number was if Brandt had given it to her. "What's up, Zee?"

"I hate to ask you to do this, but is it possible for us to meet today?"

He hesitated for a few seconds. "Sure. Um . . ."

"I just got a call from a client that her teenage son was arrested for a DUI. They're not going to release him until he's arraigned on Monday, so I want to meet with her Saturday to let her know what to expect."

"No problem, Aziza. I'm on my way."

Jordan ended the call. He reversed his actions when he turned off the stereo, computer, retrieved his jacket and turned out the lights. Half an hour after walking into the offices of Chatham and Wainwright, he was back in his car, leaving Manhattan for Westchester County.

CHAPTER 5

Aziza chided herself for asking Jordan to drive to Bronxville when she read the crawl along the bottom of the television screen. A winter weather alert was in effect for the tristate area. The day before, temperatures had been in the upper 40s, and within twenty-four hours it was now in the mid-twenties with a forecast of sleet and, in some of the northern counties, snow.

It had been an hour since she'd called him, and during that time rain had changed over to sleet, and now it was snowing — heavily. Maybe, she thought, he'd changed his mind about driving up once he'd seen the weather forecast. She picked the receiver off the cradle in the kitchen and hit redial. It rang three times before his sonorous voice filled her ear.

"This is Jordan."

She smiled. "And this is Aziza. I'm calling to tell you that if you haven't left the city, then don't. It's snowing like crazy up here."

A deep chuckle caressed her ear. "It's too late. I'm pulling into your driveway as we speak."

Her stomach did a flip-flop. "Don't turn off your car. I'm going to raise the garage door so you can park inside." She hung up, walked over to the door that led to an attached garage and pressed a button. The automatic door slid up and a racy sports car maneuvered next to her late-model Nissan SUV.

Aziza wasn't aware of how fast her heart was beating until she saw Jordan Wainwright emerge from his car. She'd spent all day trying to remember what he'd actually looked like. It was one thing to observe a person one-on-one, and another when they were around the other people. Even sitting with him in Brandt's library had proven to be a distraction, because at any time someone could've walked in. What she hadn't forgotten were his eyes. They were dazzling.

"Where's your coat?" she asked, stepping back when he walked into the kitchen.

Jordan smiled. "It's in the car." Leaning over, he kissed her cheek. "How are you?" His eyes swept over her. Aziza Fleming was a chameleon.

The night before she had been a sexy siren

in a revealing dress and stilettos, and today she'd morphed into the girl next door in a pair of fitted jeans that showcased the womanly curves of her body, long-sleeve tee and black suede ballet-flats shoes. A few wisps had escaped from her dark hair that she'd pinned up off her neck.

Aziza inhaled his warmth and the lingering fragrance of a man's cologne that was as bold and dramatic as the man standing in her kitchen. Jordan Wainwright appeared taller and larger than he had the night before. His tailored attire had artfully concealed a toned body that was incongruous with someone who spent hours sitting behind a desk. He hadn't shaved, and the stubble on his lean jaw enhanced rather than detracted from his patrician face. In fact, she liked seeing him in jeans and a shirt, because it made him look less formal.

"I'm good. I'm sorry you had to drive up here in the snow."

He waved a hand. "I learned to drive in snow after living in New England for seven years." Raising his chin, he sniffed the air like a large cat. "Something smells good."

Slipping her hand in his, Aziza steered Jordan over to a table in a corner of the large eat-in kitchen. "It's roast chicken. I decided to cook today because I'll be tied up tomorrow. I'm forgetting my manners. Would you like something to drink?"

Jordan was going to tell her coffee, but he'd already exceeded his normal two cups trying to counter the effects of the tequila shots he'd downed at the party.

"I'll have tea with lemon."

Aziza peered closely at him. "Are you feeling all right?"

"Sure," he said much too quickly. "Why would you ask that?"

"You look a little queasy."

Jordan swallowed. Kyle had mentioned he looked a "little green around the gills." Did he really look that hungover? "I'm afraid I did overindulge last night," he admitted.

"You seemed okay when I left."

He closed his eyes. "It was *after* you left that I got into a competition where the guys were doing shots."

"That's frat boy craziness," she spat out.

"You sound like my law partner."

"Then he must be a very wise man," Aziza countered.

"I'll tell him you said that when I see him again."

She rolled her eyes at him. "Come with me." Jordan stood up, and again she took his hand. "You can relax on the back porch while I make your tea."

104

"You have a nice house." The white and stainless-steel kitchen in the large well-maintained Dutch Colonial was modern and functional.

Aziza gave him a sidelong glance, smiling. "Thank you."

Jordan shortened his stride to accommodate her shorter legs. "How long have you lived here?"

"It will be three years in June."

"Did you live here with your husband?"

"No," she snapped in a harsher tone than she'd intended. "We'd shared a condo in New Rochelle." Her tone was softer, conciliatory.

Jordan felt the return of the throbbing in his temples. His headache was coming back. It was as if he hadn't learned anything in twenty years. Raiding the liquor cabinet at fourteen should've taught him a life lesson, but in a moment of recklessness he'd allowed himself to be pulled into a silly adolescent game of downing shots of liquor.

And Kyle was right when he'd mentioned football players weighing more than he did, and therefore able to consume a lot more alcohol than he could before exceeding the limit for intoxication.

"This is very nice," Jordan drawled when he entered the enclosed back porch made entirely of glass. A fire burning brightly behind a decorative screen and lighted candles along the mantelpiece created an atmosphere of total relaxation. Potted plants and ferns in decorative planters, dimmed recessed lights, chairs with matching footstools, a love seat and a sofa with overstuffed cushions were positioned to take advantage of the wall-mounted, flat-screen television. Soft jazz flowed from speakers of a home theater system.

He released her hand, walking over to stare out the wall of glass. The patio was covered with snow, and with the waning daylight, it wasn't possible to see what lay beyond the patio. "How close is your nearest neighbor?"

Aziza came over to stand beside Jordan. "The house behind mine is about two hundred feet away. Whenever I want complete privacy I pull the shades. Watch," she said, picking up a remote device. Within seconds sheer shades were lowered over the wall of glass. "I can see out, but they can't see in."

Jordan smiled at her. "Clever."

She returned his smile. "Relax, Jordan, and I'll bring you your tea."

"Do you mind if I turn on your TV?"

"Of course not. Please make yourself at home."

"You may come to regret that offer."

"I doubt that," Aziza countered.

Jordan offering to help her in building a case to sue her former employer was nothing short of a minor miracle. She would be the first to admit Jordan Wainwright breaking with his grandfather was definitely unorthodox. There weren't too many lawyers willing to do what he had done, but the action revealed something about him that would have taken her time to discern: he was his own man.

She returned to the kitchen, filling an electric kettle with water and switching it on. The savory aroma of herb-encrusted roast chicken wafted throughout the kitchen when she opened the door to the eye-level oven to test the bird for doneness. She'd put it in before calling Jordan, cooking it at a lower temperature than usual, because she wasn't certain whether she would reach him, or he would agree to come.

Aziza had grown up believing Sunday dinner wasn't dinner if chicken wasn't on the menu. It could've been fried, fricasseed, baked, stewed or broiled. It had to be chicken. And if there were leftovers, then there was chicken salad and/or soup. Her mother would tease her, saying she was going to grow a beak, sprout wings and start clucking if she didn't stop eating so much chicken. It hadn't happened, and old habits were hard to break.

She switched on the counter television to the Weather Channel. A map of the tristate area showed areas of projected snowfall accumulation. It was predicted Westchester and Orange Counties would get up to a foot of snow.

"Damn!"

"What are you damning about?"

She turned to find Jordan standing in the middle of the kitchen in his sock-covered feet. "I should've never asked you to drive up here."

"Why? Did you change your mind about my helping you?" he asked, coming closer.

"No. I still need you to help me."

"What's the problem then?"

"The weather."

Closing the distance between them, Jordan stood less than a foot from Aziza. Without warning, as if changing before his eyes, she appeared incredibly delicate, vulnerable, and he wondered if the man who'd sexually harassed her had ruined her for any man who'd express an interest in her.

"What about the weather, Aziza?"

"You may . . . you may not be able to drive back home tonight." Why, Aziza asked herself, was she stammering like a tongue-tied girl when running headlong into a boy she liked? She turned back to stare at the flickering images on the television screen. "Meteorologists are predicting a foot or more of snow before it tapers off tomorrow morning."

Taking a step, Jordan stood behind Aziza, his breath sweeping over the nape of her neck. "I have two options."

"What are they?" Her voice was low, breathless, as if she'd run a grueling race.

"I can drink my tea, leave and check into a nearby hotel or motel until the roads clear."

"Or?"

He smiled. "I can drink my tea, have dinner with you, we discuss your case, then I bed down in one of your guest bedrooms until the roads clear. Which door do I pick, Miss Fleming? Number one? Or number two?"

An expression of amusement found its way across Aziza's face as she pondered Jordan's query. "You are really slick, aren't you?"

"Isn't the term *slick* passé?"

109

"What would you prefer I call you?"

Lowering his head, Jordan pressed his mouth to the side of her neck. "You can call me whatever you want. Just answer the question, Zee. Door number one, or door number two?"

The seconds ticked off, the lighted button on the handle of the electric kettle dimmed and the bubbles in the heated water disappeared before Aziza answered, "Door number two."

Jordan's gaze lingered on the skin on the back of Aziza's neck, then moved lower to her back and to where the denim fabric hugged her rounded hips. "I'm going to get my bag."

Bag! "What bag!" The two words exploded off her tongue.

Resting his hands on her shoulders, Jordan shifted Aziza to face him, his gaze going to her sexy chin. "I always carry a change of clothes in the trunk of my car."

"Why?"

"It's a Wainwright tradition that goes back to my grandfather and his brothers. They never went anywhere without a bag with several changes of clean underwear and grooming supplies. If you were to look in the cargo area of Brandt's truck you'd find the requisite Wainwright man bag." Realization dawned when Aziza exhaled a breath. "I hope you didn't think I came here to get into your panties. Did you?" he asked when she averted her eyes. "What kind of pigs have you been dealing with?"

The pain and rage Aziza had suppressed for far too long surfaced, overflowing like molten lava. "A pig I'd loved all my life, but after he'd put a ring on my finger he also wanted to put one in my nose. Then there was the other pig who hired me before I graduated law school, paid off my student loans, offered me a salary that far exceeded my experience, then sprang the trap when he expected me to lie down and spread my legs to show my gratitude."

Jordan met her eyes. "Did you tell your husband about him?"

She emitted an unladylike snort. "I did."

"What did he do?"

"It's not what he did, but what he'd said to me. *If you didn't dress like a whore, then he wouldn't treat you like a whore.* I was too shocked to think of a comeback, so I went into the bedroom, packed my clothes, throwing suitcases in my car. Whatever I couldn't take, I left. A week later I served him with divorce papers."

Jordan tried processing what he'd just heard. Husbands were supposed to protect their wives from predators, not make them targets. No wonder she wasn't sorry she'd ended her marriage.

His respect for Aziza had gone up several rungs. She was a scrapper, unwilling to play the victim for her husband *and* employer. "What did your brother say when you told him about your ex?"

"I have three brothers and I never told any of them about what went on between me and Lamar. If they'd known they would've invited him to a blanket party."

He looked confused. "What's a blanket party?"

Aziza laughed when she saw Jordan's blank expression. "A blanket party is when you throw a blanket over someone's head, then beat the hell out of him."

Throwing back his head, Jordan laughed loudly. "I see," he drawled once he recovered from his laughing jag.

"No, you won't see," she teased, "because you'll be so lumped up you'll be lucky if you can see to make an escape."

He sobered. "I have a sister, and if some dude decides to lose his mind and hurt her, then he'd better make funeral arrangements."

"How old is she?"

"Sixteen."

"Is she dating?"

"No. She's not allowed to have a boyfriend until she's a senior. She tells everyone she's on lockdown, because most of the girls at her school are dating."

"Tell her to take her time. Men are like trains. There's always one leaving the station."

Jordan smiled, attractive lines fanning out around his eyes. "I'm sure she doesn't want to hear that."

Aziza returned her attention to the kettle. "The water cooled while we've been talking."

Jordan leaned a hip against the granite countertop, watching Aziza as she took a cup and matching saucer from a cupboard. Working quickly, efficiently, she placed two teabags in a hand-painted teapot and filled it with hot water.

"Are you going to have a cup with me?" he asked.

"No. I usually have a cup before going to bed at night. Chamomile. It helps me to sleep."

Tilting her chin, Aziza studied her house-guest's face. A hint of laughter played at the corners of his strong, sexy mouth. And despite her silent protests to the contrary or her denial of not wanting or needing a man, she wanted to feel the pressure of Jordan's mouth on hers — again. She glanced downward, the demure gesture enchanting and mesmerizing.

Walking to the refrigerator, she took out a container with fresh lemon slices, feeling the heat from his gaze following her every move. "Would you like sugar or honey?"

"Honey, please." They shared a smile.

"Why," Jordan asked, "when you make a cup of tea, it becomes a ritual! You remind me of a geisha at a tea ceremony. I'm willing to wager you set the table even when dining alone."

Using a tiny silver fork, Aziza placed several lemon slices on a small dish. "Didn't you get enough of wagering earlier today when downing shots?"

"No, because wagering with you will be a lot more pleasant than with three-hundred-pound dudes with beards."

She laughed, the sound bubbling up from her throat. "You're out of luck, Jordan, because I've never been a gambler. Your tea should be steeped by now. You can take it here or on the porch."

"Will you join me on the porch?"

Aziza nodded, a sensual smile softening her mouth. "Of course. After you finish your tea, I'll show you where I meet with my

114

clients."

Jordan stood in the area outside the space where Aziza had set up her home office. Her revelation that all of her clients, with the exception of Brandt, were female was reflected in the furnishings. It wasn't a waiting room, but a parlor with creamy upholstery, pale walls and plush beige carpeting. Bleached pine tables cradled a collection of crystal candlesticks with corresponding tapers and pillars. The room was an oasis of green and flowering plants in terra-cotta and hand-painted pots. A large copper pot was stacked with wood for the working fireplace. Magazines, paperback novels and a wall-mounted television were available to her clients to enhance the room's friendly receptive atmosphere.

The furnishings in Aziza's office were a dramatic departure from those in the waiting area. Heavy mahogany furniture, leather chairs, parquet flooring, a wall of floor-to-ceiling shelves with stacks of law books and journals and an L-shaped executive desk with state-of-the art office equipment were indicators of a fully functioning law practice. One wall held diplomas, degrees and citations from local and state organizations.

"Do you have a law clerk or assistant?" he

asked her.

Pushing her hands into the pocket of her jeans, pulling the fabric taunt over her belly and hips, Aziza turned to look at Jordan. She'd tried gauging his reaction to seeing her office, but nothing in his expression revealed what he was feeling. When she'd purchased the house she'd had a contractor make major renovations: expand the attached garage to accommodate two cars, expand the front porch while putting up the addition for her office.

"No. I have four clients on retainer and I work with two real estate companies when they need a lawyer for contracts and closings." She smiled. "And before you ask — yes, I like working for myself."

"I was going to ask you if you miss working in the city."

"No." She sat down on a corner of the desk. "I grew up in New Rochelle, and for me taking the train into the city was like some people going to a foreign country. My girlfriends and I would plan our excursions meticulously in advance, so we knew exactly where we wanted to eat, where to shop and what sights to see. My parents wanted me to go to college out of the state because they felt it would make me more independent. They saw something I'd refused to see.

Lamar and I were becoming inseparable, and my dad felt I was too young to be that serious about one boy.

"In the end Daddy was right. I went to Fordham and a year later Lamar transferred from Pace University to Fordham because he claimed he missed seeing me. We graduated and went on to Fordham Law together. I was hired by a top firm, while he became a public defender. That's when our problems began, but I was too in love with him to notice the snide remarks about how women get ahead by lying on their backs. Despite all of the signs that our marriage was doomed, I still married him. My only regret is that I wasted so many years with someone whose sole intent was destroying me emotionally."

Taking two long strides, Jordan stood in front of Aziza, his arms going around her shoulders. He smiled when she rested her head on his shoulder. "But you did get out before he destroyed you." He patted her back in a comforting gesture. "Don't beat up on yourself, Zee. You're hardly alone when it comes to making bad choices in the love department."

She looked up at him. "Are you talking about yourself?"

Jordan nodded. "I had what I consider a

serious relationship. We split once we realized we were wrong for each other."

"How old are you, Jordan?"

"Thirty-three."

"You're thirty-three, single and I assume unencumbered." He nodded again. "Have you ever proposed marriage to a woman?"

"No."

"And why not?"

"Because I haven't met the woman with whom I'd want to share my life."

"Does she exist?"

"I'm sure she does."

"I felt the same way before I became Mrs. Lamar Powers. I knew I wanted to marry Lamar when our fifth-grade teacher seated us next to each other. He was the perfect boyfriend and fiancé but a lousy husband. Just make certain before you choose that special woman to become Mrs. Jordan Wainwright you look for the signs that she won't go psycho on you."

"I'll keep that in mind whenever I decide it's time for me to settle down and start a family."

Tilting her chin, Aziza saw something in Jordan's eyes that warmed her and made her feel anxious at the same time. She felt comfortable with him, almost too comfortable, given her past experience with a man

118

whom she'd loved selflessly and unconditionally. He came closer, and she knew he was going to kiss her.

"What are you doing, Jordan Wainwright?" she whispered when their mouths were only inches apart.

Jordan stared at Aziza's lush lips, feeling her moist breath on his mouth. "I'm going to kiss you, Aziza Fleming."

She needed him to kiss her because it reminded her that she was a woman with strong urges she'd denied for far too long. Lamar may have soured her on marriage, but thankfully she hadn't become a man-hater.

"Why?"

His eyebrows shot up. "I can't believe you're asking me why. Isn't it obvious?"

"Not to me," she countered breathlessly.

"I like you, Zee."

"I like you, too, but —"

He stopped her words with a soft, possessive kiss that siphoned the breath from her lungs, leaving her struggling to breathe. "You've just been overruled," he whispered against her parted lips.

Aziza's arms came up, looping around Jordan's strong neck, holding him fast as he attempted to move closer. His hands cupped her hips, he easing her between his outstretched legs, she sitting half on and half off the desk.

Somehow she found the strength to free her mouth, her chest rising and falling with her labored breathing. "Jordan!"

His splayed fingers massaged her back. "It's okay, Zee. I won't do anything you don't want me to do."

She closed her eyes. "I didn't want you to kiss me."

He smiled, staring at the dreamy expression on her beautiful face, an expression that reminded him of those on the faces of the women in the paintings of Renaissance art masters hanging in the Met.

A deep frown marred his handsome features. "If that's the case, then why did you let me kiss you?"

"I needed you to kiss me."

Jordan stared as if seeing her for the very first time. "You needed me? Why?"

"As you know, I don't date, and it has been a very long time since a man has kissed me, so why not you?"

"So," he drawled, "you see me as some kind of specimen you can put in a petri dish to see what comes of it."

"I didn't say that, Jordan."

"You didn't have to, Aziza. As an attorney you know you can say or ask the same question ten different ways, but the result will always be the same."

Her temper flared. "Don't get testy with me, Jordan, because you can't handle the truth. I like you. If I didn't, then you never would've kissed me even if you'd begged. I'm currently trying to build a case to sue a man for touching me when I'd told him not to. A man who felt so comfortable that he said things in my presence no man would have the audacity to say. A pig that used to order expensive lingerie and have it delivered to my office with a note that he would like me to model it for him. I'd asked him to stop, but he wouldn't. Then I did the unthinkable."

Jordan saw pain and grief — stark and wild — in the dark eyes brimming with unshed tears. "What was that?" His voice was low, comforting.

"I prayed something would happen to him. That he would get hit by a car or bus when crossing the street. That's when I knew I was losing it. The final straw was when I walked into my office to find him waiting for me. He handed me a small box with very pretty wrapping paper and a bow, saying it was a peace offering. I almost passed out when I opened the box."

"What was it?"

Aziza bit her lip until it throbbed like a pulse. "It was a condom."

"Why a condom?"

She swallowed in an attempt to relieve the constriction in her throat. "He told me he'd masturbated earlier that morning and before he'd ejaculated into it he'd fantasized that he was inside me."

Smothering a savage curse, Jordan caught her shoulders, his fingers tightening on her tender flesh. "You are a lawyer, Aziza." He punctuated each word. "You're trained to defend the innocent, yet you allowed yourself to be victimized by a sick son of a bitch."

Aziza pushed against his chest in an attempt to free herself, but it was like trying to move a boulder. "You think I just stood around and did nothing?"

His eyes narrowed. "What *did* you do?"

"I went to an electronics store and bought the tiniest tape recorder I could conceal on my body. I carried it with me whenever I went into the office. When I felt I had enough evidence, I handed in my resignation and a week later sued him and his firm for sexual harassment."

"What happened?"

"The D.A. refused to hear the case because he felt the tapes were used as entrapment. He claims if I'd come to his office

122

beforehand they would've authorized me wearing what would come down to a wire. A clerk in the D.A.'s office told me off the record that my boss and the D.A. went to law school together and belong to the same country club. He also has several uncles who are judges. I would've let it go, but he retaliated by refusing to give me a reference whenever I applied to another firm. That's why I decided to open my own practice."

Jordan shook his head. "It's no wonder you can't win. You're challenging the old boys' club. But there is more than one way to roast a pig without putting him on a spit."

Aziza looked confused. "You're talking in riddles."

"In some cultures people roast pigs on spits and in others they dig a pit, fill it with leaves and hot coals, then bury the pig and cover it until it's done. This is what you're going to do with your pig, Aziza. I'm going to help you bury him. By the way, does he have a name?"

"Kenneth Middleton Moore, Jr. You know him, don't you?" she asked when Jordan stiffened as if pierced by a sharp object.

"I knew his father. He was my professor. He passed away the year I graduated, and junior took over his firm. I'm willing to bet he had no idea that his boy was acting a fool. You're probably not the first woman Kenny has harassed and you won't be the last. Do you still have the tapes and the condom?"

"Yes."

"Where?"

"They're in a safe deposit box in my bank. But I do have an extra copy of the tapes here in the office."

Jordan kissed her forehead. "That's my girl. I'm not going to map out a strategy until after I hear what's on those tapes."

"Do you think we can get him, Jordan?"

"We're going to get him, Zee. We're just going to have to find the loopholes we need to bring him down."

Wrapping her arms around his waist, Aziza closed her eyes and whispered a silent prayer of thanks that Jordan Wainwright had agreed to help her stop Kenneth Moore before he victimized another woman. "I'll get the tapes for you." Jordan took a step backward and she unlocked the drawer in the desk, handing him an envelope with two minute cassettes. "Do you think your stomach will tolerate food now?"

"I thought you'd never ask. I'm starved," Jordan admitted.

Leaning into him, she kissed his stubbly chin. "Let's eat."

CHAPTER 6

Sharing dinner with Jordan felt like a date to Aziza. She'd set the table in the kitchen's dining alcove, tuned the satellite radio to a station featuring music from the 80s and 90s, and the scented votives lining the countertops created a peaceful effect when she'd turned off the lights, leaving on the hanging fixture over the table.

She hadn't lied when she'd admitted to Jordan that she liked him. In fact, she liked everything about him from his cropped raven hair, lean face, strong chin and sexy mouth to his tall, muscular lean body. Whether categorized as *fine, hot* or just plain old *sexy,* it was impossible for any normal woman to ignore him.

Was he a little arrogant?

Yes.

Brash?

Undeniably.

Confident?

Unequivocally yes.

However, as a Wainwright he had the right to be arrogant, brash *and* confident. He was a member of one of New York's most powerful and wealthy families. Even if he wasn't a Wainwright, those were necessary personality traits for a successful litigator. He hadn't given her a hint as to how he would go after Kenneth Moore, but Aziza knew he was her last resort. She'd tried contacting women who still worked at the firm to find out if they were being harassed, but they hadn't returned her phone calls.

Dinner had turned out well. The first course was a mixed citrus salad with red onions and escarole, of which Jordan had two servings. She'd added a glaze to the chicken just before removing it from the roasting pan to let it rest so the juices could flow through it. Tiny roasted red potatoes had picked up the piquant spices infused in the chicken, and wilted spinach with olive oil and garlic complemented the main dish. Keeping in mind that Jordan was still recovering from too much holiday libation, she'd blended ruby-red grapefruit punch with a piña colada mix, the pale pink fruity concoction making her yearn for the tropics.

She smiled when Jordan took a second

helping of everything. It was apparent he had a very healthy appetite. "Do you work out?"

Jordan swallowed a piece of chicken so tender it melted in his mouth. "All the time. There's a health club in my apartment building and one in the brownstone for employees."

"How much do you weigh?"

"Take a guess."

"One ninety-five."

He made a buzzing sound. "Wrong. Guess again."

"Higher or lower?"

"I'm not telling," he teased.

Pushing back her chair, Aziza stood up. "Stand up."

Jordan complied, standing and grinning. He knew what she was up to. "You can look, but not touch."

Aziza pushed out her lip, pouting. "That's not fair. Whenever I go to the store to buy a melon I have to touch it to ascertain its weight."

"Ascertain," he whispered, mocking her. "Okay, baby. You can examine the goods."

Moving closer, she ran her fingertips over his shoulders and down his chest, Jordan sucking in his breath. "Two-ten."

"You're good, counselor."

She bowed low. "Thank you, counselor."

The light, teasing mood continued as they cleared the table, loaded the dishwasher and put away leftovers. The votives were sputtering and burning out when Jordan, having retrieved his overnight bag from the trunk of his car, followed Aziza up the staircase to the second floor.

"This is your bedroom," she said, pushing open a door and touching a wall switch. "It has an en suite bath. Everything you need is in a cupboard in the bathroom — towels, soap, toothbrush and paste. If you need me to wash anything, leave it on the floor outside the door."

Jordan's mouth was smiling, but not his eyes. He'd spent more time with Alexander Fleming's sister than he'd planned, and the weather had cooperated to permit him more time with her. He didn't know what it was about her, but he'd felt an immediate and almost total attraction to Aziza. This was something that hadn't occurred with any other women he'd met or been involved with.

"Thank you, but I have everything I need."

Aziza stared at the middle of his broad chest. "I know we haven't talked about it, but I need to know how much you're going to bill me for your services."

Jordan clenched his teeth to keep from spewing curses he was certain would shock Aziza; acerbic, vitriolic curses he'd learned and that were very much a part of his grandfather's colorful vocabulary. "Did I say I was going to bill you?"

"No, but —"

"But nothing," he interrupted. "Your brother happens to be not only my cousin's teammate but also his best friend. And when friends ask for a favor they shouldn't have to pay for it."

"I'm not your friend, Jordan."

"If I'm not your friend, then what am I? I can't be your lover because I make it a practice not to sleep with a woman until I've dated her for at least a month. And you don't date."

Pinpoints of heat dotted Aziza's face. "You're right."

Jordan leaned closer. "I'm right about what, Zee?" There was a hint of laughter in his voice.

"You're my friend."

"Good. Now that we've settled that I'll let you know how you can repay me."

She balled her hands into fists in frustration. "But . . . but I thought you said friends don't pay friends for —"

"Hold up, baby. Don't go off on me until

129

you hear what I'm proposing."

Crossing her arms under her breasts, Aziza glared at Jordan. His flip-flopping as to their relationship was becoming more confusing with each passing second. "What?"

"I'll accept a hug, a kiss and an occasional dinner and brunch meeting to discuss your case."

Her jaw dropped. "That's it?"

"That's it?" he repeated. "If you want more, then we can always throw a little sex in the mix, because I know it's been longer for you than it has been for me."

Aziza's mouth opened and closed several times, then she said, "Good night, Jordan."

Throwing back his head, Jordan laughed, the rich warm sound filling the hallway. He realized Aziza wasn't expecting his comeback. He hadn't lied to her when he'd said he did not sleep with a woman until they'd dated a month. That time frame allowed him to ascertain whether he wanted to take their relationship to another level or end it amicably. Sleeping with a woman translated not only into a physical commitment but also an emotional one — something he did not take lightly.

"Good night, Zee."

Turning on her heels, Aziza walked to her

bedroom and closed the door. She sat on the padded bench at the foot of the bed, closing her eyes. She'd told Jordan things she'd held close to her heart. When Alexander had initially asked why she'd resigned her position, her response to him had been she didn't get along with her boss.

However, when she realized Kenneth Moore had set out to sabotage her career, she'd told Alexander of her intent to sue her former boss and his firm. Her brother had said he was willing to wait for her to go the legal route to seek justice, but if justice proved not to be impartial or blind, then he was going to rain holy hell down on Kenneth Moore.

Aziza had also made Alexander promise not to tell their parents or their brothers about her legal dilemma. After her beloved Nana passed away her parents had sold their house in New Rochelle and moved to a gated retirement community in central Florida. Her older brothers had attended college in California and Arizona respectively, electing after graduating to put down roots in the western states. To embroil the Flemings in something which should've never occurred was certain disaster.

She opened her eyes, her delicate jaw tightening when she recalled Jordan chastising her for permitting the harassment to continue. What he would uncover, once he listened to the tapes, was the time frame.

Her dark mood lifted like quicksilver, the beginnings of a smile tilting the corners of her mouth when she recalled his method of payment: a kiss, hug, dinner and brunch. What he wanted was more than doable.

The clock on the mantelpiece chimed the hour. It was ten o'clock. She would take a leisurely bath, brew a cup of tea, then crawl into bed and read until falling asleep. That had become her nightly ritual for the past two years.

Ribbons of sunlight slipped through the partially closed drapes in Aziza's bedroom. Swinging her legs over the side of the bed, she walked on bare feet over to the window. Wet heavy snow lay on shrubs and grassy surfaces, but it was melting quickly on sidewalks and the macadam. It was an indication the mercury was above freezing, and she would be able to meet with her client. Thinking of her client reminded her of the man sleeping in her guestroom. Normally she would've lingered in bed, but not this morning.

Making her way to the en suite bath, she completed her morning ablution in half the time it normally would've taken her. Dressed in a pair of sweats and running shoes, she walked out of her bedroom. She hadn't taken more than a dozen steps when she saw it. There was sheet of paper on the floor outside the room where Jordan had spent the night. Leaning over, she picked it up, reading the bold scrawl: *Thank you for your hospitality. Had to leave early. Need to go into the office. Will call you after I listen to the tapes. Your friend, JWW.*

For some reason Aziza felt let down. She'd wanted to see him before he left. Folding the single sheet of paper in half, then in half again, she left it on the side table in the hallway. Skipping down the staircase, she made her way across the living room, opened the front door and stepped out onto the front porch. The sounds of snow blowers and shoveling created a cacophony that shattered what would normally be Saturday-morning silence. Her neighbor was calling to her teenage son to come and shovel out her car so she could go to the store.

"Good morning, Aziza."

She waved to the schoolteacher, Julie, who complained constantly about her son. Julie had to threaten her son before he would help out around the house. Many of the chores her husband used to do before he was deployed were now the responsibility of the teenage boy.

"Good morning, Julie.

Pulling a sweater tighter around her body and walking to the end of her porch, Julie Rennick shook her head in exasperation. "That boy isn't worth the money it takes to feed him or shoe him. All he wants to do is sit in front of a computer and play video games." A rush of color suffused her normally pale face. "It's all going to come to a crashing halt when his father comes home."

Aziza knew her neighbor was in a constant state of apprehension because her career officer husband was on his second tour of duty in the Middle East. Julie and Francis Rennick had been the first people to welcome her to the neighborhood within days of her moving in.

"Have you had your coffee?" she asked Julie.

Julie shook her head. "Not yet. I've been trying to get my lazy son out of bed."

"I'm going to put up a pot and make breakfast. I'd appreciate some company."

Aziza knew Julie was lonely and at her wits end when it came to her son, so to give her a respite, Aziza invited the woman to join her on an occasional shopping spree and out to the movies. They'd gone to see *Twi-*

light and *New Moon* together, gasping and sighing along with the other adolescent girls crowding the theater when Edward or Jacob appeared on the screen. They had been thirty-something women who'd reverted to screaming, hysterical teenagers.

Julie smiled. "I'll be over as soon as I change out of my slippers. Lucky for you your friend shoveled your drive and walkway."

Aziza froze. "My friend?"

"Don't tell me you didn't know the delicious-looking man."

Suddenly it dawned on her that it hadn't been the landscape company who maintained her lawn during the spring and summer and removed snow during the winter months, but Jordan who'd shoveled out her driveway, sidewalk and the path leading to the house. Of course he'd had to shovel the driveway if he'd wanted to drive his car out, but he didn't have to do the street.

"Yes, I know him," Aziza admitted. "Come on over when you're ready. I'll leave the door unlocked." Stepping off the porch, she closed the door, leaving it slightly ajar.

She was surprised she hadn't heard Jordan shoveling because her bedroom looked out over the front of the house. She would thank him when she spoke to him again.

135

■ ■ ■ ■

Aziza handed her client's mother a box of tissues, waiting for the single mother to compose herself. She'd changed out of the sweats into a pair of black wool slacks, a white tailored blouse and low-heel black patent leather pumps. With her hair fashioned into a sleek chignon and a light cover of makeup, she had morphed into her attorney mode. And despite working from home, she always felt the need to appear professional.

"Do you really think they're going to put him in jail this time?" Benita White sniffled.

"I'm not certain, Ms. White. This is your son's second offense, so the judge may decide to go hard on him. But if you tell me that he has a substance abuse problem, then I'm going to ask that he be mandated to go into treatment."

Red-rimmed eyes widened. "I don't understand."

"Are you aware your son has a drug problem if he smokes marijuana every day?"

She sniffled again. "It's only a little weed. I smoked weed. His father smoked weed and we never went to jail."

Aziza stared at a spot over Benita White's

shoulder rather than glaring at a mother who was in complete denial when it came to her precious baby boy.

"Ms. White, I'm not going to sugarcoat it. Your seventeen-year-old son is going to serve time if you don't acknowledge that he has a problem and he needs to go into treatment. *Weed* is illegal, and getting behind the wheel of a car after smoking weed is a lethal combination. What if he got into an accident and killed someone? Would you say to the family of the victims that it was only weed?

"You were referred to me because you believe I can keep your son from going to jail." Aziza paused, watching for a reaction from the woman with flawless dark skin who'd become a mother much too young, and believed because she and her boyfriend had gotten high that it was all right for their son to get high. "If you believe that, then you're wrong, because I'm not going to defend someone who is a potential menace. I would never, ever live with myself if I get him off, and then he goes out and kills someone because he's under the influence. I'm very sorry. You're going to have to look for another attorney because I will not walk into that courtroom and lie so he can get high again." She stood up, extending her hand. "Good luck."

Benita twisted the tissue around her finger, shredding it, the pieces falling like confetti in her lap. "If my son does go to jail, how much time do you think he'll get?"

Aziza lifted her eyebrows, unable to fathom how a mother would consider incarceration for her child rather treating his obvious drug problem. "Probably anywhere between three and six months. It all depends on the judge. I've known judges to give longer sentences if only to send a message. Six months is a long time for a teenage boy to be locked away from his family and friends."

"Okay, Ms. Fleming. He'll go into treatment."

"It's just not *you* saying he'll agree to go into treatment. He has to agree to go. And if he skips his meetings or comes up with dirty urine, then Probation is going to violate him and he will be locked up. Do you understand what I'm saying?"

Benita nodded, rising. "I understand."

Aziza escorted her to the door, promising to meet her at the courthouse on Monday morning. It wasn't until Benita White drove away that she realized the woman might still be using. If that was the case, then mother and son needed outpatient treatment.

Turning off the light in the office, she opened the door leading into the main house. The temperature had climbed into the forties again, and clumps of snow fell from trees and rooftops. Aziza knew she had to hurry and change into something comfortable, or she would miss the beginning of the game. Her brother's team had made the play-offs for the second consecutive year. They'd lost the Super Bowl the previous year by a single point. They'd vowed it would not happen again.

CHAPTER 7

"When are you guys going home? It's after ten."

Jordan and Kyle glanced up from the files spread out on the conference table. The rape case was pushed up on the docket, and Jordan had two days to prepare his defense.

Kyle glanced at his watch, wincing. He hadn't realized it was that late. He exchanged a glance with Jordan. "We're almost finished."

Dr. Ivan Campbell walked into the conference room, flashing a rare smile. A dark gray tailored suit artfully concealed the solid bulk in his tall, muscular body. If it had been summer, then he would've worn his favored colorful tropical print shirts over a pair of slacks or jeans. Ruggedly handsome with a distinctive widow's peak, Ivan had been the last of the trio to commit and the first to marry. He'd preempted Kyle and Duncan when he and his photographer girlfriend had a Christmas wedding after a whirlwind romance that had shocked family and friends.

Reaching into the pocket of his suit jacket, Ivan removed two tickets. His teeth shone whitely in his mocha face when he placed them on the table. "I think you gentlemen would be interested in these."

"Hot damn!" Jordan shouted.

"Super Bowl tickets!" Kyle crowed loudly.

Ivan crossed his arms over the front of his chest, the light glinting off the gold band on his left hand. "Didn't I tell you that I'd come through?"

"Did you get one for DG?" Kyle asked.

"Yo, man. If I didn't get a ticket for Duncan, do you think I'd be standing here? The number man does have a dark side."

Jordan waved his ticket. "L.A., here we come."

"I'm so ready for a little R & R," Ivan admitted. "There're times when I feel as crazy as some of my patients."

"Yeah, right," Kyle drawled. "Now, you know we're not going to rest or relax."

Jordan slipped the ticket into the pocket of his shirt. "You know we're going to have to leave a few days before the game to recover from jet lag."

Ivan gave Jordan a layered look. "Keep

141

running off at the mouth, Jordan. You're the only single dude here."

"Hey. I'm still single," Kyle chimed up. "At least until next month."

It was Jordan's turn to look at Kyle. "Keep talking, buddy. Ivan's right. I'm the only single dude in the bunch. You're getting married next month, and Duncan and Tamara in June, so you're really not single."

"Speaking of couples. Nayo and I are giving a little get-together this coming weekend," Ivan announced. "It will be our first soiree as a married couple. DG said Tamara switched her shift with another doctor, so they're coming."

Kyle nodded. "I think I can answer for Ava. Count us in."

"Wainwright?"

Jordan gave Ivan a steady stare. There had never been a time when Kyle, Ivan and Duncan hadn't included him when they gathered at one another's house to watch a sporting event. He'd surprised the longtime friends when he'd presented them with tickets to the last World Series. He'd had to endure the wrath of their women when they'd attended all seven games, but all in all, it had been worth it.

"Count me in, too."

Ivan smiled again. "Good. It will be

Saturday at my place. Cocktails at seven. Knowing Nayo, she will design invitations, so expect to see them by midweek. I'm going to leave you to your work. Good night."

Jordan waited for Ivan to leave and then said to Kyle, "Why don't you head on home to Ava? I can finish up here."

"Are you certain you can handle it?"

"Man, go home to your woman."

Kyle gave his junior partner a sidelong glance. Making Jordan a partner in the firm had turned out to be a brilliant move. Jordan went the extra mile for their clients, as if he had to prove he was completely invested in the lives of the people in the Harlem community. He treated everyone with the utmost respect, and they in turn gave him the respect he deserved.

Since the celebrated television exposé, Chatham and Wainwright had been forced to turn away clients because they were unable to give each case the undivided attention it warranted. He and Jordan had talked about bringing in a law clerk to pick up the slack but hadn't found one willing to work in Harlem.

Kyle smiled. "One of these days I'm going to tell you to go home to your woman."

"Maybe."

Kyle sobered. "What's the matter, partner?

Are you still trying to get over Natasha?"

"No. Natasha and I never pretended that what we had was going to go beyond the summer." Jordan had yet to tell Kyle that the woman with whom he'd shared a summer romance was married.

"Are you saying you're ready to move on?"

Jordan smiled. "I've moved on."

"Good for you. If you need a date for Saturday I'm certain Ava or Tamara can hook you up with one of their friends."

"Lighten up, Kyle. What makes you think I can't get a woman?"

Kyle held up a hand. "I'm not saying you can't get a woman, because I know you can. It's just that your taste in women seems different now from when we'd worked at TCB."

"How many women have you seen me with?"

Kyle's expression stilled. "Actually, not that many."

"I rest my case, counselor."

Pushing back his chair, Kyle stood up. "On that note, I'm leaving. I'm going to be in court tomorrow and you're scheduled for Wednesday, so we probably won't see each other until the end of the week."

"Good luck, and thanks for giving me what I need to keep Robinson Fields from going to jail."

"No problem, Jordan. I'll set the alarm on my way out."

Jordan knew when Kyle left he would be the only one in the building until the cleaning company arrived. His eyes were burning and he was stiff from hunching over the table reading every word in the case file, but he had to finish what he'd begun.

He'd become so engrossed in NY v. Fields that he hadn't listened to the tapes Aziza had given him. And he knew he wouldn't listen to them when he got home. He'd promised her he would help her, but that wasn't possible because he'd taken a case that was scheduled to go to trial. She'd accused him of not keeping his promises, but he'd prove her wrong.

Reaching for his cell, he scrolled through the directory and punched the button for Aziza's number. It rang two times before there was a break in the connection.

"Hello, Jordan."

He smiled. He loved hearing her voice. "How are you?"

"Delirious. I managed to keep a seventeen-year-old out of jail when I got the judge to mandate he go into an outpatient drug rehab program."

"Good for you." Jordan prayed he would

be as successful with his case. "I'm calling to ask if you're busy Saturday evening."

There was a pause. "What's happening Saturday?"

"Some friends of mine are getting together and I'd like you to come with me."

There was another pause. "Are you asking me out on a date, Jordan?"

"Yes, I am."

"You know I don't date."

"I know. But are you willing to make one exception?" Jordan could hear her soft, even breathing coming through the earpiece.

"Yes, Jordan. I'm willing to make one exception."

He blew out a breath. "Thank you. I'll pick you up at five-thirty. Barring traffic delays, that should give us enough time to make it back to the city by seven."

"What if I meet you?"

"What?"

"I'll come into the city. Just let me know where I should meet you."

"Okay. But I'll send a driver to pick you up. He can bring you to my place, and then we'll leave together."

"That sounds like a plan."

"Zee, I haven't listened to the tapes because I'm preparing to go to trial."

"Jordan, please don't stress yourself out

over them. Get to them when you can."

"Thanks, baby. I'm going to hang up, because I'm still working."

"You're still at the office?"

He nodded, and then realized she couldn't see him. "Yes. But I should finish up in about forty-five minutes to an hour."

"Weren't you the one who talked about burnout?"

"Most days I'm out of here before eight, so tonight's the exception rather than the norm. I have an attempted rape case that's going to trial Wednesday."

"Good luck."

He smiled. "Thanks." Jordan wanted to tell Aziza that his client needed all the luck he could garner. He was confident he could present enough evidence to discredit the plaintiff's charge, but no one could predict how a juror would react once he began his cross-examination.

"What time do you get in?"

"It varies. Why?"

"Just curious. By the way, I want to thank you for the caviar and shoveling the snow."

"After all, I did promise to give you the caviar. And I had to shovel the driveway to get my car out."

"FYI — I have a contract with a landscaping company for snow removal."

"Knowing that, the next time it snows I'll hang around long enough to let them do their job."

"Good night, Jordan."

"What's the matter, Zee? Does the notion of my hanging out at your place make you uncomfortable?"

"Good night, Jordan," she repeated.

He laughed softly. "Good night, Zee." Pressing a button, he ended the call. It was apparent Aziza Fleming wasn't that unaffected by him because he knew for certain that she affected him — in a good way.

Forcing his attention back to the file, he read and reread the defendant's deposition until the words were imprinted on his brain. Only then did Jordan put away the file before placing a call to a car service to pick him up in front of the brownstone to take him home.

Donald Ennis sat across from Raymond Humphries, watching his reaction to the photographs he'd given him. Raymond's head popped up.

"Who is she and what is her connection to Wainwright?"

"She's a lawyer."

"So is he," Raymond interrupted, visibly annoyed that the private investigator appeared intent on playing cat and mouse when he was expecting a television film crew to come to his offices within the hour. "What's the connection?"

Donald frowned. "Her name is Aziza Fleming. Her brother is pro football defensive tackle Alexander Fleming. She's the woman Wainwright put into the limo the night of the party. I —"

"Where does she live?" Raymond asked, again interrupting him.

"Slow your roll, Slick."

For a reason he couldn't fathom, this morning Donald enjoyed toying with Raymond Humphries. Maybe it had something to do with Robert Andrews officially announcing his candidacy to challenge a popular state senator for his seat in the upcoming election. Or maybe it was because he'd tired of Raymond's god complex. However, he would continue to play along with the megalomaniac if only to get his apartment.

Raymond's eyes narrowed. "You forget yourself, Ennis."

"And you keep forgetting that I am not your employee. I am an independent contract worker, and whether you're willing to admit it, you need me. From now on, whenever I come to you I want you to let me have my say before you start the interrogation. If there is anything you don't understand, then please wait until I'm finished and I'll answer all of your questions."

If Raymond didn't need Donald Ennis, he would've had the man physically thrown out of the building. The flipside was that the scruffy little cretin *knew* that he needed him. "Go on."

Donald felt as if he'd won a small victory. "She lives in Bronxville and has a private practice which she runs from home. Ms. Fleming is thirty-one and a divorcée with no children. Her ex-husband works as a Bronx County public defender. Yes," he said, smiling, "it appears as if the lady likes hooking up with lawyers."

He sobered quickly. "She'd worked for a Manhattan law firm for a couple of years before she quit and set up her own practice. I have someone checking why she gave up a six-figure position to run what translates into a mom-and-pop operation. It looks as if she and Wainwright are more than associates because he did spend the night at her home. My people will continue to keep tabs on Wainwright and Ms. Fleming, but I'm going to need a little extra to find out what I can on her."

"Come by tomorrow morning. Ms. Jackson will give you what you need." Raymond always paid the P.I. in cash. Checks meant a paper trail neither man wanted to be bothered with. "Thank you, Ennis."

Donald bowed his head. "You're welcome." He stood up and walked out of the office, closing the door.

Raymond stared at the photos, taken with a long-range lens, of the very attractive woman standing on her front porch. He didn't know who the people were in Ennis's employ, but they were very, very good when it came to surveillance. There came a soft rap on the door. "Come in."

Minerva Jackson stuck her head through the slight opening. "The camera crews are setting up in the large conference room."

"Is everyone here?"

"Your wife just arrived with your grandchildren. Diane and Robert are with the makeup specialist."

"Let me know when they're ready to begin."

Minerva smiled at her lover. "Okay."

The incessant ringing of the telephone jolted Jordan from a deep sleep that had been a long time coming. Reaching for the receiver of the annoying instrument on the bedside table, he mumbled a sleepy greeting.

"Turn on the television," Kyle said, his voice filled with tension. Jordan was suddenly alert. Swinging his legs over the side of the bed, he walked to the sitting area in the bedroom and flicked on the television. The grim face of the mayor, surrounded by the police, fire commissioners, head of the city council and other city officials filled the screen.

An underground explosion had shut down a large swath of downtown Manhattan. Manhole covers had become missiles, shattering windows of vehicles and buildings, including those in the Manhattan Criminal Court building. There were more explosions when flames had engulfed parked cars, hampering firefighters' efforts to contain the area. The fire commissioner took the microphone, announcing all buildings in the area affected by the explosion were evacuated and no one would be allowed to return until they were inspected and deemed structurally sound.

Jordan whistled softly. "I'm willing to bet the people who live down there had flashbacks of 9/11."

"I'm sure they did," Kyle agreed. "With the courthouse closed, the calendar will have to be revised. Take the rest of the week off and relax. You've been working nonstop since you've joined the firm."

"But —"

"But nothing, partner," Kyle said, cutting him off. "You have nothing on your schedule because you thought you were going to be in court, so I'm pulling rank and ordering you not to come into the office. I'm certain you can find something fun to do in your spare time."

Jordan knew Kyle was right. Even though the firm closed down for a week from Christmas to New Year's, he still had gone into the office. "I'll see you Saturday at Ivan's."

"Bet."

Jordan hung up, turned off the television and went back to bed. He was going to take Kyle's advice and relax.

CHAPTER 8

"Mr. Wainwright, this is Sergio. I will be there in two minutes."

Aziza opened her eyes and stared out the side window. The driver had turned down East 98th Street, slowed and double-parked beside a high-rise facing Fifth Avenue. Jordan had called earlier to say he'd listened to the tapes and they had to talk. There had been warmth in his voice when he'd asked if she'd had anything planned for the next two days. When she'd answered in the negative, he'd ordered her to pack enough clothes to last through the weekend and that he was sending a driver to bring her into Manhattan.

Aziza did not and could not fathom what he'd found on the tapes that she'd missed. Her wanting to sue Kenneth Moore wasn't about money, but stopping a predator.

She didn't need the money because she didn't live an extravagant lifestyle. She was able to pay her mortgage every month. Her vehicle was paid in full, and she had zero credit card debt.

Her hourly rate was less than what she would've charged if she'd had a practice in the city because her overhead for operating the practice was negligible. The fee she'd earned from negotiating Brandt's contract netted a six-figure commission, and Alexander had asked her to handle his contract when it came time for renewal.

What she wanted was revenge *and* retribution. Men like Kenny went through life using their power, money and influence to do whatever they wanted without a hint of a sense of right and wrong. The instant she'd given Jordan the tapes, Aziza had vowed to make it her life's crusade to make Kenneth Middleton Moore, Jr., pay for his crimes *and* his sins.

The rear door opened, startling her. Jordan had appeared like a specter. He slipped in beside her, reaching for her hand. Smiling, her eyes met and fused with his, wondering if he was as pleased to see her again as she him. They were going out to eat, then return to his apartment.

"Missed you," Jordan whispered in her ear. He took off his suit jacket, hanging it on a hanger suspended behind the front passenger seat.

A shiver shook her from the repressed passion in his voice to the warmth from his body when he pulled her close. "I've missed you, too." The admission was ripped from somewhere she hadn't known existed.

"Are you cold?"

"No," Aziza said much too quickly. It was impossible for her to be cold. She'd selected a magenta silk surplice blouse, black wool slacks and a reversible three-quarter black suede swing coat lined with sheared mink. Pink-hued pearl studs and a matching strand around her neck complemented her simple but elegant outfit.

"I like your hair." Jordan pulled a spiral curl, smiling when it sprang back like a tight spring. Her hair was her crowning glory. Full, lush and framing her face like a beautiful doll's.

Aziza gave him a sidelong glance. "Thank you."

Her favorite stylist had called earlier that morning to inform her that she had a cancellation, and if she wanted to come in to relax her roots and trim her ends she would take her. What normally would've been a twenty-minute drive was accomplished in ten. She'd missed her standing appointment six weeks ago because she'd flown down to Florida to celebrate Thanksgiving with her parents.

She silently admired his dark gray suit with a faint pinstripe. A stark white shirt, silk silver tie and black slip-ons pulled together his winning look. The scales of justice tie tack was a match for the gold cuff links in the shirt's French cuffs.

"Nice cuff links."

Jordan glanced at his wrist. "They were a gift from my dad when I graduated law school. The tie tack is from my law partner." Reaching for her hand, he laced their fingers together.

The warmth and the smooth rolling motion of the car lulled Aziza into a state of total relaxation. "Do you like working in Harlem?" she asked after a comfortable silence.

"No."

"No?"

Looking out the side window, Jordan stared at the passing landscape. "I love it. I love the neighborhood and the people. I don't know how to explain it, but working in Harlem feels like a homecoming."

Aziza laughed softly. "It could be that in a parallel universe you'd lived there."

Jordan gave her hand a gentle squeeze. "If you had the option of living or working in a parallel universe, where would you choose?"

"That's easy. It would have to be a tropical island where I'd wear a minimum amount of clothes, eat exotic foods, drink fruity concoctions and dance half-naked on the beach under the moonlight."

"Are you serious?"

"Very, very serious," she drawled.

"I can make it happen for you."

Shifting to her right, Aziza stared at Jordan, seeing an open invitation in his hazel eyes. "Talk to me, Jordan Wainwright."

"Kyle and Ava, whom you'll meet Saturday, will marry in Puerto Rico next month. I'd like you to come with me as my guest."

Aziza wanted to tell Jordan to hold up, that he was moving much too quickly, that they'd known each other barely a week. Did he believe, because he'd offered his legal services, she would agree to everything he proposed?

"I'll let you know."

"When will you let me know?"

Taking a deep breath, Aziza forced herself to relax. There was something in Jordan's tone and line of questioning that reminded her of Lamar. Whenever he asked a question he'd expected an immediate answer.

"If we're going to remain friends, then you should know I don't react well to being

158

pressured. I can't commit or give you an answer until I check my calendar."

Jordan brought her hand to his mouth, dropping a kiss on her knuckles. "I'm sorry. There're times when I can be a little too overbearing."

"A little?" she teased.

"You don't have to agree with me," he countered, smiling.

"Okay, I won't."

Jordan pressed his mouth to her fragrant curls. "You just have to have the last word, don't you?"

"That's what you get for dating a lawyer."

"Didn't you tell me you don't date?"

Aziza rolled her eyes upward. "Yes, I did. But what do you call going out to dinner together?"

"A business meeting."

"We're going to discuss business?"

"Yes."

He closed the partition, concealing the driver from view. "What are you doing, Jordan?"

Staring at Aziza under lowered lids, Jordan found himself transfixed by her stunning beauty. "We're going to discuss business."

He knew she was apprehensive about collecting evidence or finding a loophole in the law where Kenneth Moore would pay for causing her emotional pain and suffering, but it was going to take time and planning.

"I listened to the tapes. I want to cross-exam you as if you were on trial. We'll tape our sessions, then transcribe them. Once we review the transcripts, word by word, line by line, it will be up to us to find a case or cases with decisions we can use to bury the pig. It may be a lengthy process, so you need to exercise patience."

Aziza ran a finger down the length of his nose. "I promise to be very, very, very patient." She kissed his chin. "How can I thank you?"

"You already are. Didn't I tell you a hug and kiss is thanks enough?"

"But the question is when will a hug and kiss stop being enough?"

The air in the rear of the limo felt charged, electrified as if a storm — a very passionate storm — was just beyond the horizon. Aziza knew she and Jordan were playing a game, a very dangerous game wherein once they crossed the line there would be no turning back.

"I don't know, Zee. You being with me is more than I could've ever expected."

More than I'd expected. As soon as the admission had rolled off his tongue Jordan knew he'd revealed a little too much about how he felt and was beginning to feel about Aziza Fleming. He liked her. That she knew, but what she did not know was how *much* he liked her.

Kyle thought his taste in women had changed since he'd come to work in Harlem. He hadn't wanted to debate the issue with his partner. He'd always liked a particular *type* of woman. Whereas some men were attracted to a woman's overall physical appearance, it hadn't been that way with Jordan. For him it was usually her intelligence and ambition.

His relationship with a legislative assistant had begun when he'd asked her for directions during a trip to D.C. He'd driven to Washington to attend the wedding of a former law school friend and had gotten lost. Tapping his horn, he'd managed to get the attention of a young woman in the car next to his. When he'd explained his dilemma, she'd told him to follow her because she lived blocks from where the wedding was scheduled to take place.

Jordan had handed her a business card, telling her to contact him if or when she came to New York because he would take her out for a night on the town. He'd forgotten the incident until she'd called him six weeks later. She was in New York on business, and wanted him to make good on his promise to show her a good time.

Kirsten was exceptionally intelligent, ambitious and completely uninhibited. What had begun with dinner dates, Broadway plays and trips to museums escalated into a deepening relationship where Jordan had found himself inexorably in love with her. They'd alternated weekends when he would drive down to D.C. with her coming up to New York.

What had surprised Jordan was his willingness to accept a long-distance relationship. Everything had changed when his workload at TCB increased and his trips to Washington became less and less frequent. He knew their relationship had reached a point where it had to be resolved. He had asked Kirsten to move to New York, and she had refused. She didn't want to resign her position with an up-and-coming U.S. representative, and she could never see herself living in New York. Their two-year liaison had ended as smoothly as it had begun: amicably.

Jordan had waded back into the dating pool with a condition that he not sleep with a woman until they'd dated at least a month. It had worked with some women, and the others who wanted sex on the first or second date, he'd quickly relegated to his past.

Perhaps Kyle mentioning his taste in women had changed since he'd come to work in Harlem was because Natasha Parker was the first African-American he'd seen him with. What his partner hadn't and didn't know was she wasn't the first and probably wouldn't be the last. After all, he *was* a Wainwright, and like his brother Noah, he, too, liked diversity.

"Where are we going?"

Aziza's sultry voice shattered his reverie. The driver was attempting to maneuver into a lane leading to the Robert F. Kennedy Triborough Bridge.

"Long Island City. Have you ever eaten at the Water's Edge?"

"No."

He smiled. "Good. Then you're in for a real treat."

Aziza settled back to watching the passing scenery. She wasn't familiar with the restaurant, and she'd never been to Long Island City. She was born and raised in the suburbs, still lived in the suburbs, and the only borough she was familiar and completely at home with was Manhattan. Jordan mentioning eating in another borough was an indicator that she needed to get out more and that Manhattan was only one-fifth of New York City.

"Would you ever consider moving out of Manhattan?" *Now where did that question come from?* she asked herself.

Stretching out his legs, Jordan shifted into a more comfortable position. "It would depend where. If it were Long Island or Westchester, then I would consider it because I could commute directly into Manhattan by taking the Metro-North or the Long Island Railroad."

"What about the other boroughs? Just say . . . Brooklyn?"

"No."

"Why not?"

"Why leave Manhattan for Brooklyn, the Bronx or even Queens? It's almost like making a lateral move. Besides, I don't like being packed into a subway car with a thousand other people all jostling to get to work on time. And forget about standing on a corner and waiting for a bus."

"You sound like an elitist, Jordan. You live in the city, yet you eschew public transportation. How did you get to school as a kid?"

"I was driven to school."

"I know you didn't take the cheese bus because you don't do buses."

Jordan gave her a puzzled look. "What the

164

heck is a cheese bus?"

"It's what kids call a yellow school bus."

"No, I didn't take the cheese bus."

Aziza stared, speechless. Jordan had come back at her like a rabid dog, snarling and snapping. "Dial it down, Jordan. There's no need to be so defensive."

"I'm not defensive, and I never make excuses for my family's wealth or my lifestyle. It is what it is."

"If I've insulted you, then I apologize."

The sweep hand on his watch had made a full revolution when Jordan said, "Apology accepted."

He felt Aziza withdraw from him, although she hadn't moved, and that was the last thing he wanted. Talking about his family was not high on his discussion list. Every family had its secrets, but the closely held secret surrounding his birth had become an explosive topic between him and his grandfather.

Jordan would've never known the truth if he hadn't overheard the heated verbal exchange between Wyatt and Edward Wainwright. The two men were unaware that he'd walked into the room until he'd interrupted the argument, saying things to the patriarch he never would've said under another set of circumstances.

165

The adoring bond between the elderly man and his first grandchild had evaporated in a blink of the eye, mistrust rearing its ugly head to keep them at a distance.

Wyatt was no longer Grandpa, but the more formal Grandfather. His visits to the mansion had become sporadic, and it was months at a time before he'd stop by to see his mother. Whenever Jordan called her, he'd always ask if Wyatt was there. Christiane had called him immature and unreasonable, that he couldn't change or control the past.

Jordan didn't tell Christiane she was right, that he couldn't change what had happened in the past. But as someone in control of his own destiny, he would never lie to his child or children. He would tell them the truth whether it hurt or if they chose not to accept it.

Estrangement from Wyatt had served one purpose — it had put the tyrannical reprobate on notice. He could not and would not control Jordan Wyatt Wainwright.

CHAPTER 9

The tension that had filled the Town Car until it was palpable was missing once Jordan seated Aziza at a table in the restaurant with panoramic views of the East River and the buildings along Manhattan's east side. When he'd called to make the reservation for dinner, Jordan had requested a table near the window. The fluctuating early January temperatures had returned to normal, a brisk cold wind had swept clouds from the nighttime sky, and stars littered the heavens like a sprinkling of diamonds on black velvet.

Rounding the table, he sat, watching Aziza staring out the wall of glass.

"Beautiful."

She turned and smiled at him. "Yes, it is."

"I wasn't talking about the view."

Aziza hesitated, replaying his compliment. It was apparent he was referring to her. She looked away again. "Thank you."

Jordan leaned over the table. "Did I embarrass you?"

"No."

"If I didn't, then why won't you look at me?"

Her gaze swung back, and she gave him a long, penetrating stare. "What are you doing, Jordan?"

"What do you mean?" He waved away the waiter approaching their table.

"Why are you sending me double messages? We claim not to be dating, yet you tell me to wear something nice because you're taking me out to dinner. To me that translates into a date. You also tell me you want to spend the next four days together so we can plan strategy for my case, but one of those nights we'll attend a dinner party together. Please answer one question for me."

"What do you want to know?"

"What role do you want me to play, Jordan? Are you going to introduce me to your friends as your girlfriend or just a *friend?*"

The beginnings of a smile lifted the corners of his mouth. "I'll leave that up to you. If you feel comfortable enough with me to pretend I'm your boyfriend, then boyfriend it is. Otherwise a good friend will do."

Propping an elbow on the table, Aziza

rested her chin on the heel of her hand. "I've never been good at pretense. What you see is what you get."

Jordan's expression stilled, becoming almost somber. "I like what I see, Aziza."

"Aren't you coming on a little strong, Jordan?"

"No, Zee. You just don't know how hard it is for me to keep my hands off you. And because I know what you went through with Kenny Moore, I'm in a quandary how to pursue you."

Lowering her arm, Aziza reached across the small space separating them to hold Jordan's hand. "How would you pursue me?" Her voice was barely a whisper.

Reversing their hands, Jordan's thumb caressed the silken skin on the back of hers. "I would court you, Aziza Fleming. I'd call and ask you out to dinner and escort you as my date to fundraising events. I like museums, walks in the park, drives in the country and watching action movies. You say you love tropical islands. We could visit one where we'd wear next to nothing, sip tropical concoctions and dance on the beach under the stars. I'm not the world's best cook, but I can make breakfast and serve you in bed. Does that answer your question?"

Aziza fought to control her swirling emotions. A man she'd known less than a week was willing to give her what a man she'd known all her life hadn't or couldn't.

She and Lamar had become an unofficial couple in junior high school, joining kids their age when they hung out at the mall or went en masse to the movies. It wasn't until she was a high school junior that her father had permitted her to date. And what he'd meant by dating was her seeing other boys and not Lamar exclusively.

But it was not to be. She'd continued to see Lamar, lost her virginity to him the night of prom and believed herself totally and inexorably in love with him. They had been inseparable throughout college and law school. Eight months after passing the bar, they'd exchanged vows. However, that was when her world as she'd known it at that time had changed forever. Instead of a fairy-tale romance, it had become a macabre horror show.

"What you're proposing sounds wonderful but . . ."

Jordan lifted his expressive eyebrows when she hesitated.

"What's bothering you, baby?"

Aziza smiled. The endearment had rolled off his tongue as naturally as breathing. "I'm not looking for anything that's too serious." And by serious she meant declarations of love that would lead to marriage.

"We don't have to get serious. All I want is for us to have fun. A lot of fun."

"Is that a promise?"

Jordan stared at the lowered lids, sweep of lashes grazing silken cheeks and the lush parted lips that called to him like a beacon on a moonless night at sea. She was like a powerful magnet that pulled him in, refusing him respite from her hypnotic sensuality. He'd met a lot of women, known some intimately, but none had affected him the way Aziza Fleming did. Within minutes of meeting her for the first time he'd known there was something special about the tall, attractive woman who'd become an unwilling victim for a predator boss.

He'd promised Alexander Fleming that he would help his sister prepare and win her lawsuit, but what he hadn't anticipated was being captivated by her wit, ambition and sensual warmth.

"I know you don't put much stock in my promises," he said in a quiet tone, "but this one time I know I can follow through. We're going to have crazy fun together."

Aziza lowered her gaze, staring at their entwined hands. She felt a shock of electricity sweep up her arm when the pad of Jordan's thumb made circular motions on her palm. She'd lied when she'd told him that she wasn't a good actress, because she'd given an award-winning performance when interacting with Jordan Wainwright.

Coming face-to-face with him for the first time had been not only exciting but also shocking. Television cameras had failed to capture the sexual magnetism that made him so self-confident. They also hadn't revealed the brilliant colors of his eyes or how he looked as good as he smelled. The cologne was clean, subtle and undeniably masculine like the man who wore it.

When Jordan admitted not being able to keep his hands off, it was as if he'd been reading her mind. Although she'd been alone for several years, she wasn't lonely. Aziza had filled the empty hours decorating her home, setting up a private practice, visiting her parents in Florida, nieces and nephews in California and Arizona and socializing with friends from her childhood.

Most of the girls she'd grown up with were either married, divorced or a few had elected to remain single. The tightly knit trio planned a Girls' Week each summer and for the past two years had piled into cars and driven to New Jersey's Cape May, reverting to teenage girls when they "acted a fool." They returned home tanned, exhausted and a lot heavier than when they'd arrived. Everyone complained about going on a diet or undergoing detoxification from the calorie-laden foods and alcoholic libation, but no one said they wouldn't do it again.

Yes, her life was predictable and uneventful, and the only thing missing was a man. Aziza was aware that if she wanted to meet a man, she knew where to go. Al was a professional football player, and if she'd asked him to set her up with somebody, he would. Dating Jordan wouldn't change her mind about marriage, but he would serve to fill up some of the empty spaces on her social calendar.

"I want to warn you about one thing, Jordan Wainwright."

"What's that, Aziza Fleming?"

She leaned closer. "I'll let you know when it stops being fun."

"What are you going to do if it does?"

"Walk away and not look back."

Jordan stared, complete surprise on his face. Aziza hadn't issued a warning but a challenge. The proverbial ball was in his court, and he was expected to play hard or go home. But that wasn't to going happen because he wasn't going home. Not when he'd gotten Aziza to agree to come out and play.

"Point taken, baby." He let go of her hand and signaled their waiter. "I don't know about you, but right about now I'm hungry enough to eat half a cow," he drawled. The server approached the table, placing menus in front of them.

Aziza stared at Jordan's head as he studied the menu. The black hair covering his head reminded her of the silky black feathers she'd seen on a raven. It wasn't jet-black but blue-black.

You could do a lot worse. The voice in her head was right. Jordan Wainwright was a rare find, and if she'd wanted something more permanent, then a keeper.

He'd been blessed with jaw-dropping good looks, a hot body, intelligence, excellent taste in clothes, and he wasn't a baby daddy. Jordan had everything women looked for in a man and then some.

Without warning, he looked up and caught her staring. "Do you see anything you like?"

Aziza wanted to say *you* but glanced down at the menu instead. "The macadamia nut crusted wild salmon looks good."

Jordan smiled. "It is."

"What are you having?"

"I have to decide between the duck and halibut. Would you mind if I order a bottle of wine and appetizers?"

"Not at all."

The waiter returned and Jordan ordered a bottle of white zinfandel, crispy rock shrimp, fanny bay oysters, baby spinach Caesar salad and their entrées. He'd decided on the duck breast.

"That's a lot food, Jordan," Aziza whispered when the waiter left to put in their order.

He winked at her. "I told you I was hungry. I got so wrapped up in listening to your tapes that I didn't stop to eat."

"Do you cook for yourself?"

"Not really."

She gave him a narrowed look. "What do you mean by not really?"

"Last summer I hired someone to cook for me. Occasionally we would cook together, and I learned to make a passable brunch and how to grill meat, chicken and fish."

"Where is your personal chef now?"

Jordan wondered how much he should tell Aziza about Natasha before divulging they'd also become lovers. "She went back to culinary school. She had a year before graduating."

"After she graduates, will you hire her back?"

"No."

"Why not, Jordan?"

"She'll probably look for a position in New Jersey where she can be close to her husband who was seriously injured in a vehicular accident with a drunk driver."

Aziza blinked. "So, she's married?"

Jordan stared at the smirk on Aziza's face under hooded lids. "Why would you say it like that?"

"Something in your voice changed when you mentioned that you'd cooked together. I'd thought perhaps you'd been a couple at one time."

Jordan wanted to tell Aziza that she'd thought right. He and Natasha had been a couple, albeit temporarily, but still a couple. He'd brought her with him to backyard cookouts at Kyle's and Ivan's homes, and he had invited Kyle and his fiancée to his place where Natasha had prepared dinner, while stepping in as his hostess for the night.

"We weren't a couple in the real sense of the word." He decided to be truthful. "I didn't know she was married until she told me about the accident. It came as quite a shock because there's one thing I don't do, and that is sleep with a married woman."

"Were they living together?"

"No. They'd been separated for years. I suppose I would've felt better if she'd been divorced."

"If she was, would the two of you still be together?"

Jordan shook his head. "No. We knew it was going to be just for the summer."

Aziza wanted to ask him how he'd been able to sleep with a woman, then walk away completely detached from what he'd had with her. Maybe it was different for a man? Or maybe it was because she'd only slept with one man that she wasn't as open-minded about sex as she should've been.

"Were you in love with her?"

Leaning back in his chair, Jordan crossed his arms over his chest, a gesture she interpreted as defensive.

"No, Aziza. I wasn't in love with her. If I had been, then I wouldn't have let her go." It was the same thing he'd said to Noah.

"For richer or poorer. In sickness and in health," Aziza intoned.

"Why so cynical, Zee? Don't you believe in the institution of marriage?"

"I'm ambivalent. Most of my cases over the past two years have been divorces. All but one involved women who were married to extremely wealthy men, who were prisoners because their husbands were quick to remind them that he'd bought them."

She told Jordan about a client whose millionaire husband couldn't achieve an erection unless he physically abused her. Her screams and moans had become a sexual turn-on for him. However, he'd always countered the violent act when he'd come home with a diamond necklace, emerald ring and other expensive baubles. He'd compounded his physical brutality with emotional abuse when she was expected to come to him on hands and knees to ask for money.

It all had come to an end when he'd beaten her so severely that her mother had called the police when she'd shown up unexpectedly and saw the welts and bruises.

"I took on another case when a former client pleaded with me to save her cousin, who was too frightened and intimidated to press charges. A ninety-minute consult at the woman's hospital bedside ended when I got her to press charges against her husband for assault. I also talked her into asking for a restraining order. As soon the restraining order was executed, I started divorce proceedings asking for sole custody of their preschool twin sons.

"The benign-looking batterer was arrested as he chaired a board meeting, led out in handcuffs and charged with multiple counts of assault and battery. The judge set his bail at two million and he was ordered to surrender his passport because he posed a flight risk. He was given half an hour to pack what he needed from his four-million-dollar home and ordered to stay away from his wife and children until his trial or his bail would be revoked and he'd be remanded to the Westchester jail to await trial."

"Was he indicted?"

"He took a plea and was given two years probation and a thousand hours of anger management."

"Did she get what she wanted in the divorce?"

"Oh, yes," Aziza drawled, grinning. "There was no pre-nup, so she cleaned the sucker out. She was granted sole custody with supervised visitation."

"Good for her. She's lucky she had you to represent her."

Aziza sobered quickly. "I was dealing with Kenny coming onto me and my own divorce, so transference was in full effect. Every man who'd done a woman wrong had become Lamar Powers and Kenneth Moore.

If a man looked at me or ignored the scowl on my face and attempted to talk to me got the straight no-chaser *business* from me." Her eyelids fluttered wildly. "But when I think about some of the things I said to those guys, I wish I could find them and apologize."

The approach of the waiter and a sommelier carrying an ice bucket with a bottle of wine preempted their conversation. The appetizers arrived and they toasted each other with an excellent vintage of the pale rosé. Over the next ninety minutes, they dined on delicately prepared appetizers and delicious entrées, and they talked about everything but themselves.

Aziza didn't miss the stares from other women as they walked past their table. Several were bold enough to stop completely until garnering Jordan's attention before moving on. They only validated what she'd known. Her dining partner and date for the night was so hot he sizzled!

Jordan shook Aziza gently in an attempt to wake her. They were finally back in Manhattan and in front of his building.

She'd fallen asleep when they'd encountered bumper-to-bumper bridge traffic. A ride that should've taken about twenty minutes, barring delays, had stretched into more than an hour. He'd enjoyed the warmth of her body draped over his and the sensual scent of her perfume. He'd alternated between watching the slow-moving traffic with staring at the woman asleep in his arms. To say Aziza Fleming was an enigma was an understatement. She was soft and feminine, but there was also an edge to her that said, "Don't mess with me."

What had shocked him when he'd listened to the tapes was there were only four incidents where Kenneth Middleton Moore, Jr., had crossed the line, blatantly sexually harassing Aziza. All of the other encounters were open to interpretation. Four incidents in hundreds of hours of taping.

Kenneth's initial undertaking to get Aziza into his bed had been subtle, beginning with compliments on her work and appearance. Then a year later and within two weeks, his behavior had changed, escalating into an all-out campaign to pressure her to give into his demands.

Aziza woke, disoriented, looking around her. "Are we there yet?"

He ruffled her curls. "Yes, we are."

Stretching and covering her mouth with a hand to smother a yawn, she closed her eyes. "I'm sorry about falling asleep on you."

Smiling, Jordan stepped out of the car when the driver came around and opened the door. Turning, he assisted Aziza out while the driver retrieved her luggage from the trunk. His arm went around her waist, following Sergio as he carried the bags to the side street entrance. The driver handed off the bags, then turned and walked back to his vehicle.

Aziza walked into the Fifth Avenue maisonette, her eyes widening in amazement at the size of the duplex Jordan called home. Rather than enter through the lobby, he'd used the entrance on 98th Street, leading into a small kitchen and maid's room and bath.

"I've turned the maid's room into a home office," Jordan said, standing off to the side when Aziza peered in.

"No law books?" she teased.

He shook his head. "We have a law library at the office." Reaching for her hand, he pulled her gently down a narrow hallway and into an area with a pantry and a laundry room with a washer and dryer.

"Do you do your own laundry?"

"I don't know how to turn the damn things on."

Aziza rolled her eyes at him. "Then why do you have them?"

"The lady who cleans my apartment also does laundry."

"I see."

"What do you see?"

"As the French say, *c'est la vie.*"

Jordan placed her overnight and garment bag on the floor. He turned back to face her. "Do you have a problem with something?"

With wide eyes, Aziza stared up at him. "There's no need to get defensive, Jordan," she said quietly. *"Chacun à son goût."*

A smile spread over Jordan's face like a ray of sunshine. "So, the beautiful woman speaks fluent French. You are just full of surprises."

"And it's apparent you understand the language."

"Yes. My mother taught me."

"Who taught her?"

"Her mother."

"What did I say?" she asked.

"Everyone to his taste," he translated. Supporting his back against the wall, Jordan closed his eyes. "I grew up with live-in housekeepers, a butler, chef and chauffeur, all who were available 24/7." He opened his eyes. "I never had to concern myself with having clean clothes or what to eat because someone was always there to take care of my basic needs."

Aziza leaned closer, bracing her hands on his chest, feeling the warmth from his body through the custom cotton shirt. "What did you do when you went away to college?"

He smiled down at her. "I rented an apartment off campus and hired someone to come in to clean and do laundry. I contracted with a caterer who prepared what I wanted and delivered it in containers I could freeze for several weeks."

Rising on tiptoe, she pressed a kiss to his throat. "You know you're spoiled."

"No, I'm not."

"Yes, you are," she crooned, her mouth inches from his. "You always get want you want, which means I'm very fortunate to have you helping me with my lawsuit."

Jordan held his breath until he felt a band tightening across his chest. Was that all he was to Aziza? Someone to help her build a solid case where she could sue Kenneth Moore? What she didn't know was that he wanted to be more — much more.

"You're wrong, Zee. I don't always get what I want." *I want you,* he added silently.

Aziza leaned closer, her breasts pressed to his chest, her arms going around his trim waist. "Okay," she whispered. "Perhaps I should rephrase that. You get almost everything you want."

Jordan smiled. He lowered his head, burying his face in her curls. "True." Pressing his palms to the wall, he splayed his fingers. "You can't push up on me like this."

"I'm just hugging you. Can't I get a hug from my friend?" His hands came off the wall, as if in slow motion, and he rested his hands on her back over her coat.

Jordan knew if they continued to stand there with Aziza's full breasts pressed to his chest, if he continued to hold her, then he didn't think he would be able to control the growing heaviness in his groin. She was fully clothed, yet he'd become so aroused he feared she would feel his erection.

"Baby, please, you're going to have to get off me before something happens."

It was too late. Something did happen when Aziza felt the solid bulge against her thigh. Dropping her arms, she took a backward step, her gaze locked with Jordan's. His breathing had quickened, the skin over his cheekbones tightening. Without warning, her body reacted to his arousal; breasts warm, heavy, panties wet, the flesh between her legs pulsing uncontrollably.

"What's the matter? I can't hug you?"

For the tiniest fraction of time, they froze, sharing the space and the sexual magnetism that made it impossible for them to move or speak. The chaste kisses, casual hugs, the inane repartee had served as cover for what had been an instantaneous attraction.

Not that he'd condone Kenneth Moore's behavior, but Jordan understood why he'd come onto Aziza. She was completely unaware of her sexiness. She had a habit of lowering her lids and peering up through her lashes. The demure gesture was natural and innocent, and given her limited sexual experience, it was a lethal combination. And what she'd called hugging wasn't that at all. Not with her breasts crushed against his chest — instead of easing his erection, it grew harder. Sexual tension gave way to anger.

"Don't get it twisted, Aziza. I may have played a frat boy game when I did shots the other night. But let me warn you I'm hardly a boy when it comes to sex. The next time you rub up on me, I'm definitely not going to apologize when I put you on your back and go inside you." He leaned over and picked up her luggage. "Now I'll show you to *your* room."

CHAPTER 10

When Jordan saw the gamut of emotions cross Aziza's face — shock, horror and anger — he wished he hadn't said what he'd said to her, but the acerbic words were out and impossible to retract. Her eyes narrowed, reminding him of a cat as it went into attack mode.

"I've asked you to help me put away a sexual predator, and you have the audacity to come off sounding like one when you talk about putting me on my back." She took a step, going on tiptoe and thrusting her face within inches of his. "Don't *you* get it twisted, Jordan. If I lie on my back for you, it will because *I* want to feel you inside me, not the other way around. Now, I'm ready to see my bedroom."

Jordan felt properly chastised. For a reason he couldn't fathom, he'd expected Aziza to order him to call a driver to take her home. But it was apparent her drive to bring down the man who'd harassed her to the point of almost destroying her career was stronger and more passionate than her reaction to his off-color sexual remark.

"I'm sorry, Zee."

She waved a hand. "You've said what you felt, and I've had my say. So let's not beat a dead horse."

Aziza followed Jordan, staring at his broad shoulders under the exquisitely tailored suit jacket as he led the way into the main living area of the duplex; she wanted to tell him if he'd been anyone other than Jordan Wainwright she would've walked out and had the doorman hail a taxi to drive her back to Bronxville. But she hadn't because her passion to make her former boss pay for his sins and his crime had reached a fever pitch. After she'd handed in her resignation, she'd felt sheer and utter relief that she hadn't had to gird herself before walking into the building where the firm was located. It was during the ten-block walk from Grand Central Station to Thirty-Second Street that she'd given herself a pep talk, that she hadn't been imagining that the married man with teenage boys was coming onto her, that she'd misinterpreted Lamar's claim that she was looking for attention because of the way she dressed.

Each time she'd interviewed for another position and received a rejection, it had upped her frustration meter. It was only when she'd made the decision to open a private practice, working from home, that she'd relegated the macabre episode to the deepest recesses of her mind. But then without warning, it had surfaced again when viewing a television news segment about sexual harassment in the workplace. A victim of sexual harassment had pleaded with others who were experiencing what she'd gone through to take action to stop the predators. Not doing anything was tantamount to empowerment.

It'd taken Aziza a week of sleepless nights before she'd worked up the nerve to tell Alexander. He had been enraged, threatening to take the man's head off, but she'd had to remind her brother that murdering Kenneth Moore would be interpreted as capital murder and that he would probably spend the rest of his life in prison.

Talking to Alexander had made her aware of her acceptance of the D.A.'s opinion that her attempt to gather evidence on Moore was entrapment and had empowered him to go after another woman. That was when she'd decided — not again. She'd tried taping and calling other women who worked at the firm but with no success. Jordan was her last and only hope for justice.

Jordan breathed out an inaudible sigh as he climbed the circular staircase leading to the second-floor bedrooms. It was apparent Aziza had declared a truce — a very fragile truce. She'd drawn a line in the sand, and he had to be very careful not to cross it again. She was right when she'd told him he said what he felt. He wanted to make love to her. He was willing to forego his inane month time frame before becoming involved in a sexual liaison. Even when he'd stuck to dating a woman for a month before sleeping with her, it wasn't a guarantee they would have a long and lasting relationship.

He and Kirsten had dated for two years, yet nothing had come of it except they'd enjoyed each other's company. Jordan didn't know what it was, but now he wanted a woman for more than company. Seeing Kyle with Ava, Duncan with Tamara, and Ivan with his wife, Nayo, made him feel like an outsider now that Natasha had returned to school *and* probably her husband. She'd contacted him once, and that was to send him a thank-you note for underwriting the cost of tuition to complete her education. To Jordan it was only money, but for Natasha it meant fulfilling her dream to become a chef.

Offering his legal expertise to help Aziza stop a predator would mean a personal victory for her. And for him it would mean exposing a criminal who'd used his powerful connections to circumvent the law and to prove to Aziza that not all men were like her ex-boss and husband.

What he didn't want to acknowledge was that interacting with the beautiful lawyer had him fantasizing about making love to her. And he wanted to prove to her that he could be trusted to care for and protect her.

He walked into one of two facing bedrooms at the end of the long hallway. A runner had muffled their footsteps. "This will be your bedroom. You'll have your own bathroom, so we don't have to run into each other."

Waiting until Jordan turned a ceiling fixture radiating light onto white-on-white furnishings, Aziza entered a space that reminded her of layouts in *Architectural Digest.* Unknowingly, a slight gasp escaped her parted lips. "How beautiful!" she said, recovering her voice.

The room was decorated in shades of white, ranging from milk-white to eggshell and oyster. The linen headboard on the king-size bed matched the cushioned bench at the foot of the bed and the fabric on a corner sofa. Oyster-hued silk drapes hung from tall windows that overlooked Central Park. Framed photographs of tropical birds were positioned above the bed and fireplace. Lamps with milk glass bases and matching silk shades were set on bleached pine bedside tables.

Jordan pointed to a closed door at the opposite end of the room. "Behind that door is a walk-in closet where you can hang up your clothes."

"How large is this place?" she asked, smiling.

Attractive lines deepened around Jordan's eyes when he returned her smile. It was obvious her former annoyance with him had vanished. "It's a little over five thousand square feet. There are two more bedrooms on the first floor, but I prefer sleeping up here because of the views of the park." He picked up her luggage and placed on the carpeted floor next to the door. "I'll leave you to get settled in. If you'd like coffee or tea before you turn in, then just let me know."

"Is the coffee instant?" she teased.

He gave her an incredulous look. "Even if I couldn't boil water or make toast without burning it, I could always brew a decent cup of coffee." Grinning and winking at her, he said, "What do you want? Latte, cappuccino, espresso or a frappé?"

"It's like that, Jordan?"

"Hell, yeah, it's like that, Zee Fleming."

She flashed a sexy moue. "Let me change into something more comfortable and I'll let you know how good your coffee is."

"Which one do you want?" Jordan asked.

"The weather's not warm enough for a frappé, so I'm going to go for the cappuccino."

He glanced at his watch. "I'll give you half an hour. Is that enough time?"

Aziza nodded. "Yes." She planned to take a quick shower and slip into sweats.

Jordan winked at her again. "I'll see you downstairs in half an hour."

Waiting until Jordan left the bedroom and closed the door behind him, Aziza opened her luggage and took out a quilted case with her grooming supplies, then headed for the bathroom. Asian-inspired, minimalist and decorated on the principles of feng shui, the cool colors and pale-toned materials created a haven for balance and total relaxation. A profusion of pink and white orchids flourished in glazed pots decorated with Asian characters and overflowed from hanging baskets, reminding her of the loggia in a

193

villa when she'd vacationed in the Virgin Islands.

Jordan had invited her to go to Puerto Rico as his guest at his law partner's wedding. Going to the tropics in February was more than tempting. If she checked her planner and discovered she didn't have anything scheduled, then Jordan Wainwright could look forward to a very willing companion.

She dabbed an oil-free solution onto a cloth and, using circular motions, removed the makeup from her eyes and face. Her skin felt clean and tingly as she went through the motions of brushing her teeth.

Undressing and leaving her clothes on a bench in an area that also functioned as a dressing room, she walked up one step to the shower area. Sliding ash doors fitted with light-filtering frosted glass screened a low tub and shower stall.

Tucking her hair under a bouffant cap, Aziza turned on the water in the stall, adjusted the temperature, then stepped in under the warm spray.

Aziza's sock-covered feet were silent as she descended the staircase, walked along a wide hallway and stopped to peer into formal living and dining rooms. The furnishings in Jordan's maisonette reflected everything that was Manhattan: energy, glamour, edginess and chic. The architect had painted the walls in neutral colors, but remaining baseboards and cornices were a classical white. The parquetry was stained dark to contrast with the light carpeting throughout the entire duplex. She smiled. The pale carpets were definitely not child-friendly.

She found the gourmet kitchen, a chef's dream with state-of-the art Miele appliances: double ovens, cooktop range and grill, built-in refrigerator/freezer and wine storage. The distinctive smell of coffee filled the kitchen. An espresso machine made whirring sounds as Jordan aerated cream until it was light and frothy. He'd spared no expense when he'd renovated and decorated his home.

Jordan had also changed. A pair of low-rise jeans, a white T-shirt and socks had replaced his suit and imported footwear. Her gaze lingered on his muscular arms. His bulging biceps were a testament to his claim he worked out regularly.

"That really smells good."

Jordan spun around, smiling when he saw Aziza standing in the entrance to the kitchen. His gaze traveled slowly from the narrow headband holding curls off her face, down to a gray pinstriped long-sleeved tee and gray sweatpants. "Please come in and sit down." He pulled out a tall stool at the cooking island, seating her. "What are you wearing? You smell delicious."

Aziza smiled. "Chance. It's from Chanel."

"My mother named my sister Chanel because it's her favorite perfume. She also named one of my brothers Rhett because she'd fallen in love with Rhett Butler after reading *Gone with the Wind.*" Reaching for a shaker filled with ground cinnamon, Jordan sprinkled it lightly over the layer of hot cream he'd ladled into mugs filled with coffee.

"Does she like her name?"

Placing a tall mug in front of Aziza, Jordan sat beside her. "She claims she hates it because a group of girls at her school refer to her as Number Five. When she introduces herself to anyone, she tells them to call her Charlie."

"But that's also the name of a fragrance."

"Go figure. I'm totally confused when it comes to today's teenagers. It's as if they're superglued to their cells and computers. If it's not texting, it's tweeting, blogging, Facebook or MySpace. Chanel was averaging more than three thousand text messages a month. When her grades started slipping, my mother had a mini-breakdown after her accountant told her Chanel had exceed her mandated seven-hundred-fifty-a-month limit. It was my sister's turn to have a breakdown when she lost phone privileges for two months.

"My sister tried to get me involved in the fray because I've always taken up for her, but that was one time I stood behind our parents. We'd discovered a classmate was sending her threatening messages and she was responding in kind. My father, who is as benign as they come, extended the loss of her phone privileges to six months. No cell, no texting, no bullying."

Aziza took a sip from the cup, savoring the warmth sliding down her throat and spreading throughout her chest. "Cyber-bullying has become so insidious among teenagers. My older brothers have five preteens between them and they tell me how lucky I am I don't have children."

Jordan stopped drinking as he gave Aziza a sidelong glance. "You don't want children." The statement was a question.

She took another sip. "Excellent coffee."

"Why are you skirting the question?"

Shifting slightly on the stool, Aziza turned and looked directly at Jordan. He was right. She was skirting the issue only because it reminded her of how she'd spent more than half her life pinning her hopes and dreams on a man who'd harbored resentment so deep that it'd become impossible for him to repress it any longer. And when given the opportunity, his passive-aggressive behavior had whittled away the love she'd had for him until loathing was all that was left on her part.

Lamar had talked about starting a family right after they'd married, but Aziza had wanted to wait until they'd been married for at least three years. It would've given them time to adjust to married life and to jump-start their careers. That was when Lamar had claimed she'd loved her career more than him. She'd denied it, unaware that he'd spoken the truth. Less than six months into their marriage, she'd fallen out of love with him.

"I don't know," she said truthfully. "There was a time when I was certain I wanted to become a mother, but that dream ended with my marriage."

"What about now?"

"What about now, Jordan?"

"Do you still want children?"

Aziza leaned closer, her shoulder pressing against his muscled one. "Why do I get the impression that you're cross-examining me?"

Jordan kissed the end of her nose. "Tonight I'm asking questions. The cross-examination will come tomorrow. We're going to set up our own mock court where I'll become opposing counsel and it will be my job to discredit you. I want to identify everything that can't be proven before we redirect what you've recorded."

"But the D.A. wouldn't accept the tapes as evidence," she argued quietly.

"We're not going to submit them as evidence," Jordan countered. "We're going to build our defense from what's on the tapes." He kissed her nose again. "You're going to have to trust me. Do you trust me, Ms. Fleming?"

"I do trust you, Mr. Wainwright." Aziza trusted Jordan, but she wasn't certain whether she trusted herself whenever they were together. He was too urbane and much too sexy to ignore. She continually told herself Jordan wasn't her type, that she wasn't interested in becoming involved with the man, but knew it was all a lie.

She'd lost count of the number of times she'd cried herself to sleep whenever her body betrayed her. Those were the times when she *did* need a man, if only to remind her why she'd been born female.

The urges became less frequent over the years before they stopped altogether. But now they were back, stronger than they'd been when she and Lamar were dating. Leaning against Jordan, her body pressed to his, feeling his erection had brought everything back. The spontaneous orgasm had happened before she was able to stop it.

"What are you thinking about, baby?" Jordan's mellifluent voice broke into her reverie.

"Sex."

"Sex?"

It was obvious she'd shocked him with her response. "Yes, Jordan, sex." Wrapping her hands around the mug, she enjoyed the warmth against her palms. "I can't remember the last time I've had sex."

Jordan didn't know how to react to the unexpected disclosure. Was she telling him because she wanted him to do something to end her self-enforced celibacy, or because she wanted him to know she didn't sleep with men?

"Is it by choice?"

A hint of a smile softened her mouth. "Of course it's by choice."

"Do you miss it?"

"At times," she admitted. "Like tonight.

When I hugged you and . . ."

"And I wound up with a hard-on," he said, completing her words.

"Yes, Jordan. When you had a hard-on it reminded me of what I'd missed and . . . and what I'm missing."

Jordan forcibly pried her hands from around the cup, tightening his grip when she attempted to pull free. "Look at me. Please look at me, Aziza," he demanded, enunciating each word. She met his eyes. "What do you want me to do?"

Biting on her lip, Aziza stopped the words poised on the tip of her tongue. "I'm not going to ask you to make love to me because it would complicate everything. I'm not going to ask you to make love to me because it would mean I'm using you to assuage a need I've denied for longer than I can remember. I'm not . . ."

Jordan stopped her words with a soft, gentle kiss that stopped her breath. "Don't say anything else, baby. I envy you."

"Why?" she whispered against his firm mouth.

"I envy you because you're more forthcoming about your feelings than I could ever be. You had me — all of me — the moment I saw you. I didn't lie when I told you how hard it is for me to keep my hands off you. Seeing you, smelling you, hearing your voice and hugging you under the pretense that I *can* touch you without you going off on me — it's like celebrating Christmas every day of the year."

Aziza rested her forehead on his shoulder. "Christmas is my favorite holiday."

"It happens to be mine, too." Jordan ruffled her hair. "It appears as if we both want the same thing, but I'm not going to do anything until you tell me I can."

"What about your thirty-day rule about sleeping with a woman?"

"What about it, Zee?"

"What if we make love before the month is up?"

"Rules and laws were made to be broken. If not, then we'd never get any clients." She laughed, the throaty sound sending a warming shiver up Jordan's back. He couldn't believe he was talking about making love with Aziza if they were discussing a case. "I want you — now — but I don't want it to be something we talk about, then execute."

Aziza traced the curve of Jordan's eyebrows, the ridge of his cheekbones and jaw with her forefinger. "You want spontaneity?"

"Spontaneity, passion and tenderness."

"In other words, we'll become friends with

benefits."

He smiled. "I promise benefits beyond your wildest dreams."

"I know about you and your promises, Jordan."

"I can't believe you still aren't going to cut me some slack about eating your caviar New Year's Eve."

Aziza pressed her mouth to his throat, feeling the strong pulse beating there. "I can't believe I'm having this conversation with you."

"No more than I can believe you're here with me."

Jordan wanted to tell Aziza it was as if he'd waited all his life for someone like her. He hadn't known what he'd wanted in a woman until he'd shared the same space with Alexander Fleming's sister.

How a woman looked wasn't a priority. How she related to him topped his list of requisites. He'd never dated a lawyer, and interacting with a woman who shared his passion was an added bonus. Aziza claimed she didn't want anything serious, and Jordan was more than willing to go along with her assertion. However, if he found himself getting in too deep, then he knew he would have to be the one to end it.

The sound of the phone ringing shattered

the silence and the spell pulling Jordan and Aziza together in a cocoon of desire.

He went still. The house phone rarely rang, and it usually meant a member of his family was attempting to reach him. "I have to get that," he said after the second ring. Rising from the stool, he walked over and picked the cordless receiver off the cradle. "This is Jordan," he said with his usual greeting.

"Jordan, this is your grandfather."

A slight frown appeared between his eyes. It'd been more than a year since Wyatt Wainwright had dialed any of his numbers. Jordan glanced at the clock on the microwave. It was almost eleven — an hour past the time when Wyatt usually retired for bed. Anyone familiar with the habits of Wyatt knew if they didn't reach him before ten at night, then they would have to wait until eight the following morning. His habits were as predictable as the change of seasons.

"To what do I owe the honor of this call at this ungodly hour?" he drawled sarcastically.

"Watch your mouth, son!"

"Remember, Grandpa, you called me, not the reverse. What do you want?"

"I need your help with something."

Jordan turned his back when he saw Aziza,

with wide eyes, staring at him. "Does it have anything to do with Wainwright Developers?"

"Yes."

"I'm sorry, Grandpa, but I can't help you. I'm no longer involved with the family business."

"This became your business when you called me out on television. I'm certain you remember that little show of bravado."

"Grandpa, do you mind if we talk about this at some other time?"

"When is that?"

"Tomorrow. I'm not going to be in the office for the rest of the week, so I'll get in touch with you."

"You're not sick, are you?"

Jordan smiled for the first time since hearing his grandfather's voice. He and Wyatt were like oil and water, but he knew the older man would give up his life for his first grandchild. Jordan knew he would do the same for his grandfather, but he wasn't about to let Wyatt know that.

"No, Grandpa, I'm not sick. My schedule was rearranged because of the fire and explosion near the courthouse, so I decided to take a few days off from the grind. I'll call you on your private line tomorrow morning and we'll talk." Although Wyatt had stepped down as CEO of Wainwright Developers Group, he still went into the office.

"Thank you. Good night, son."

"Good night, Grandpa."

He hung up and exhaled a sigh. Jordan didn't know if the rift that had begun when he'd inadvertently discovered the circumstances of his adoption and that Wyatt had been the mastermind behind the scheme would ever heal. The things he'd said to his grandfather had come from a place inside him he hadn't known existed, yet once the acerbic words were out, they could not be retracted. The act of betrayal had spilled over to his parents and they'd had to endure his wrath.

Christiane Wainwright had collapsed and had to be sedated and that was when Jordan realized she'd been forced to become an unwilling participant in a game not of her choosing. He'd apologized to her, and Christiane had held him to her bosom sobbing that she understood his anger. It'd been two years and he and his mother had never broached the topic again. She was his mother and he her son.

Once he rethought his words and actions, Jordan had come to the conclusion that not only did he physically resemble the man who'd ruled his family and his real estate empire with an iron fist, but he'd also shared similar negative psychological characteristics with Wyatt Wainwright. It'd become a daily struggle not to become his grandfather's clone.

"What you doing?" he asked Aziza when she walked over to the sink.

"I'm rinsing my cup before I put it in the dishwasher. I'm ready to turn in."

"But it's still early."

"Not for me," Aziza said. "You city folks dress in black and stay up all night like vampires. I'm sorry, but this country girl is early to bed and early to rise." The glass of wine she'd had with dinner had made her sleepy. She didn't know why Jordan had ordered a bottle of wine when he'd only taken a couple of sips before setting his glass aside.

"What time do you want breakfast?" Jordan asked.

"What if we play it by ear? I doubt if I'm going to be hungry, so instead of breakfast I'll probably want brunch."

Jordan closed the distance between them, leaned down and kissed her cheek. "Sleep well."

Aziza felt her pulse quicken when the warmth of his body swept over her. Everything about Jordan was so compelling, his sensuality so magnetic, that it was all she could do not to beg him to make love to her. She wanted him, he wanted her and it would only be a matter of time before the sexual tension would have to be resolved. And she prayed it would be soon rather than later.

"Thank you, Jordan." Turning on her heels, she walked out of the kitchen, feeling the heat from his gaze on her back.

She knew she'd turned a corner, leaving her past behind, when she'd told him that she wanted *and* needed a man to make love to her. It'd taken years, but now she knew what her father had been talking about when he'd insisted she see other boys. Committing to and knowing only one man so early had stunted her growth emotionally.

When she should've gone out with other boys at her high school and college, she had become so fixated on Lamar that she'd forgotten they existed. In the end, it had become her undoing when she had unknowingly surrendered her will in order to please him.

However, Lamar Powers hadn't known Aziza Fleming as well as he'd thought he had. Growing up surrounded by males had given her an advantage. She'd had to fight in order to assert herself.

Her father and brothers had always had her back, and that was what she'd expected Lamar to do. But when he'd failed to protect her, she'd known she had to go it alone.

It was as if her carefully constructed world had come crashing down on her. She'd filed for divorce at the same time she was fighting a harassment case that threatened to destroy her career.

Meeting Jordan Wainwright would serve a twofold purpose: he would help build a case to bring down a predator, *and* he was the perfect candidate with whom to have a no-strings-attached affair.

She smiled as she climbed the staircase to the second floor. For her it would become a win-win situation.

CHAPTER 11

Jordan's internal alarm clock woke him at five. Groaning, he lay on his stomach, punching the pillow under his head. It'd taken hours for him to drift off to sleep and now that he was awake he knew it was impossible to go back to sleep.

If it had been a normal workday he would've taken the elevator to the building's basement-level health club and swum laps in the Olympic-size swimming pool before returning to his apartment to prepare to go into the office.

During the summer months he walked to the brownstone, working out in the street-level gym. Employees in the brownstone utilized the workout equipment in lieu of a costly Manhattan health club membership. He kept a supply of shirts, slacks, jackets and suits on hand in a closet in his office to change into after using the showers set aside for the men and women.

But today was different. He wasn't going downstairs or going into the office. Kyle had insisted he take the three days off because since he'd joined the practice in July he hadn't taken a day off. The firm usually closed the week between Christmas and New Year's, so he didn't consider that a vacation. He usually arrived at the office around six and tried to leave most nights around six. Late nights were for clients who were unable to come to the office during the day.

Working with Kyle at the Harlem-based practice was different than when they'd worked for TCB because they hadn't had to juggle so many cases then. At any given time, Jordan had no less than six or seven open cases. Most he sought to settle before going to trial to save money for his clients. He'd realized early on that Kyle Chatham hadn't opened a practice in Harlem to make a lot of money but to advocate for those he represented. The glaring difference between the clients at Chatham and Wainwright and those at Trilling, Carlyle and Browne was the number of zeros in their bank balances. The clients at TCB had pockets so deep they could buy an island with a single stroke of the pen. And unlike the partners at C & W, those at TCB always went to trial where billable hours sometimes exceeded six figures.

Turning over, Jordan stared up at the ceiling. It would be another two hours before sunrise and he loathed getting out of bed. He would've been content to remain in bed if he hadn't been alone, but the woman he wanted in his bed was in a room across the hall. Her revelation that she wanted and needed to be made love to had kept him from a restful night's sleep. Images of undressing her, seeing her completely naked and picking her up and taking her to bed had invaded his head, swirling around like a sirocco until he felt as if he were losing his mind; the erection that had refused to go down made him feel as if he was coming out of his skin.

Jordan's body betrayed him again, he was groaning as if in pain. Sitting up and swinging his legs over the side of the bed, he walked on bare feet to the en suite bath. He lingered long enough to brush his teeth and rinse his mouth with a peppermint mouthwash before standing under the spray of ice-cold water beating down on his head and body. His lips had taken on a bluish hue and his teeth were chattering uncontrollably before he attempted to adjust the water temperature. He may have caught hypothermia, but at least his hard-on had gone down.

Patting the moisture from his body with a thick towel, Jordan tucked it around his waist and returned to the bedroom. He entered a walk-in closet, opening drawers to select underwear, socks and a long-sleeve tee. Moving farther into the closet, he selected a pair of khakis. Racks, like those in a department store, held slacks, jackets, shirts, suits and ties. They were arranged according to fabric and color. Jordan used the services of his father's personal tailor to fashion his wardrobe, and the result was sartorial sophistication. Most of his suits were in varying shades of blue and gray, his shirts predominately white with French cuffs and silk ties in solids, stripes and checks ranged from snow-white to midnight-black. Other shelves were lined with footwear with styles from running shoes to dress patent leather slip-ons. His casual attire was conservative, reflective of the Americana style adapted by Ralph Lauren. Wearing a uniform to school from grades one through twelve had set the stage for suits, shirts, ties and shoes.

Jordan dressed quickly, slipping his feet into a pair of running shoes, and walked out of his bedroom. The door to Aziza's bedroom was closed, and he didn't break stride as he headed for the staircase.

He took a quick glance out the window. The sky had brightened and the sound of cars and buses along Fifth Avenue was a signal that the city was wide awake and readying itself for another day of bustling activity. Walking to the front door, he opened it, retrieving a copy of the *New York Times.* Tucking the newspaper under his arm, he retreated to the kitchen to drink several cups of coffee while he perused the paper.

The caffeine was what Jordan needed to jolt him into awareness as he turned on the small flat-screen television on the counter-top and half listened to the commentary from a news journalist as he read the articles that garnered his attention. His head popped up.

Images of Robert Andrews, his wife and daughters filled the screen as the businessman-turned-politician announced his intent to challenge popular incumbent New York State Senator Billy Edwards in the upcoming election. With wide eyes, he peered closely at the extremely attractive woman standing beside her husband. She had to be at least fifty or fifty-one, but appeared at least a decade younger. Her daughters, who looked to be in their twenties, were a mirror image of their tall, slender mother.

"Good luck, Robert," Jordan said to the television.

Although approaching eighty, Billy Edwards was wildly popular with the Harlem community. His constituents had suggested he run for mayor, governor and/or a U.S. Representative, but Billy's concern for his assembly district exceeded his ambition to become a political juggernaut.

Jordan wasn't as concerned about Robert Andrews winning or losing the election as he was about the man's wife and children, who would now be subjected to public scrutiny. What was the man thinking? Had blind ambition overshadowed common sense?

Maybe he doesn't know. The thought popped into Jordan's head as the television journalist faced the camera to identify herself and her station's call letters. He wanted to believe that Robert knew everything he should know about his wife before becoming a public figure. Family secrets thought to be buried had a way of coming to the surface at the most inopportune time. He prayed that this wouldn't be one of those times. Putting aside the newspaper, he left the kitchen and headed for his home office.

The twelve-by-twelve space had been the bedroom for the live-in maid of the former tenant. Jordan, who'd grown up with live-in household staff, hadn't wanted a repeat of that, so he'd contracted with a bonded cleaning service to have someone come in twice a week to clean and do laundry.

Picking the receiver off the cradle, he sank down in to a tobacco-brown suede love seat and pressed speed dial for Wyatt's private line. It was answered after the first ring.

"Wyatt."

Jordan smiled. The single word was pregnant with power. "Good morning, Grandpa. How can I help you?" There was a pause before Wyatt's voice came through the earpiece. No doubt, he was shocked that Jordan had offered to help him without hearing what it was he wanted him to do.

"I need you to handle a situation for me. Someone has been shakin' down tenants in the buildings on 114th."

"What do you mean by shaking down, Grandpa?"

"Several tenants have complained that since the violations have been removed, someone from the tenants' committee is pressuring them to make a monthly *donation* to a special fund to defray the monies they had to pay out for legal fees."

Jordan wanted to tell his grandfather there were no legal fees because Kyle had taken on the case pro bono. "Did they say who was hustling them?"

"No. They said something about 'snitches get stitches.' "

"If they're not willing to give up a name, then what do you expect me to do?"

"I heard one of them mumble about 'red dreads and fly shit.' Whatever the hell that means."

"I know who they're talking about."

"Who?" Wyatt asked.

"I can't tell you, Grandpa. But, I promise to take care of it."

There came a beat. "Thanks. I don't need any more negative talk coming out of Harlem, not when we're trying to buy several abandoned parcels near 118th and St. Nicholas."

"Good luck with that. Meanwhile, I'll handle this extortion situation."

"Thanks, Jordan."

"No problem, Grandpa." He wanted to ask his grandfather if he'd seen the news segment where Robert Andrews was throwing his hat into the political arena but decided to let sleeping dogs lie. Wyatt would find out soon enough, and then all hell was certain to break loose.

Jordan knew exactly who his grandfather was referring to. He ended the call and phoned Kyle, repeating his telephone conversation with his grandfather. "You didn't charge the tenants' committee for representation, but the president of the committee decides to shake down his own people."

"Did they actually identify Joseph Mills by name?" Kyle asked.

"No. But Wyatt said someone mentioned 'red dreads and fly shit.' And that could only be Mills because he does have reddish dreadlocks and freckles."

Kyle laughed. "What do you know about fly shit, partner?"

Jordan also laughed. "I'm not that removed from cultural vernacular as you'd like to believe I am."

"You keep hanging out in Harlem and you'll be a certified brother before you know it."

Jordan's expression became a mask of stone. "I thought I already was a *brother,* brother."

"You are. Forget it, Jordan. I'll handle Joe Mills. I'm going to tear him a new one, because he's ripping off people who trusted him."

"Are you sure you don't need me to

confront him, Kyle?"

"No, Jordan. The man's a bigot and I don't want him to say something slick and end up looking for his teeth. I'll be certain to let him know that you've dislodged more than a few speed bags *and* you're not too shabby with the heavy bag."

Jordan, seeing movement out of the corner of his eye, swiveled in the seat. Aziza had come into the office without making a sound. Leaning against the door, she'd crossed her arms under her breasts. He couldn't pull his gaze away from her fresh-scrubbed face. "He's not worth me knocking him out."

Jordan had hired a personal trainer who'd put him through a strenuous martial arts workout that included lifting weights and a boxing regimen of hitting the speed and heavy bags. The workout had increased his endurance and overall body strength.

"After I talk to Mills, I'll give you an update."

"Thanks." He hung up, his gaze fusing with Aziza's as he came around the desk and sat down on a corner. "Good morning."

Aziza smiled. "Good morning. Who are you talking about knocking out?"

"Some clown who's not worth the time of

day. How was the bed?"

It took Aziza several seconds before she realized Jordan was asking how she'd slept. "The bed is wonderful, although I found myself tossing and turning." She smothered a yawn with her hand. "Sorry about that."

Jordan wanted to tell her that he'd done the same tossing and turning when he usually fell asleep within minutes of his head touching the pillow. Pushing off the desk, he reached for her hand. "Come with me. I'll show you where you can relax while I bring you a cup of coffee."

Aziza followed Jordan, walking into a large room that was sports bar, game room and lounge. Wall-mounted flat-screen TVs could be viewed from every angle, foosball and pool tables were set up in opposite corners, and a neon jukebox, pinball machines and arcade games offered something for everyone. A quartet of matching leather love seats were positioned for ultimate viewing.

"This is better than Coney Island," she teased. "It's been ages since I've played Pac-Man, Ms. Pac-Man and Donkey Kong. I still have one of the highest Pac-Man scores at an arcade in my old neighborhood. But what I excel at is pool."

Jordan rested a hand at the small of her back. "Do I hear a challenge?"

"Yeah, you did."

"We'll play later. But I only think it's fair to warn you I've been known to make grown men cry."

"That's their first mistake. They're men."

"Oh, so you're going to rely on your feminine wiles?"

"Whatever works, Wainwright."

"You're going down, Fleming."

"We'll see," Aziza drawled.

Jordan told Aziza he was going to begin his cross-examination using his trademark technique. He introduced himself as if gaining the witness's confidence with a gentle voice that soothed rather than antagonized or put them on the defensive. He asked and she revealed how a recruiter had approached her six months before graduation, based on the recommendation of one of her professors, who was an associate of Moore, Bloch and Taylor. She was interviewed twice — once by one of the partners and then by Kenneth Middleton Moore, Jr., who'd seemed genuinely impressed with her grades.

Kenny, as he'd asked her to call him, offered to pay off her twenty-thousand-dollar student loan and promised to give her a generous raise if she passed the bar on her first attempt. Kenny kept his promises, and her first year working at the firm had exceeded her expectations.

Jordan turned off the tape recorder. Their first session had lasted forty-five minutes, Jordan stopping before she got to the part where she'd begun to suspect that Kenny's interest in her was more than professional.

"I'm going to fix you something to eat, then after I transcribe our session, we'll play that game of pool."

"Do you mind if I make a suggestion?" she asked.

He gave her a direct stare. "Of course."

Aziza met his eyes. The stubble on his lean jaw made him look dangerous, less urbane. "What if I prepare brunch while you transcribe the tape? That way we can accomplish two tasks at the same time."

His lids lowered. "Are you sure you don't mind cooking?"

"Of course I don't mind."

"I didn't invite you here to work."

"If I'd stayed home, I still would have had to prepare something to eat," she argued quietly.

"Okay," Jordan said after a pregnant pause.

"Don't worry, Jordan. I'm not going to burn down your kitchen."

He made a face. "Very funny, Zee."

Jordan knew she was right about saving time. It wouldn't take that long for him to transcribe her responses because he'd already input his questions into the computer. All that remained was his typing in her responses — most of which he could repeat verbatim. He extended his arms, and he wasn't disappointed when Aziza moved into his embrace. "I don't want you to worry about Kenny. We're going to take him down. Down where he'll pay for what he did to you and probably countless other women."

Aziza nodded. She wasn't as concerned about herself as she was with other women who either were forced to endure his harassment because they felt they didn't have any recourse, or those who were too frightened to speak up. Exposing Kenneth Moore would give those frightened and silent ones a voice — a voice that said they were sick and tired of the harassment and that they weren't going to take it anymore.

"How long will it take you to transcribe the tape?" she asked.

"Probably a couple of hours. Why?"

She smiled up at him. "I need to know in case I decide to make something a little more complicated than bacon and eggs."

■ ■ ■ ■

Aziza loved cooking in a kitchen twice the size of hers. She discovered an abundance of fresh fruit and veggies in the refrigerator but not much meat or fish in the freezer. The pantry provided a treasure trove of gourmet jams, preserves, pure flavor extracts and several varieties of flour: cake, wheat, bread and bleached. Reaching for a straw basket among a collection on a shelf, she filled it with ingredients she needed to put together an elegant brunch.

It was exactly two hours later when she'd set the table with china, silver and crystal glassware and covered dishes when Jordan walked into the kitchen. She smiled at him. "Perfect timing."

He shook his head. "No, you didn't." He laughed, pointing to the flowering plant. Aziza had taken a potted orchid from the bathroom, placing it on the table as a centerpiece.

"Yes, I did. Don't you think it looks nice?"

"Is this your way of telling me that I should have fresh flowers in the house?"

"Loud and clear," she retorted. "Come and sit before everything gets cold."

Pulling out a chair at the table, Jordan

seated Aziza, then came around and sat opposite her. A wide grin split his face when she removed a covered dish to reveal eggs Benedict. She handed him a basket filled with croissants dusted with confectioners' sugar and slivered almonds. A glass bowl was filled with diced cantaloupe, apples, orange sections, green grapes and strawberries. Crystal goblets were filled with fresh-squeezed orange juice.

"You did all this in two hours?"

"It would've taken even less if I didn't have to wait for the yeast to rise."

"Give me your plate, sweetheart, and I'll serve you."

Aziza handed him her plate, and he carefully ladled an English muffin topped with crisp bacon and a lightly poached egg smothered in a rich, buttery hollandaise sauce onto it.

"You know we can't eat this too often," Aziza warned. "Talk about cholesterol overload."

"Once a week is all right."

"How about once a month, Jordan?"

"Uh-huh, baby. There's no way I'm going to wait thirty days to eat like this again."

Aziza took a sip of orange juice, savoring the feel of pulp on her tongue. "Okay. Twice a month."

Jordan raised his goblet in a salute. "Twice a month it is."

"If you want more coffee, then you'll have to make it. I don't know what you do to make the coffee taste so good, but I'm not even going to attempt to challenge you in that department."

"It's the beans and water."

"What about them?"

"I grind the beans and use distilled water."

"They can't be just ordinary coffee beans, Jordan."

"It's Jamaica Blue Mountain. I get it at a gourmet shop on Madison Avenue in the 80s. I purchase enough to last about a couple of months. Even when stored in airtight canisters they tend to lose some of their flavor over time. I buy my caviar at the same shop."

"Speaking of caviar, you're going to have to help me eat it once I open the tin."

Jordan bit into the croissant, shocked to find it filled with almond paste. "Damn! This is good."

"It's nice to see someone appreciate food."

He swallowed a mouthful of the delicious pastry. "I've always had a good appetite. That's why I have to work out or I'd end up with a nice little paunch."

Aziza sucked her teeth. "Yeah, right. You

probably have less than three percent body fat, so stop playing, Jordan Wainwright."

"Come on, babe. You know I spend most of my day sitting behind a desk."

"Desk or no desk, you probably would never have a weight problem."

"How do you stay so thin?" Jordan asked Aziza.

"I'm *hardly* thin." She was five-nine and weighed one-forty, but she wasn't about to reveal her weight to Jordan. "What I do is go to a dance studio several days a week."

"What type of dancing?"

"Al got me hooked on ballroom dancing after his stint on *Dancing with the Stars*."

"You're kidding, aren't you?"

"No, I'm not, Jordan. A couple hours of the samba, mambo and cha-cha equal a strenuous workout."

"It looks as if you like the Latin dances."

"I love them because they work the entire body. I keep promising myself that I'm going to Rio for Carnivale and samba until I drop from sheer exhaustion."

"A couple of years ago I went to Trinidad for Carnivale."

"How was it?" she asked.

"Awesome. Do you want to go with me?"

"When, Jordan?"

"This year. Ash Wednesday isn't until the

last week in February, so if you want to come with me, then don't schedule anything the weekend before."

"When is your partner's wedding?"

"The second weekend in February."

"That's a lot of partying in the Caribbean in February," she said teasingly.

"It's usually the coldest and snowiest month in the Northeast, so it's the perfect time to leave for warmer climes. What say you, counselor? Will you come with me?"

Aziza smiled, although her mind was a jumble of confusion and contradiction. A week ago she hadn't met Jordan Wainwright and now he was making plans for her to accompany him to Puerto Rico and Trinidad. Was he moving too fast, or was she too slow? The lawyer had unknowingly overwhelmed her with his unabashed masculine charm that left her fighting for control of emotions gone awry.

Her inexperience with men had left her totally unprepared for someone like Jordan Wainwright. She was certain she could hold her own with him when it came to the law, but unfortunately, she was still an ingénue in matters of the heart.

"I'll let you know after I've checked my calendar." It was the same thing she'd told him when he'd asked her to accompany him to Puerto Rico.

"Do you get seasick?"

"Not usually." She gave him a quizzical look. "Why, Jordan?"

"I've made arrangements for some of us to sail down to Puerto Rico for the wedding."

"It sounds like fun."

Jordan winked at her. "I did promise that we're going to have fun."

Aziza nodded as she ate her eggs. To say Jordan Wainwright was full of surprises was putting it mildly. Sailing to Puerto Rico and celebrating *Carnivale* in Trinidad. What else, she mused, could she look forward to sharing with him?

CHAPTER 12

"What's the matter, baby?" Aziza drawled, chalking the tip of her cue. "Why the tight jaw?"

She knew what had Jordan out of sorts without asking the question. She'd beat him in Pac-Man, foosball and Donkey Kong, and the final challenge was a game of billiards. She'd beat him handily, while not pretending to give him an edge.

With a deathlike grip on his cue, Jordan glared at the woman who'd trounced him soundly in every game. It wasn't as if she hadn't warned him, but he hadn't wanted to believe she was *that* good. What bothered him was not her beating him, but how coolly she'd reacted after each victory. It was if there was ice water in her veins.

What shocked Jordan at times was how detached and unaffected she appeared when talking about her ex-husband and boss. As if she'd turned a switch to tune out the ugliness. Even when he'd taped their first session, her answers were direct and delivered in a monotone. If he'd been a juror, he would've thought her rehearsed.

However, he was about to salvage what was left of his ego. He'd been taught to shoot pool by someone who'd learned from his father: Wyatt Wainwright. His great-grandfather had schooled Wyatt in the game in the same manner a teacher her students. By the time Wyatt was twelve he'd been earning enough money to pay the rent on his parents' cold water Lower East Side flat.

Christiane complained bitterly that her father-in-law exposed his grandson to low-life riffraff whenever he'd taken Jordan with him to pool halls, but the older man had tried to reassure her no harm would come to the boy as long he was with him. Wyatt had carried a registered firearm on his person at all times, and his driver, who doubled as his bodyguard, was also armed.

You're going down, baby — hard. Jordan forced a smile that stopped before it reached his eyes. "Instead of two out of three, let's play a single game." He took a step, bringing him closer to the table.

Her eyebrows lifted. "Are you sure you don't want a second chance?"

He slowly shook his head. "No, Zee.

231

You're going to need a second chance. What if we make a little wager?"

Aziza went completely still. Jordan had changed the rules. She'd wanted to wager, and he hadn't. Why now had he changed his mind? "What do you want?"

"You've heard of strip poker?" She nodded. "Well, I propose a game of strip pool. For every ball you miss, I'll remove an article of *your* clothing. The same rule applies to me."

"What about socks and shoes?"

"Shoes and socks are included."

She went back to chalking her cue. "When I'm finished you're going to be butt naked. And to show you that I'm a good sport, I'm going to let you break first."

Jordan moved into position, resting the cue between the fingers of his left hand. Bending slightly from the knees, he recalled everything his grandfather had taught him. He went still, then in an action too quick for the eye to follow, the white ball made contact, scattering colorful balls over green felt, all finding a home in the pockets.

Placing the cue stick on the table, he raised his arms in victory. "How you like *that?*" he taunted, enunciating each word. Winking, he beckoned her. "Come, darling.

232

Let's see what you're hiding under that shirt."

Aziza backed away from the table. "You're a ringer!"

"No, Zee. You're wrong. What I am is a winner. Now it's time to pay the piper."

She set her cue next to Jordan's, then turned and sprinted out of the room, he in pursuit. She'd gotten as far as the door when he swung her up, her feet leaving the floor so quickly she almost lost her breath.

"No fair, Jordan!"

He cradled her to his chest. "Yes, fair, Zee. I won, and now it's time for you to adhere to the rules."

Aziza put her arms around his neck in an attempt to keep her balance. His eyes bored into hers, seemingly reading her thoughts. She wasn't afraid to take her clothes off for Jordan. What was frightening was her inability to remain indifferent around him.

"Okay. But let me go." One minute she was in Jordan's arms and the next she stood in front of him, her hands going to the top button on the tailored shirt she wore over a pair of jeans. A slight gasp escaped her when Jordan stopped her, his fingers tightening around hers.

"It's all right, Zee," he said softly, "you don't have to undress for me."

"What kind of game are you playing?" There was no mistaking her confusion and annoyance.

"I was testing you to see how far you would go."

She gave him a wild-eyed stare, her chest rising and falling heavily. "Test me, Jordan? Who the hell do you think you are to test me? Is it because of the tapes? Did you hear something that made you believe that I'd perhaps said or done something to Kenny Moore that would make him turn on me like a predator stalking prey?"

Jordan shook his head. "No. You've got it all wrong."

"No!" she flung at him. "*You've* got it all wrong. I thought I'd never be able to trust another man again. And I was beginning to trust you. But then you come out of nowhere with the bait and switch. You laid the ground rules for the game and when I follow through you tell me it's test."

Reaching out, Jordan pulled Aziza to his chest, one hand cradling the back of her head. She was trembling. "Are you angry with me, baby?"

"I'm more than angry," she mumbled against his chest. "I'm livid."

He smiled. "Good."

"Good? What the hell are you talking

about, Jordan?"

"I want you enraged because it is that passion and thirst for revenge that will help me bring Moore to justice. You've told me you want to make him pay for nearly ruining your career, but they are just words, Zee. When we talk about charging Moore with sexual harassment, you sound as if we're talking about the weather. You showed me more emotion when you talked about your clients."

"It's not only because of my career, Jordan."

"Then what is it?"

"What he did to me — what I'd allowed him to do to me — made me feel dirty. At first I kept asking myself what did I do or say that would make him turn on me. Then I began to second-guess myself when I thought about what Lamar said about the clothes I wore. Were they too provocative? Perhaps I couldn't see what others saw.

"I lowered my hemline, made certain all the buttons on my blouses were buttoned and even wore long sleeves in the warmer weather so as not to show too much skin. I did all of that and the SOB still came after me. So, if you want to know if I'm ready to take him down, then the answer is yes. I'm tired of playing the victim. I let Kenny

235

Moore victimize me. I let Lamar victimize me. And I became a three-time victim when the D.A. threw out the tapes as inadmissible evidence, then asked if I'd bought my law degree because I should've known better than to waste his time with bogus nonsense."

Jordan went completely still. "You keep mentioning the tapes, but what about the condom?"

Pushing against Jordan's chest, Aziza met his eyes. They were more gray than green. "What about it?"

"Had you told him about the condom?"

"No. I'd decided it was my trump card just in case he decided to go forward and charge Kenny. We know DNA doesn't lie."

"You, my darling, just gave me what we need to bury the pig."

Aziza's heart was beating so fast it made her feel lightheaded. Her first reaction when she'd seen the condom had been to throw it away in disgust. But, like the results from a rape kit, it could be used as admissible evidence. "I can't believe it."

He brushed a kiss over her parted lips. "Believe it. I have a few connections at the Manhattan D.A.'s office — someone I know who would love to prosecute a case like this. And she happens not to be a member of the

236

old boys' club."

Aziza looped her arms around Jordan's neck, pulling his head down. Twin emotions of joy and relief raced through her as she kissed him with a passion she hadn't known existed. The silent expression communicated trust, appreciation and repressed passion that had long been denied.

Jordan deepened the kiss, his tongue finding its way into her mouth. He knew they were treading into dangerous waters, but not only was it too late, he no longer cared. He wanted Aziza Fleming in his life and in his bed. But he didn't want her to come to him out of gratitude, but because she wanted and needed him as much he needed and wanted her.

"Make love to me."

He heard her entreaty, believing he'd imagined it. It was what he wanted to hear her say more than anything else. "Tell me again."

Aziza pressed closer, her breasts flattening against his chest. "Don't make me beg you."

Jordan's hands were busy, searching under her shirt. He covered one lace-covered breast, feeling the rapid pumping of her heart through the delicate fabric. "Tell me, Aziza," he repeated.

"Please, make love to me."

Needing no further prompting, he swung her up in his arms. Taking long, determined strides, he carried her out of the room, down the hallway and up the staircase to his bedroom. He was about to break every rule he'd made for himself, yet was willing to accept the consequences.

Jordan placed her on the twisted sheets where he'd spent a restless night tossing and turning, fantasizing about making love to a woman who'd become an invisible itch he hadn't been able to scratch. He followed her body down, supporting his greater weight on his arms.

Burying his face along the column of her neck, he breathed a kiss there. "Will you allow me to make love with you because you want me? Not because you need me."

Aziza closed her eyes. She was so overcome with emotion that she felt like sobbing. The man holding her to his heart was offering her a second chance to live her life without doubt and mistrust. It no longer mattered how long she'd known Jordan. She'd known Lamar for more than twenty years, yet she hadn't really known him. What mattered was that the man in whose bed she lay had reached out to help without asking for anything in return.

"Yes, you may."

Jordan smiled. "You probably don't have any condoms in your handbag, so we're going to have to use mine."

She pounded his back with a fist. "That's not funny."

He raised his head, his expression sobering. "What isn't funny is an unplanned pregnancy."

"That can't happen."

"It won't, Zee, if I use protection."

"Thank you very much," she whispered.

Jordan kissed her again. "You're very welcome."

Aziza's eyelids fluttered closed, and she was more than content to lie with Jordan without moving or talking. She breathed in his body's natural scent mingling with his cologne. Everything about Jordan Wainwright seeped into her, making them one without him being inside her.

Foreplay was something with which she was totally unfamiliar. The peace she usually felt following an orgasm was what she was now experiencing. She lay, completely clothed, in bed with a man languishing in a fulfillment she hadn't thought possible, and at the moment she realized making love wasn't two naked bodies slamming into each other. It wasn't about moans, groans, sweat and the ribald utterances that would leave her feeling dirty and cheap.

Her breathing slowed and deepened until she found herself drifting off to sleep. Jordan must have moved, because she woke up with a start. "What's the matter?"

"Nothing's the matter," he said in her ear. "I'm going to get up and take off my clothes."

Now Aziza was fully awake. Jordan had moved off the bed. He kicked off his shoes, removed his socks and then his hand went to the hem of his shirt, pulling it up and over his head. She managed to smother a gasp when she saw what had been concealed by tailored suits and custom-made shirts. Well-defined pectorals, rock-hard abs and a flat belly were a testament to a diligent workout regimen. Jordan Wainwright's body equaled his face when it came to perfection. Her gaze lingered on his when he reached down to remove his jeans and underwear. She hadn't realized she'd been holding her breath until the side of the mattress dipped slightly when he sat down beside her. She sat up, her hands going to the buttons on her shirt.

Jordan leaned closer, his hand covering hers. "Please, let me." Not dropping his gaze, he undid the buttons on her shirt, pushing it off her shoulders. But he was forced to look down when she exhaled an audible breath. A swath of heat shot through his groin when he stared at the soft swell of brown flesh rising and falling under white lace as she breathed out through her parted lips.

Aziza was right. She wasn't thin. She was womanly, curvy and as lush as ripened fruit. He slid the straps to her bra off her shoulders, then, reaching around her back, unhooked the lace garment.

"Oh, sweet —" He bit down on his tongue, stopping the blasphemous word that would've been certain to make his mother gasp in horror before she lit a candle for his wayward soul.

He knew of some women who'd paid thousands to a plastic surgeon to achieve the breasts Aziza had been blessed with. They were full, firm and perched high above her rib cage. He cradled them as if they were fragile glass, then his mouth replaced his hands, tasting and placing kisses around the nipples until the areola hardened like tiny pebbles.

Jordan had wanted to get into bed and lie with Aziza until she was completely comfortable with him, mindful that she'd had only one prior lover and ever mindful that she'd been sexually harassed. And he did not want her to come to him out of a sense of gratitude; he wanted her to want him because they complemented each other as male and female and shared a love and passion for law. Both had walked away from high-paying positions and well-heeled clients to represent the indigent and underserved.

The most glaring difference was that at thirty-one, Aziza Fleming knew who she was and where she'd come from.

However, when Jordan Wyatt Wainwright had been thirty-one, he had discovered for the first time in his life who he was and where he'd come from.

Placing his first two fingers between her breasts, he traced an invisible line down her ribs and flat belly to the waistband on her jeans. Jordan felt the shudders racing through her body under his fingertips.

An audible sigh filled the silent room at the same time Aziza rose several inches off the bed. "Please, don't tease me," she pleaded.

She was pleading with him not to tease her when that was what she'd been doing since their initial introduction. Each and every time she lowered her lashes to glance up at him — it was teasing. When she'd pressed her breasts to his chest the night before — it was teasing.

Jordan slid a hand under her buttocks, while the other unsnapped her jeans, easing the denim fabric down her hips to her thighs. White bikini panties were decorated with tiny red hearts. "Cute," he drawled, smiling.

Aziza wanted Jordan to stop talking and make love to her. It was becoming more and more difficult not to move her hips. She felt the blood, hot and sluggish, sluice through her lower body and the arousing passion she'd locked away long before she'd ended her marriage.

Then, he did stop talking, removing each article of clothing in what seemed like a stylized ritual. Her blouse was first, then her bra, socks and jeans. The only thing that remained was her panties. Jordan moved over her, her gaze going from his face to the area below his waist. She smothered a gasp. Although he was semi-erect, Jordan was large — much larger than she could've imagined. Just the thought of his rigid sex inside her resulted in a rush of moisture, followed by a soft pulsing where it was impossible not to move her hips. She did gasp when his hand cupped her mound through the layer of silk. His eyebrows lifted a fraction. He knew. He knew by the dampness that she was aroused and ready for him.

Jordan forced himself to go slowly. Leaning over, he opened the drawer to the bedside table and removed a condom. He hadn't realized that his hands were shaking until it took two attempts to open the packet and roll the latex sheath down the length of his fully erect penis.

Smiling, he removed the remaining article of clothing that had kept him from viewing all of Aziza's beautifully proportioned body. He'd found her perfect with flawless brown skin the color of chocolate mousse, full, lush breasts, hips wide enough to carry children without difficulty and long legs with curvy calves, slim ankles and slender arched feet that seemed to go on forever.

"You are more than I could've ever imagined." His voice was filled with awe.

Aziza wanted to tell him that he'd shocked her, too. He *had* a lot more between his thighs than she could've ever imagined. "Thank you," she said instead. Extending her arms, she invited him into her embrace *and* inside her body.

She thought she was going to climax when his fingers searched the folds at the apex of her thighs, finding the swollen nub and applying pressure with the pad of his thumb. "Oh, my! Oh . . . oh . . ." She was babbling like an idiot.

Jordan answered her, positioning his sex at her wet vagina, pushing gently. His own groan echoed hers as he felt her body opening, stretching to accommodate the length and girth of his blood-engorged penis. Aziza was tight, tight enough to make him feel as if he were deflowering a virgin.

He hadn't slept with so many women that he hadn't been able to remember their faces or their names, but for a reason he was unable to fathom he wanted Aziza to be the last woman in his life. He wanted what Kyle, Ivan and Duncan had — that special woman with whom they planned a future that included marriage and children.

Before he was introduced to Alexander Fleming's sister he hadn't known what had been missing in his life because growing up wealthy had provided him with whatever he wanted, not necessarily what he needed. He'd known her a week, but it was long enough time for him to admit he was willing to fight to hold on to her.

Jordan rolled his hips, pulled out an inch and then with a sure thrust he found himself fully sheathed inside Aziza. They shared a sigh and a smile. "Did I hurt you, baby?"

"No. You feel good. Real, real good, Jordan." And he did. He hadn't begun to move and she felt him so deep inside her it was as if he'd touched her womb. Curving her arms under his shoulders, she held him tightly, as if he were her lifeline.

He moved again, this time establishing a strong rhythm that Aziza followed as if they'd choreographed the steps to an intricate dance. He felt her heat, her flesh close around him in a long, measured pulsing at the same time his own passions quickly spiraled out of control.

Jordan covered her mouth with his, cutting off the whimpers heating his blood; he quickened his thrusts. She felt so good. The rising scent of sex, mingling with her perfume, had become an aphrodisiac. He wanted to pull out and taste every inch of her body, but didn't want to shatter the sensual spell making them one.

"Jordan!" Aziza breathed out his name when the first ripple of release held her prisoner before easing. The pressure in her vagina built steadily as Jordan's sex swelled to enormous proportions until there was no more room.

"Yes, baby. I feel you." His breathing was deep, labored. "You're going to have to let it go."

Her head thrashed from side to side. "I

don't want to let it go. I don't want it to be over."

Closing his eyes and gripping the pillow beneath her head, Jordan clenched his teeth so hard his jaw ached. "It's not going to be over, baby. Not for a long, long time."

And during the nanosecond where time stood still, before he ejaculated into the latex covering, Jordan vowed to hold on to Aziza Fleming at the risk of losing his own life.

Aziza cried out as the walls of her vagina contracted around Jordan's rigid flesh; she felt as if she were floating outside herself as the orgasms grew stronger and stronger, overlapping one another in what had become freefall. She lay motionless, breathing heavily and savoring the aftermath of complete fulfillment.

When she did move it was to trail her fingertips over his damp back. "Thank you."

Jordan smiled into the pillow. "No, baby. Thank you." He wanted to tell Aziza that she was exquisite — in and out of bed. He loathed moving, but he had to get up and discard the condom. "I have to get up."

Aziza moaned in protest when he pulled out. She missed the weight pressing her down to the firm mattress and his warmth. Turning over on her side, she pulled the

247

sheet and lightweight blanket up and over her body. She giggled like a little girl when Jordan returned, got into bed and pulled her hips to his groin.

"What are you doing?" He was simulating making love to her again.

"What does it look like? I'm humping you."

"Don't start something you can't finish, counselor."

He caught the tender flesh on the nape of her neck between his teeth. "You think I can't get it up again?"

"I don't know."

"What don't you know?" Jordan asked.

"If you're not taking something for erectile dysfunction."

Jordan reached between her legs, his fingers working their magic until Aziza was moaning and writhing as she felt the familiar flutters that signaled she was going to climax again. Then, without warning, he withdrew his hand and turned over.

With wide eyes, she sat up, staring at his broad back. "You can't leave me like this."

"Oh, yes, I can. It appears as if I've just run out of my pills."

The seconds ticked. "I'm sorry," she apologized.

He turned and smiled at her. "I'm not,

Zee. I haven't spent a sorry moment since I've met you."

Curving her arms under Jordan's shoulders, she pressed her mouth to the side of his strong neck. "I think I'm going to enjoy being your girlfriend because you're so good for a woman's ego."

Jordan wanted to tell her it wasn't about boosting her ego but about falling for her — hard. It also wasn't about spouting the flowery phrases — phrases she'd probably heard before. What he intended to do was show her. Show Aziza how important she'd become to him.

CHAPTER 13

"This is Jordan." He'd picked up the receiver before the second ring.

"Jordan, darling. This is your mother. Wyatt told me you were taking time off from work, so I thought perhaps you weren't feeling well."

Cradling the receiver between his chin and shoulder, he executed tying his tie without looking in the mirror. He had less than twenty minutes to finish dressing before the driver arrived to take him and Aziza to Ivan's brownstone, which was within walking distance of their offices.

He would've taken his car, but trying to find a parking space in Manhattan during the winter months was like finding a needle in a haystack. However, from the Memorial Day weekend through the Labor Day weekend, many residents left the city for Long Island's East End, the Berkshires or the Jersey Shore. Every Fourth of July weekend,

Christiane closed up the Fifth Avenue mansion and relocated her household, including the live-in staff, to the family compound at Chesapeake Ranch Estates, Maryland.

"I'm quite well, Mother."

"I got a call from Deborah Westerbeck earlier this morning. She's in charge of seating arrangements for the museum's midwinter fundraiser, and she wants to know if you're coming unescorted. If you are, then she will pair you up with her niece."

"Tell Mrs. Westerbeck I'm bringing a guest."

"Who is she, darling? Do I know her?"

Jordan tightened the knot before turning down the shirt collar. "No, you don't. But I think you'll like her."

"Do you like her, Jordan?"

"Yes, I do, Mother. I like her a lot." A distinctive beep came through the earpiece. Jordan glanced at the name and number on the display. This was the call he'd been waiting for. "Mother, I'm going to have to ring off. I have a very important call coming through. I'll see you Friday night."

He tapped the flash button. "Melody, thanks for getting back to me. I'm going to make this quick, because I know you don't like to talk shop when you're not working." He'd called the A.D.A. at her office, but had been told Melody Harvey was away from her desk and would return his call. It had taken her more than twenty-four hours to get back to him.

"No problem, Jordan. What's up?" It took him less than ten minutes to give the prosecutor the details about Aziza's harassment case. "If Bonner tossed it out before, what makes you think he won't do it again?"

"She has what translates into a rape kit." Jordan told Melody about the condom.

A beat passed before she said, "She's got him, Jordan. If you're representing her, then you can guide her through the process. The tapes are inadmissible, but the content of the condom isn't. I'd love to handle this case, but I just discovered that I'm pregnant again, so I'm planning to leave in a couple of weeks to work part-time for Jeffrey. I told him that he can fire me as an employee, but he can't fire me as his wife and the mother of his children."

Jordan laughed softly. He and Melody were law school classmates. "Congratulations on the new baby. Jeffrey is a lucky man to have you as a law partner, wife and the mother of his children. When it comes to this case, I've made a decision not to revisit the same well," he said cryptically. "Ms. Fleming lives in Bronxville, so I'm going to

252

have the Westchester County's D.A.'s office handle the case."

"Good move, Jordan. I hope you string the bastard up by his *cojones*."

"I'll take a felony conviction and the revocation of his license for starters. Thanks again, Melody. I'll keep you updated."

He'd replaced the receiver in the cradle when Aziza walked into the bedroom. She was stunning in a black pencil skirt, matching hip-length jacket with a shawl collar and white tailored blouse. Sheer black stockings and a pair of black-and-gray variegated snakeskin stilettos pulled her elegant look together. She'd brushed her hair off her face into a loose chignon. Expertly applied makeup accentuated her best features: her eyes and mouth.

Walking across the room, he closed the distance between them, cradling her face. "You look absolutely beautiful." Diamond hoops had replaced the pearl studs.

Aziza lowered her lids and smiled up at him. She hadn't known what to expect when she'd asked Jordan Wainwright to make love to her, but it wasn't the warmth, ecstasy and fulfillment that had lingered for hours. She'd consciously not compared Jordan's lovemaking to Lamar's because there had been a time when she was so

253

inexorably in love with her ex-husband that making love with him had been an extension of her deep affection.

Aziza wasn't in love with Jordan, but there was something special about him and between them. To say the sex was good was an understatement. She'd thought she would've held back, unable to rid herself of the hang-ups she'd held on to because the man with whom she'd pledged her future had disappointed her and the man who'd offered to shepherd her professional career had shown her another side of his personality — deviance.

"Thank you. I hope what I'm wearing isn't too casual."

Attractive lines fanned out around Jordan's incredibly luminous eyes when he smiled. "You're perfect."

"And you're biased."

"You've got that right," he crooned, kissing the end of her nose.

Jordan wanted to tell Aziza what he'd gleaned from his conversation with Melody but decided to wait, not wanting to spoil the mood that had begun when he woke with Aziza huddled close to his length. He'd watched her sleep, wondering if she was dreaming, what she had dreamt about. When she finally did wake, she'd given him a shy smile, slipped out of bed to the bathroom, then returned and lay in his embrace until nature had forced him to seek out the bathroom.

They'd lingered in bed, making slow, passionate love, and when it had ended he'd known their relationship had changed. He'd held her, waiting for her respiration to return to normal, and they'd gone back to sleep. When they'd finally left the bed, the sun was high in the sky.

Aziza stepped around Jordan, picking his suit jacket off the bench at the foot of the bed while he fastened the cuff links in the French cuffs. Doubling as his valet, she held it as he pushed his arms into the sleeves of the dark blue garment.

"Turn around, Jordan, and let me check your tie."

He complied and stared at Aziza while she straightened the navy-blue silk tie with minute white squares. Was this what she'd done with her husband before they'd gone out? Helped him into his suit jacket? Adjusted his tie?

I'm not going to ask you to make love to me because it would mean I'm using you to assuage a need I've denied for longer than I can remember. Was she, Jordan mused, using him? Had he becoming a willing replacement for her husband — a man she'd loved but couldn't trust to protect her from a sexual predator? He wanted to tell himself that he was thinking too much, overanalyzing a new relationship when he should be enjoying it.

He forced a smile he didn't feel. "Are you ready?"

"I just have to get my coat and handbag."

Looping an arm around her waist, Jordan led Aziza out of the bedroom to the hallway where she'd left her coat and bag on the chair near a side table. He returned the favor when he held her coat. Hand-in-hand, they descended the staircase, he leading her to the front door and out into the lobby.

The doorman came to attention with their approach. Aziza averted her gaze from the man in the dark gray greatcoat and cap. He was staring at her as if she had a zit in the middle of her forehead.

"Good evening, Mr. Wainwright."

Jordan nodded in acknowledgment. "Good evening, Hector."

"Shall I call a taxi for you and your lady?"

"No, thank you. I've called for a car."

Hector clasped his gloved hands together. "It's best you wait inside where it's warm. It's very cold tonight." A sweep of headlights lit the sidewalk under the building canopy.

"I think your car is here," he said, opening the door as a sleek black Lincoln, with its engine running, parked in front of the building.

Sergio was standing on the sidewalk with the rear door open when Jordan and Aziza left the building's warmth. Aziza got in, sliding over on the leather seat to make room for Jordan. She sank into his embrace when the door closed with a solid slam.

"It is frigid," she whispered. She and Jordan hadn't left the duplex in three days.

Jordan pressed a kiss to her temple. "I don't mind the cold. It's the snow that bothers me."

"You don't ski?"

"No. I don't like cold weather sports." He closed the partition and then anchored her legs over his thighs. "Do you want Sergio to turn up the heat?"

"You're all the heat I need," she whispered. "What are you doing?" Jordan's hand had found it way between her thighs.

Throwing back his head, Jordan laughed, the warm, rich sound filling the interior of the vehicle. "I'm trying to keep another part of you warm." He lowered his voice to a whisper.

"*That's* never cold."

He laughed again. "I can attest to that."

■ ■ ■ ■

Less than ten minutes after they'd gotten into the car, the ride ended in front of a brownstone in Harlem's Mount Morris Park Historic District. Lights blazed from windows in the four-story building. Aziza barely had time to feel the cold when Jordan, holding her to his length to share his body heat, led her up the stairs to the entrance of the century-old structure. The solid oak door with lead-paned glass opened within minutes of the soft chiming of the bell to the first-floor apartment.

A tall, solidly built dark-skinned man with a widow's peak, wearing a black pullover and slacks, flashed a warm smile. "Welcome, folks. Come on in out of the cold."

Welcoming heat wrapped around them like a comforting blanket when Aziza and Jordan stepped into the spacious vestibule. A mahogany staircase with carved newel posts led to the upper floors. An antique credenza table held a Tiffany-style table lamp, and a leather chair with decorative walnut trim complemented the furnishings in the space.

Jordan exchanged a handshake with psychotherapist Dr. Ivan Campbell before they pulled each other close in a strong embrace. "Thanks, Doc." Easing back and extending his hand, he drew Aziza to his side. "Zee, this is our host, Ivan Campbell. Ivan, Aziza Fleming."

Ivan stared at the woman with Jordan, his eyes widening in appreciation. She was the perfect counterpart to the always well-dressed attorney who'd become his best friend's law partner. She was stunning!

He offered his hand, smiling when she placed her groomed one in his. "It is indeed a pleasure to meet you."

Aziza's head was level with Ivan's. Four-inch heels had put her over the six-foot mark. "Thank you."

Ivan shared a surreptitious wink with Jordan. "Come on in and join the others. We're serving cocktails before dinner. Jordan, you probably know everyone here, so I'll leave you to introduce your lady."

Aziza gave Jordan a sidelong glance, wondering if he was going to abstain. He'd told her about his first attempt to sample alcohol at fourteen. He'd admitted it had taken another ten years before he drank again and always in moderation.

She exhaled an inaudible sigh when she realized she wasn't over or underdressed for the gathering. Most of the women had chosen the de rigueur little black dress or slacks with dressy tops and the men suits with shirts and ties. The ubiquitous New York City black was in full effect.

A young man dressed in black with a white waistcoat bowed slightly. "May I take your coat, miss?"

Jordan helped Aziza out of her coat, handing it to the man assigned to coat check. She leaned close to him. "Do you know everyone here?"

His eyes scanned the small crowd standing and sitting in the expansive entryway in front of roaring fire in a minimalist-designed fireplace. A bartender had set up a portable bar between the entryway and the formal living room. He'd met most of the Campbells' guests over the summer when they'd gotten together either at Ivan's or Kyle's house for outdoor cookouts.

Jordan had been as shocked as Kyle and Duncan when Ivan had announced that he was getting married. The older of the trio by several months, Ivan had the reputation of "love them and leave them," but when he'd met and fallen in love with the exceptionally talented photographer Nayo Goddard, he hadn't hesitated to give up his carefree social lifestyle to settle down with her.

"Practically everyone," he said in her ear. "Can I get you something from the bar?"

"I'll have club soda with a twist."

Jordan pressed his mouth to her hair. "Are you sure I can't get you anything stronger?"

"No, darling," she drawled, smiling up at him.

"Damn, partner. You and your lady need to get a room."

Jordan turned to find his law partner standing a few feet away. "Mind your neck," he quipped, touching fists with Kyle Chatham. Placing an arm around Aziza's waist, he pulled her close. "Aziza, this Kyle Chatham, partner, mentor and soon-to-be ex-bachelor. Chat, this is Aziza Fleming."

Aziza extended her hand and was rewarded with a light kiss on her fingers. *So, this is the dynamic Kyle Chatham,* she mused. Jordan's law partner was tall, very dark and strikingly handsome. His cropped hair was salt-and-pepper, but it was his slanting gold-brown eyes that drew her rapt attention. The woman who'd managed to get Kyle to commit was more than lucky. She was blessed.

Kyle stared at the tall woman beside Jordan, silently congratulating his partner on having exquisite taste in women. He'd observed Jordan with women over the years

261

they'd come to know each other, but none had surpassed Aziza Fleming. He knew he was staring at her, but so were the other men in the room.

"It's truly a pleasure to meet you," he said, smiling.

Aziza returned his smile. "Congratulations on your upcoming wedding."

Kyle released her hand. "Thank you. Are you coming with Jordan?"

Knowing Kyle had put her on the spot, Aziza narrowed her eyes at Jordan, wondering what he'd told his friend about her. She'd stopped the practice of inputting her appointments in her cell phone once she'd set up the home office. Now that she'd committed to dating Jordan, she would have to go back to it.

"Yes." She was certain she didn't have any court appearances in February, so that meant whatever she'd scheduled for the Valentine's Day weekend could be rescheduled.

"Hey, Jordan," crooned a sultry voice. A petite woman wearing a white tailored blouse, black pencil skirt and a pair of Louboutin black patent leather pumps wended her way through those standing around drinking and nibbling on hors d'oeuvres set out on low tables.

Smiling, Jordan reached out and scooped Nayo Goddard-Campbell off her feet. He planted a noisy kiss on her cheek. There was something about the photographer's face that reminded him of the prototype for a black Barbie doll.

"Happy New Year, Nayo."

Nayo hugged him. "Thank you. Happy New Year to you, too. And thank you for the case of champagne."

Jordan set her on her feet. "Enjoy." Whenever he was invited to a soiree he usually ordered a case of champagne or their favorite wine and had it delivered to the host or hostess's residence.

The sparkle of the diamonds in Nayo's ears competed with the ones in the eternity band on her left hand. "Did you bring a date because I've arranged seating by couples?"

Aziza bit back a smile. Jordan's friends asking him if he'd come with a date spoke volumes. They were aware that he wasn't currently involved with a woman. And given his looks, money and social standing he could have a harem of women at his disposal. It was apparent he was just as discriminating about whom he dated as he was in his choice of attire.

"Nayo, this is Aziza Fleming. Zee, Nayo

263

Campbell, our gracious hostess for the evening."

Nayo peered at the tall, beautiful woman with Jordan Wainwright, wondering where she'd seen her before. "I know you."

"I don't think we've ever met," Aziza countered.

"Why then do you look so familiar?" Folding her hands at her tiny waist, Nayo closed her eyes for several seconds. "I know," she said excitedly. "Are you related to Al Fleming?"

Conversation ceased and all eyes were directed at Aziza. "Uh. Yes. He's my brother," she admitted reluctantly in a quiet voice.

Nayo applauded. "I knew it. I took a photograph of Al when I had an assignment to photograph as many sports figures I could find in a month. You and your brother were coming out of a restaurant on Third Avenue when I was waiting on the corner to catch a bus. I think he'd just come over from the Bears to play with the Giants. Unfortunately, the shot wasn't that good, so I couldn't use it."

"You have a very good memory," Aziza said.

"My memory is only as good as the images I'm able to capture on film. When you speak to your brother again, tell him I would like to take an updated photograph of him." She frowned at Jordan. "And don't stand there looking like the cat that swallowed the canary, Jordan Wainwright."

He spread out his hands. "What did I do?"

"Why did I have to find out secondhand that the Viking is your cousin?"

"I didn't know you followed football."

"What about football, doll face?" Ivan had come over to join the conversation.

"Don't you dare doll face me, Ivan," Nayo said between clenched teeth. "You know I'm still pissed off about you, Kyle, Duncan and Jordan going to the Super Bowl without even bothering to ask your women whether we wanted to come along."

Aziza stared at Jordan. "You're going to the Super Bowl?"

A flush darkened his face. "Well . . . um . . . you know —"

Nayo waved a hand in front Jordan's face. "Save it, counselor. It appears as if your girlfriend is as much in the dark as the rest of us." She reached for Aziza's hand. "Come with me, girlfriend. We need you to help us plan strategy."

Jordan exchanged a confused look with Ivan. "What the hell was that all about?"

Ivan shook his head. "Man, you don't

want to know."

"But I *do* want to know. What's wrong with us going to a ballgame?"

"When DG told Tamara he was going, she got on the phone with Ava, who in turn called Nayo." Ivan ran a hand over his face. "I don't understand women, Jordan. We get together for a game every Sunday, and they walk around with major attitudes. I tried to tell Nayo that it is the shortest season for any sport, yet they mumble, grumble and push out their lips like spouts on a jug."

"Have you invited them to watch the games with you?" Jordan asked.

"Yes."

"Then what's the problem?"

"They don't want to watch it with us. Yet they bitch and moan about not going to the Super Bowl."

Resting an arm on Ivan's shoulder, Jordan shook his head. "It's not about the game, but the parties and the hype. I'm willing to bet if you took your wife with you, she'd end up on Rodeo Drive shopping her brains out."

Ivan blinked. "You think?"

Jordan nodded. "I know."

"Talk to me, Wainwright."

"I took a girl to Arizona for Super Bowl XLII and she spent the entire trip hanging out at a spa in the desert. I didn't see her again until it was time to fly back to New York."

"Damn, man. That's wrong."

"Tell me about it. That was the last time I invited *any* woman to go along with me to a sporting event."

"What about Aziza? Is she into football?"

"Not really," Jordan confirmed. "She'll only watch when her brother is playing."

Ivan blew out a breath. "I suppose that lets you off the hook."

Kyle joined them, handing Jordan a glass with tomato juice, lime wedge and celery stalk. "There's no vodka in it."

"What's up with you, gangsta? I heard about you downing shots," Ivan teased.

Jordan laughed. He'd gotten used to people calling him gangsta or sheriff, viewing them as an affectionate sobriquet. "I wasn't thinking straight that night."

Pushing his hands into the pockets of his slacks, Kyle rocked back on his heels. "That's what happens when your woman looks like Aziza."

"I hear you, brother," Ivan intoned. "I don't know if I'd be able to handle dating a model. I really don't like other men gawking at my woman."

Jordan swallowed a mouthful of the piquant virgin cocktail. "She's not a model."

"What is she?" Ivan and Kyle chorused in unison.

He held back laughter when he saw the expectant expressions on his friends' faces. "She's an attorney."

Groaning and shaking his head, Ivan closed his eyes. "Why do I have a house full of lawyers? What are of the odds of Nayo and I inviting six couples and five of the twelve being attorneys?"

"That's because we got it like that," Kyle bragged, bumping fists with his junior law partner.

Aziza followed Nayo Campbell through the kitchen where a caterer and his staff were braising, sautéing and chopping different ingredients for the evening's dinner party, past a well-stocked pantry and laundry room and then down a flight of stairs to the street level. Framed movie prints covered the walls of a home theater with an authentic popcorn machine. Two women, both wearing diamond engagement rings, seated on leather love seats, were talking quietly to each other.

"Please sit down, Aziza," Nayo said, indicating a facing love seat. She sat on a matching club chair. "Let me introduce you to Tamara Wolcott and Ava Warrick. Ladies, this is Aziza Fleming, Jordan's girlfriend. Ava is engaged to Kyle and Tamara to Duncan Gilmore, who you'll meet later. Right now he's upstairs looking at photographs."

Aziza smiled at the two attractive women. "Please call me Zee. It's less of a tongue-twister than Aziza."

Nayo rested folded her hands in her lap. "I like your name. It's African, isn't it?"

"Yes. It means *beautiful* in Swahili. Is yours African, too?"

Nayo nodded. "It's *our joy* in Yoruba. I guess you're wondering why we're meeting."

Aziza stared at the three women. She assumed they were all around her age — early thirties. When she'd asked Jordan about his friends' girlfriends, he'd said Ava was a social worker and Tamara a trauma center doctor. Jordan had also revealed that Kyle, Duncan and Ivan, who'd grown up together in public housing, had made a boyhood pact to own a Harlem brownstone. The three friends had realized their dream when they purchased an abandoned brownstone, renovated it and set up their businesses under the same roof. Ivan and Kyle owned property in Harlem, while Duncan had purchased a condo in Chelsea.

"I did give it some thought."

Tamara leaned forward. A mane of heavy dark hair framed her tawny-brown face. *Lush* and *voluptuous* were adjectives most people used when describing Dr. Tamara Wolcott. A black stretch-knit top and matching slacks hugged her curves like second skin. Strappy stilettos added another four inches to her statuesque figure.

"Let me explain why we're upset," she said to Aziza. "Our men usually get together once a week during the football season, and we don't have a problem with that. It's their time to bond and it is our time to get together to test our cooking skills. What has us so pissed off is that Kyle, Duncan and Ivan promised if they were able to secure Super Bowl tickets, they would take us with them. I want to know one thing, Zee. Has Jordan mentioned taking you to L.A.?"

Aziza could feel waves of resentment coming off them. They were football widows who had expected their men to take them to football's big dance — the Super Bowl. She could identify with them. If one looked up *sports fanatic* in the dictionary they would find Ezekiel, Omar and Sheridan Fleming. Her father and brothers took spectator to another level. They watched football, baseball, basketball, golf, hockey *and* soccer.

"He didn't say a mumbling word."

"I'd hoped he'd be different, but Jordan is just like the rest of them," Ava complained, waving her hand. Recessed light reflected off the cushion-cut diamond on her finger with blue-white sparks.

"What did you do during last year's Super Bowl?" Aziza asked.

Tamara, Ava and Nayo exchanged glances. "We didn't know them last January." It was Nayo who'd spoken.

Aziza mentally did the math. A year ago none of the women knew their fiancés, or husband, which meant they hadn't had, or wouldn't have, long engagements. "Have any of you been to a Super Bowl?" They shook their heads. "Well, I have, and if given the choice, I'd rather watch and celebrate in the comfort of my own home. That way I don't have to deal with unruly, intoxicated fans *and* the frustration of spending hours in an airport waiting for a flight home."

Tamara grimaced. "So it's not as glamorous as it looks?"

"It's fun if you're really a fan. I only watch it when my brother is playing."

"Her brother just happens to be Al Fleming," Nayo stated proudly.

"No!"

"You're joking!"

Ava and Tamara had spoken at the same time.

Aziza smiled. "He's my baby brother."

Nayo moaned under her breath. "A baby brother I'd love to photograph. I've taken a few photos of athletes, but I don't have enough for a showing. Can you help a sister out and ask him for me?"

"I'll ask him." Aziza would ask her brother, but what she couldn't promise Nayo was that he would agree. Alexander Fleming had managed to keep a low profile despite his A-list status.

"Some of my girlfriends and I usually take turns hosting a Super Bowl gathering each year," she continued. "You're welcome to join us."

Ava angled her head. "Where do you live?"

"Bronxville."

Ava smiled. "That's not far. I'm willing to drive if y'all want to come with me," she said to Nayo and Tamara.

Nayo stood up. "Sounds good to me. I better get upstairs before everyone will think I'm a neglectful hostess."

Aziza and the others followed their hostess into the living room. More couples had arrived, and the bartender was doing a brisk business pouring and mixing drinks.

A shiver raced over the nape of her neck when the scent of familiar cologne wafted in her nostrils. "How was your strategy meeting?" Jordan asked softly.

"It was wonderful."

"Should I be concerned?"

"Nope."

"Should Ivan, Duncan or Kyle be concerned?"

Aziza smiled. "They have to ask their women."

"Are you saying you're *my* woman, Aziza Fleming?"

She turned to face Jordan, her smile still in place. "I'll let you know."

"When, baby?" Jordan caught his breath when he saw the open invitation in the eyes of the woman who'd ensnared him in a sensual web from which he didn't want and couldn't escape.

"When we dance together on the beach in the moonlight."

Jordan resisted the urge to kiss her with a room filled with people. "I can't wait."

He couldn't wait to take her to Puerto Rico, but that was more than six weeks away. One thing he didn't have to wait for was making love to Aziza. He'd broken his own rule about not sleeping with a woman until they'd dated at least a month. But

CHAPTER 14

A smile softened Aziza's mouth when Jordan reached for her hand under the tablecloth. At the conclusion of the cocktail hour everyone was escorted into the formal dining room. Couples were seated together with the host and hostess at either end of the table.

Ivan had exchanged his sweater and slacks for a tailored dark gray suit, white shirt and aubergine silk tie. All eyes were trained on him as he stared across the table at his wife.

"Nayo and I would like to welcome you into our home and kick off what will probably become a very active social year with weddings and new births. The two empty chairs are for a couple who'd planned to attend, but at the last minute were forced to cancel. For those of you who are familiar with Signature Cakes, I would like to inform you that pastry chef Faith Whitfield-McMillan and her husband, Ethan, are now the proud parents of a healthy baby boy." Applause followed his announcement.

Nayo's dark eyes sparkled like onyx. "When Ivan and I decided to host this gathering we decided to compromise. I invite my friends and he invite his, and before everyone leaves we all will be friends. This is a little unorthodox, but I'd like to go around the table and have everyone introduce themselves." Her smile widened. "I'll break the ice. I'm Nayo Goddard-Campbell, a freelance photographer and as soon as Ivan and I get the necessary permits to install an elevator, I plan to open a gallery on the top floor." She turned to her right. "Geoff."

A slender young man with shaggy blond curls and cool gray eyes smiled at Nayo. "Geoffrey Magnus. I own an art gallery in the Village. I'm proud to say that some of the photos in this magnificent home once hung in my gallery."

The woman beside Geoffrey rested a hand on his shoulder. Her blunt-cut dirty-blond hair was swept off her face with a velvet headband. She wore the quintessential little black dress with a single strand of pearls and matching studs. "I'm Bethany Lawry. I just joined my dad's law firm as a junior partner."

All eyes shifted to Jordan. "Jordan Wainwright, junior partner at Chatham and Wainwright."

"Aziza Fleming. I'm an attorney with a private practice in Bronxville, New York."

"What's up with the lawyers?" Ivan quipped.

An incredibly handsome man with sable coloring and salt-and-pepper hair cleared his throat. "Micah Sanborn, former NYPD. I'm currently an A.D.A. with the Kings County D.A.'s office." Everyone laughed.

A woman with short curly hair and shimmering catlike eyes smiled at Micah. "I can assure you I'm not a lawyer. Tessa Whitfield-Sanborn, wedding planner for Signature Bridals." A smattering of applause followed her announcement. Tessa's wait list had gone from twelve to eighteen months after she'd coordinated the wedding of an A-list actress.

"Duncan Gilmore, accountant, financial analyst and in another two years I'll add tax attorney to the list." His olive coloring, cropped curly hair, chiseled features and beautifully modulated voice garnered the rapt gaze of every woman in the room. "All my friends call me DG."

Tamara rolled her eyes at him. "You say that as if you're a playa from the Himalaya."

She pantomimed putting her hand over her eyes the way the mime did when he executed the routine.

Kyle laughed loudly. "It was Jordan not DG who was a playa when he first came to work with us," Kyle teased. "He couldn't get a lick of work done because the *ladies* from Ivan and DG's offices found every excuse to come to the second floor — and it wasn't because they wanted legal advice."

Aziza gave Jordan a sidelong glance. "Were you a playa, baby?" she asked innocently. The entire table erupted in laughter, some pounding the table so hard glasses and silver rattled.

Jordan glared at Kyle. "TMI, brother."

"No it's not, brother," Kyle drawled. "Your woman has a right to know that the Harlem honeys like JW."

Aziza looped her arm through Jordan's. "If that's the case, then I definitely have to hold on tight."

"That's right, girl," Nayo crooned. "Hold on to your man."

There was chorus of amens from the women in attendance before introductions continued.

"Tamara Wolcott. And no, I'm not an attorney but an E.R. doctor."

Kyle waited until the snickers subsided.

"Kyle Chatham, senior partner at Chatham and Wainwright, Attorneys-at-Law," he announced smugly. He and Jordan executed a thumbs-up simultaneously.

"Ava Warrick, social worker. I don't know why y'all hatin' but I happen to like my lawyer." She winked at Kyle. He angled his head and brushed a kiss over her mouth.

"Hear, hear," Geoffrey intoned, raising his water goblet, and was rewarded with an adoring look from Bethany.

Eyes were trained on the remaining couple. The man with dark blond hair and intense dark blue eyes was jaw-dropping gorgeous. "Rafael Madison, U.S. Deputy Marshal assigned to the White Plains Federal Courthouse."

"I'm Simone Whitfield-Madison, owner of Wildflowers and Other Treasures and floral decorator for Signature Bridals." The resemblance between Simone and her sister was obvious. Both had curly hair, but Simone's was streaked with reddish highlights and her eyes were a sparkling hazel.

Ivan winked at Simone. "That concludes the introductions, so if anyone needs to purchase artwork, hire an attorney, doctor, social worker, financial analyst, wedding planner or floral designer, you'll know who to contact. Sorry, Rafe, but you're the odd

279

man out. Let's hope none of us will need the services of the U.S. Marshal Service."

Tiny lines fanned out around the hunky lawman's remarkable eyes when he flashed a wide grin. "Once I put in my twenty years with the service I plan to go to law school. So that will make it even — six attorneys and six *others.*" He managed to duck when his wife threw a balled-up cocktail napkin at him. This elicited another round of laughter.

Nayo signaled for a member of the waitstaff to begin serving, and over the next two hours her guests dined on expertly prepared prime rib, herb-crusted Cornish hens and broiled flounder stuffed with lobster and crab.

The wines flowed, the conversations were lively as the seven couples exchanged pleasantries and anecdotes that kept everyone laughing. The conversation shifted to Kyle and Ava's upcoming wedding in the Caribbean and the process of coming up with baby names after Tessa and Micah announced they were expecting a daughter in mid-April.

It was minutes after midnight when Ivan and Nayo's guests began to take their leave; those who didn't have cars had contracted with car services to take them home. Aziza barely had time to settle back and relax in the warmth of the car when the ride ended. The temperature had dropped to single digits, and when Jordan helped her out of the car, she ran to the building, startling the doorman when he rushed over to open the door for her.

Within seconds of closing and locking the door, Jordan swept Aziza off her feet and carried her up the staircase to his bedroom. The sound of clothing being tossed aside, the escalating moans and groans that accompanied their undressing each other echoed with the rising passion threatening to explode.

Somewhere between madness and sanity, Jordan remembered he had to protect Aziza from an unplanned pregnancy. He snatched open the drawer to the bedside table and grabbed a handful of condoms. Light from a full moon silvered the bed and bedroom through half-open drapes.

Aziza felt a burning in the back of her throat where she'd choked off the screams building there. There was something so feral and unbridled about making love without the pretense of foreplay that it excited and frightened her at the same time. Moisture flowed from her like an unchecked faucet when she stared at Jordan sheathing his tumescence in latex. The condom was so thin she was able to feel the heat of his sex when he penetrated her. She extended her arms and opened her legs as Jordan loomed over her. He lowered his body until her breasts were crushed to his hard chest.

"Love me, Jordan," she whispered in his ear.

Jordan wanted to do more than love Aziza. He wanted to brand himself on her body, heart and mind. His mouth covered hers in a soft kiss that belied the fire raging in his groin. "I love your mouth," he whispered. His mouth moved lower as he fastened his teeth to the tender flesh at the base of her throat. "I love your sweet neck."

Continuing his downward journey, he placed kisses all over her firm breasts, catching the hardened nipples between his teeth. "I love your beautiful breasts." She gasped when he increased the pressure, worrying the hardened flesh between the ridges of his teeth. He'd bitten her, but it wasn't hard enough to hurt her or break the skin.

He slipped down the bed, his tongue marking a trail over her belly. Inhaling, Jordan blew out his breath over the mound covered with moist tangled curls. Then, without warning, he grasped her legs, anchoring them over his shoulders.

Aziza screamed once and then swallowed the sobs of rising ecstasy when she felt Jordan's tongue searching between her legs to find the opening that brought her so much sexual pleasure. She wanted to tell him to stop but it felt so good, too good. Heat, then cold swept over her, her skin beading with gooseflesh.

"Please." She heard a voice, but didn't recognize it as her own.

Jordan heard the entreaty. He rested a hand on Aziza's belly and felt her muscles contracting under his touch. He wanted to make love to her with his mouth until she climaxed, yet feared if he continued he would come without being inside her.

Pulling his mouth away, he moved up her trembling body and kissed her deeply, his tongue plunging in her mouth over and over and simulating his making love to her. "Touch me," he whispered hoarsely.

Reaching between his legs, Aziza held his hardened flesh, feeling the heat and the blood rushing to his erection. Spreading her legs, she lifted her hips and eased him inside her inch by every delicious inch, sighing when he was fully sheathed up to the root of his penis.

Slowly, deliberately, they moved together, she arching to meet his strong thrusting.

Things they never would've said out of bed they communicated wordlessly with their bodies. Just when she felt the soft tremors that indicated the onset of an orgasm, Jordan slowed and stopped without pulling out. And when he started moving inside her again, the pulsing increased. He continued stopping and starting up again until she felt as if she were going crazy.

Her fingernails made half-moon imprints on his back with her increasing frustration. She felt as if she was standing on a precipice, unable to move because she feared falling.

"Jordan!" His name came out in a strangled cry. She couldn't hold back any longer. An orgasm seized her, followed by another one and then one more. She'd fallen off the precipice, shattering into a million little pieces of pure ecstasy.

Burying his face between Aziza's neck and shoulder, Jordan bit his lip to smother the groans when he felt his scrotum tighten. He couldn't hold back any longer. Grasping the pillow under her head, he surrendered to the pleasure holding him captive.

They lay joined, enjoying the sensations that had made them one with the other. Jordan would've fallen asleep where he lay if Aziza hadn't tried to push him off her. He'd become dead weight.

Somehow he garnered enough strength to roll off her body. He knew he had to get up and discard the condom but found that his limbs refused to follow the dictates of his mind. And for the first time since sleeping with a woman, Jordan Wainwright pulled off the condom and dropped it to floor beside the bed. Turning back to Aziza, he pulled her hips to his, closed his eyes and within minutes had fallen asleep.

Aziza sat in her office going through the mail that had accumulated during the time she'd stayed with Jordan. She separated junk mail, magazines and bills, putting them into piles.

Jordan had taken her out for Sunday brunch, then when they returned to his place he'd told her about the conversation he'd had with the district attorney who had been his classmate at Harvard Law. She'd agreed that the tapes were inadmissible, but not the condom with Kenneth Moore's DNA.

As her legal counsel, he'd also decided to sue Kenneth Moore in the Westchester County federal court for violation of her civil rights based on sex and race. In several of the taped conversations Kenneth admitted hiring her because she was a "sexy

African-American woman," "his firm needed more color," and "he'd always fantasized about making love to a black woman." In cross-examination he would use Kenneth Moore's words against him.

Aziza now knew what rape victims went through when they had to face the person that had violated them in the most violent way possible. Kenneth Moore hadn't physically violated her, but she felt as if she'd been violated nonetheless by his innuendoes, sexual overtures and finally with the condom. Rape was rape, whether physical or emotional, and the pervert had to pay for his crimes.

It would be another week before Jordan would be available to accompany her to file charges against Kenneth Middleton, Jr., and she'd decided not to go to the safe deposit box until that day. She wasn't superstitious or paranoid by nature, but Aziza didn't want any unforeseen event or accident to destroy the only evidence she needed to prove her assertion.

Flipping the pages on the planner on her desk, she perused the notations for the next month. She had one court appearance — a hearing for a thirteen-year-old who had begun staying out at night after her mother caught her with an eighteen-year-old boy.

With the exception of two projected house closings, she was available to go to Kyle and Ava's wedding, attend a museum fundraiser at the end of the week and plan her girls-only Super Bowl party. She'd exchanged phone numbers with Tamara, Ava and Nayo.

Aziza had enjoyed interacting with Jordan's friends, finding them friendly, and what she valued most was they were unpretentious, notwithstanding the lawyer jokes. She did find it odd that there had been so many lawyers at the dinner party.

She turned on her computer and, while waiting for it to boot up, she scribbled on a To Do pad: pay bills online, email "girls" about Super Bowl party, order food for party.

Her brother's team had one more game before making it to the big game. She also had to go through her closet to find something to wear to the museum fundraiser. Instead of going through her closet, she would go shopping. It'd been a while since Aziza had felt the thrill of trying on dresses and shoes.

"No shoes," she whispered. Shoes to her were like crack to an addict. One pair became two, then three. But then, Aziza mused, she had to have clothes for the destination wedding, and the timing was

287

perfect. It was January, and boutique and department store racks were filled with cruise wear. A satisfied smile parted her lips when she added shopping to her To Do list.

Donald Ennis muted the television, put the chilled bottle of beer to his mouth, took a deep swallow and belched loudly. The studio apartment was so hot he'd had to open several windows. He didn't intend to complain to the super because there were times when the building was so cold he'd had to get fully dressed before going to bed.

Reaching under the waistband of his boxers, he scratched between his thighs. His girlfriend hated when he did it, but because she was visiting her sister in Philly he could scratch and belch to his heart's content. He'd left a message with Minerva Jackson to have Raymond return his call, but so far he'd heard nothing from the man for more than twelve hours. He hoped the old man hadn't kicked off before giving him his apartment.

Donald wanted to tell Raymond that Robert Andrews had a snowball's chance in hell of defeating Billy Edwards. Even if Humphries spent every dollar he had for his son-in-law's campaign, and even if Billy passed away the day before election day,

Robert Andrews still wouldn't win. Billy was like Adam Clayton Powell, Jr., and Charlie Rangel. They didn't have to campaign and would still be reelected.

He took another long swallow, belched and scratched again, repeating the ritual until the bottle was empty. Slumping lower on the worn recliner, Donald closed his eyes and drifted off to sleep. The cell phone on the table chimed the distinctive ring for Raymond Humphries. Donald opened his eyes and picked up the tiny instrument.

"Humphries."

"Hey, Slick. I know why she left Moore, Bloch and Taylor."

"Didn't I tell you . . . Why!?"

Donald smiled. The old man was learning not to bark at him. "It looks as if she had a fallin' out with her boss."

"So she quit?"

"No, Humphries. She and Kenneth Moore split."

"Cut the double-talk, Ennis."

"Miss Fleming was having an affair with her boss."

"You mean she was sleeping with him while she was married?"

Donald shook his head. "I believe that's what an affair means."

"Who told you this?"

"None of your damn business. Do you really think I'm going to reveal my sources? And there's something else you should know. It appears you're right about Jordan and his grandfather scamming everyone. The two of them had dinner at Hasaki the other night. In fact, they looked rather chummy."

"What about the girl?"

"If you're asking if she's still seeing grandbaby boy, then the answer is yes. Right now she's spending more time at his place than her own."

"I think it's time Ms. Fleming took on another client. I want you to lie low and out of sight until I contact you again."

Donald's eyebrows lifted. "Are you telling me to pull my people off this case?"

"Only for now. Come by the office Friday. Ms. Jackson will have a lease for you to sign and the keys to your new apartment."

"Lease? I don't want to rent, Humphries. I want to own the apartment."

"You're not going to own any of my properties until I run the Wainwrights out of Harlem."

Donald knew Raymond had him by the proverbial short hairs, but he would go along with him until he got what he wanted. Still, he had to make one last plea. "I'm not going to work for you *and* pay you rent, too."

"I'll waive the first three months' rent. After that, you're on your own."

He smiled. "Okay, Humphries. You've got yourself a deal."

Aziza lifted the skirt of the flowing midnight-blue gown with one hand as she navigated the sidewalk along Fifth Avenue. When Jordan had told her they were attending a museum fundraiser, she hadn't thought she would walk to the event. He'd also neglected to tell her that it was the Museum of the City of New York's annual Winter Ball and the museum on Fifth Avenue between 103rd and 104th was only five blocks from his building.

Jordan covered the gloved hand tucked into the bend of his arm over his tuxedo jacket. "Are you cold?"

"No," she replied. Aziza wasn't as bothered by the crisp nighttime temperatures as she was about turning her ankle in the four-inch dark blue Christian Louboutin's leather and Swarovski crystal pumps. "If I'd known we were going to walk I would've worn flats and carried my heels."

"Don't worry, baby. I won't let you fall."

Jordan hadn't wanted to believe Aziza could improve on perfection. He'd thought her beautiful the night he saw her in his cousin's penthouse, but tonight she'd morphed into red carpet Hollywood glamour. Her hair was styled with tousled curls moving as if they'd taken on a life of their own. The bodice of the strapless gown matched the sexy heels, the toes which peeked out from under yards and yards of silk chiffon with each step. The black silk coat sweeping around the hem of her gown, lined with cashmere, provided some protection from the winter weather. However, unlike Hollywood actresses laden with multimillion-dollar jewelry, Aziza had chosen only a pair of London blue sapphire and diamond earrings.

"How many fundraisers do you attend in a year?" Aziza asked Jordan.

Jordan paused. "Probably a half dozen. Why?"

"And you expect me to go with you?"

"Yes."

"Do you realize how many outfits I have to have? I can't be seen in the same dress twice in one season."

Jordan laughed, his breath visible in the night air. "Don't worry. I'll pay for your clothes."

"I don't want or need you to pay for my clothes."

"I know what you spend for your shoes and handbags because of my mother."

"What about her, Jordan?"

"You like the same designers, and I've never seen you in the same pair of shoes twice."

"I hope you don't have a problem with me spending *my* money for what I like."

"No. After all, it is *your* money. But if I'm inviting you to go out with me, then I feel it's only fair I subsidize your wardrobe. By the way, I should tell you that you'll meet my parents tonight."

Aziza knew she would've fallen if Jordan hadn't held her up. He'd waited until they were only feet from the museum, where men and women in formal dress were getting out of cars, taxis and limos, to reveal this shocking news.

"Now you tell me."

"Don't worry. They'll love you."

You're wrong, Jordan. They don't love me. In fact, they don't even like me. Especially your mother. Edward Wainwright was polite, but appeared indifferent. He seemed more interested in talking to a group of men who'd gathered near one of the many portable bars.

Aziza leaned closer to Jordan, staring at

Christiane Wainwright across the table. Tall, slender and fashionably dressed in emerald green silk that was an exact match for her eyes, Christiane had barely acknowledged her when Jordan made the introductions. There were traces of silver in her coiffed blond hair.

"Jordan, will you please bring me a glass of wine?"

He rested a hand on her bare shoulder, then pushed back his chair. "I'll be right back. Mother, can I get you anything?"

The smile that curved Christiane's mouth did not reach her frosty green eyes. "No, thank you, darling."

Aziza stared at Jordan's ramrod-straight back until he disappeared from her line of vision. He was resplendent in formal dress. Then she turned to look at her lover's mother. "I'm sorry I'm not what you'd expected, but —"

Christiane gasped. "You understand French?"

Aziza nodded. She'd overheard Christiane tell another woman that she was disappointed in her son's taste in women. "I understand, speak and read it fluently."

Christiane looked down her thin nose at the young woman who was as stunning as she was direct. "You are not what I'd expected my son to date. However, he is an adult and I can't tell him whom he should see."

"See or like, Mrs. Wainwright? Your son and I aren't only dating, but we happen to be quite fond of each other."

The instant the admission was out of her mouth, Aziza realized what she felt for Jordan went beyond a mere liking. She'd known him all of two weeks and her feelings for him grew more intense with each encounter. And it wasn't about sex but mutual respect. He respected her as a woman and her opinion when they'd discussed his defending a young man charged with attempted rape.

"Are you saying that you and Jordan are serious?"

Aziza smiled. "It all depends on how you interpret serious."

"Do you plan on marrying my son?"

"I think that's a question you'd have to ask Jordan. Isn't it customary for the man to do the proposing?"

There was no way Aziza was going to tell Jordan's mother that she doubted whether she would ever remarry. She liked Jordan — a lot — but not enough to contemplate marrying him.

Christiane smiled. "Yes, it is. But one can

never tell nowadays. Women have changed so much since I was a young girl. Most seem so lacking in morals."

"Have things changed that much since you were a young woman, Mrs. Wainwright? I estimate you and my mother are of the same generation and she came of age during the sexual revolution. And she would be the first to admit that she'd slept with my father before they were married. So, I don't see how times have changed that much. In fact, I believe women are much more discriminating today given the number of prevalent sexual diseases."

"To say you're a very outspoken young woman is an understatement."

"I grew up with three brothers, so I had to be outspoken in order to assert myself. Then when I chose a male-dominated career, I knew that if I didn't speak up I would never succeed."

Christiane lifted pale eyebrows. "You're a doctor?"

"No. I'm a lawyer."

Jordan returned, preempting further conversation. He set a glass of chilled white wine in front of Aziza and then sat down beside her. He noticed the strained look on his mother's face, aware that he'd shocked her when he'd introduced Aziza as his date for the evening. He didn't want to tell his mother that her shock would be compounded if she knew Noah was also dating a woman of color.

"Aziza told me she's an attorney."

"Yes, she is," he confirmed. "Did she tell you she's Brandt's attorney?"

Christiane rested a pale hand against her equally pale throat. A large diamond shimmered on her slender finger. "No, she didn't. My dear, you seem to have done very well for yourself. You've managed quite a coup to have snagged two Wainwright men. Jordan, darling, you must invite Aziza to share Sunday dinner with the family in the very near future."

"Why don't you invite her, Mother?"

Christiane knew if she didn't accept her son's girlfriend, then she could risk losing her son, and that was something she couldn't fathom. "Aziza, I would like you to join us whenever you're available, so Jordan can introduce you to the rest of the family."

Aziza forced a smile she didn't feel. Not only was Christiane Wainwright pretentious, but she was also the epitome of snobbery. How had she raised a son who was the complete opposite?

"I will let Jordan know when I am available."

The need to make idle chitchat with Christiane ended when three other couples joined their table. The women were laden with so many precious jewels Aziza marveled at how they were able to lift their arms or move their heads. Most of them had drunk too much and now talked too much. The inane chatter was annoying. Edward Wainwright returned to the table when waitstaff had begun serving the first course.

Jordan was his father's son. He'd inherited Edward's height and patrician features, but not his blond hair or blue eyes. Watching Edward interact with his wife revealed one thing: she was the stronger of the two.

"You look bored, darling."

Aziza smiled, but didn't respond to Jordan whispering in her ear. What she wanted to tell Jordan was that she preferred hanging out with his friends. Maybe she was bored or jaded, but she couldn't imagine attending another four or five fundraisers with him.

She realized they were necessary to support and sustain the viability of particular organizations, but she found them to be nothing more than fashion shows where people came to preen and be seen. Photographers who tried to be inconspicuous were nothing more than paparazzi whenever they recognized a celebrity. Many of the photos would probably appear on the pages of *Vanity Fair* and *W.*

"You'd rather hang out with Kyle, DG and Ivan, wouldn't you?"

Turning her head, she smiled at him, the smoky shadow on her lids making her eyes darker and more mysterious. "How did you know?"

Jordan pressed his mouth to her curls. "You haven't laughed once since we arrived. And it's such a shame because you're the most stunning woman here."

"You're biased, Jordan Wainwright."

"Shamelessly," he confirmed. "There's going to be dancing after dinner. So I'd like you to save me at least one dance."

"Only one?"

He laughed softly. "All I need is one. After that we can go home and have our own private party. We'll have things that are not listed on the menu."

"We can't, Jordan."

He went completely still. "Why not?" Their eyes met and held.

She wanted to tell him that she wasn't as bored as she was out of sorts. She was expecting her period and the first two days usually wiped her out. "I have PMS."

He kissed her hair. "I'll bring you tea with

lemon and I promise to rub your tummy."

Her smile was dazzling. "You are definitely a keeper, Jordan Wainwright."

Jordan shuttered his gaze to keep Aziza from seeing how her words echoed his feelings toward her. She, of all the women he'd met or known, was worth fighting for. He didn't want to admit he was falling in love with her, and it was becoming more and more difficult to imagine a future without her in his life.

CHAPTER 15

"All rise. The Honorable Judge Meyers presiding."

Jordan stood with his client, waiting for the judge to take her seat, then motioned for Robinson Fields to sit. When the case of NY v. Fields had been placed on the calendar he'd expected a male judge. He'd always found himself at odds whenever a female judge presided over a rape case. But he continued to believe that justice was blind. After all, she was a woman.

"I don't want you to make eye contact with Ms. Chance until you're on the stand," he whispered to his client. He didn't have to coach Robinson or tell him to wear a suit. The bespectacled young man was highly intelligent and articulate.

He'd gone over the case file with Kyle and had decided to lean heavily on the so-called victim. There was no way Jordan was going to allow a twenty-two-year-old college graduate with his whole life ahead of him to go to jail because of a spurned, spiteful young woman.

The prosecutor began his opening statement damning men like Robinson Fields.

The D.A. sat down and it was Jordan's turn. He stood up, noticing for the first time that Aziza sat in the back of the courtroom. Forcing his gaze away from her, he approached the jury box, then turned and stared at Roslyn, who was dabbing her cheeks with a shredded tissue. "Ladies and gentlemen, I'm here to prove that Robinson Fields didn't rape Miss Chance. He didn't have to." He paused when there came gasps from those sitting in the courtroom. He turned to the judge. "I'd like to call Miss Chance to take the stand."

A soft murmur rippled through the courtroom when Roslyn stood up and walked to the witness chair. She was tall and slender with long red hair and sparkling blue-green eyes. She stated her name for the record, then clasped her hands together to still their trembling.

Jordan unbuttoned his jacket and pushed his hands into the pockets of his trousers. He glanced down at the floor for several seconds, then smiled at the witness. "Miss Chance, I know you've been under a lot of stress, so I'm going to be mindful of that when I question you. Okay?" She nodded.

Jordan angled his head and smiled. She'd unclasped her hands. "Miss Chance, when did you meet Mr. Fields for the first time?"

"It was in Atlanta."

"When and where in Atlanta, Miss Chance?"

"It was four years ago . . . no, four and a half years ago. He was a freshman student at Morehouse and I was a freshman at Spelman."

"Why did you decide to attend Spelman College?"

"Objection. Irrelevant," shouted the D.A.

"It's not irrelevant," Jordan argued. "I'm trying to prove a point as to why Miss Chance decided to attend Spelman College when she could've gone to Sarah Lawrence or Barnard."

"Overruled," the judge intoned. "Please answer the question, Miss Chance."

Roslyn lowered her head. "I don't know. I suppose I wanted to go to a college in the South."

Jordan decided to press his attack. "Why did you apply to historically black colleges, Miss Chance? Howard, Bethune-Cookman, Dillard, Wilberforce, Fisk and Hampton. All private black colleges." He paused. "Miss

Chance, is it true that you and Mr. Fields have history? In other words, you and the defendant were a couple when you were in college."

"We went out a few times," she whispered.

"Speak up, Miss Chance," the judge ordered.

"We went out a few times," Roslyn repeated.

"Just a few times, Miss Chance? I have proof that you and Mr. Fields went out more than a few times. During four years, neither of you ever dated anyone else. Is this true?"

"Yes."

"Didn't you tell your roommate that you were in love with Robinson Fields and that you expected him to propose marriage after you graduated?"

"Yes. I mean no."

"Which is it, Miss Chance. Yes or no?"

Red blotches dotted her cheeks. "We talked about getting married, but we never set a date."

"Did you continue to date Mr. Fields after you returned to New York?"

Running her fingers through her hair, Roslyn held it off her face. She glared at Robinson for the first time. "No. He told me that we had to 'cool it.' "

"How did you feel when he told you that?"

"I was very angry."

"Angry enough to . . . Let me rephrase that. You were angry, so how did you react?"

"What do you mean?"

"Did you curse at him? Throw things?"

"No. I just walked away."

"But didn't it hurt to be rejected like that?"

"Of course it hurt! I wasn't as mad at Robbie as I was with his parents. They had no right to put that kind of pressure on him. Why couldn't he marry who he wanted?"

"What about your parents?" Jordan asked, continuing with his questioning. "Did they know you were dating an African-American man?"

Roslyn looked at her parents. They sat motionless, impassive expressions frozen in place. "No. They never knew I was dating Robbie."

"What do you think would've been their reaction if they'd found out?"

"Objection. That calls for conjecture."

"Overruled. Answer the question, Miss Chance."

"They would've been very angry. My parents are racists."

Jordan frowned. "That's a very strong word, Miss Chance. Perhaps they're biased or bigoted, but not racist."

"No, they are racists."

"And despite what they'd told you, you still dated a black man?"

Resentment filled Roslyn's eyes when she glared at her mother and father. "Yes!"

"Did you ever see Robbie again after he said you had to cool it?"

"Yes."

"What's the time frame from your last encounter? One month? Two months?"

"Six months. I saw him, but he didn't see me."

"Where did you see him?"

"He was at the South Street Seaport."

"Was he alone?"

"No. He was with a woman."

"Was she a black woman?"

Roslyn closed her eyes. "Yes."

"How did this make you feel?"

She bit her lip. "I was angry."

"You were angry because you saw him with a black woman, who could've been his sister or cousin."

"She was hardly a relative. She was wearing an engagement ring and they were touching and kissing each other."

"If you and Robbie were no longer seeing each other, how did he end up in your apartment?"

"I called him and asked him to come."

"Why?"

"I wanted to ask him about the woman I'd seen him with."

"Did he agree to come?"

"Not at first, but when I started to cry he said he would."

"Where were your parents, Miss Chance?"

"They were vacationing in Europe."

"So, you were home alone?"

Roslyn slumped in the chair as she affected a bored expression. "No. A maid lives with us."

"You have a full-time live-in maid?"

"That's what I said."

Judge Meyers removed her glasses. "Miss Chance, it's yes or no."

"Yes."

"So, you invited Robinson Fields to your apartment when you knew your parents would be away. What happened, Miss Chance?"

"We talked."

"What about?"

"His girlfriend. He told me she was in her first year of medical school."

"Did he mention that he was going to marry her?"

"He said he'd given her a ring."

"What else did you talk about, Miss

Chance?"

"I asked him if he was sleeping with her and he wouldn't tell me. I started screaming at him and he just stood there, then turned to leave. I'd risked everything to be with him and I just couldn't let him walk away from me."

"What did you do, Miss Chance?"

"I hit him."

"Where?"

"Across the face."

"Did he hit you back?"

Roslyn glared at Robinson, nostrils flaring when she compressed her lips. "No. I wanted him to hit me, but he wouldn't. I made it to the door and set the alarm. He couldn't get out without setting it off. He asked me to disarm it, but I told him I wouldn't until he made love to me. He grabbed my arms and shook me and that's when I started screaming. When Sophia came I told her he was trying to rape me."

Jordan shook his head. "You accuse my client of attempted rape when all he wanted was to get away from you."

"I'd do it again and again and again!" she screamed, pointing at Robinson.

After the outburst, Judge Meyers ordered the charges dropped. "Jurors, you're dismissed."

The courtroom was in an uproar with Roslyn screaming hysterically when she was handcuffed; her mother had collapsed and her father was screaming obscenities at the judge who was trying to restore order by banging her gavel.

"Mr. Chance, you're under arrest for contempt."

Jordan gave Robinson Fields a rough hug. "Go home with your parents. I'll call you in a couple of days." Gathering his file and leather portfolio, he wove his way through the spectators and out the courtroom. He saw Aziza standing in the hallway outside of another courtroom.

She looked very corporate in a black pantsuit, white blouse and low-heeled pumps, her hair in a loose twist. A trench coat with a Burberry inner lining was tossed over her shoulders.

He lowered his head and kissed her mouth. "What are you doing here?"

"I came to see you in action."

"You did not come all this way to see me discredit a young woman."

Aziza's eyes communicated what she didn't and couldn't say. She wanted to see him before he flew out to Los Angeles for the Super Bowl. They'd spent every weekend together since the beginning of the year, and for her it still wasn't enough.

"No. I have a meeting with a potential client this afternoon, so I decided to take an early train and watch my boyfriend in action. You were really dynamic. Your client never had to take the stand."

"That's what I plan for you, darling. That you won't have to take the stand."

Aziza nodded. Jordan planned to fly into Westchester County Airport Monday night, stay over at her house, and Tuesday morning they would initiate the action to charge Kenneth Moore with sexual and racial harassment. They weren't certain how long it would take the case to go to trial — if it ever did — but at least Kenneth would be put on notice, and hopefully other women would come forward once the charges were made public.

She glanced at her watch. She had less than an hour to meet with Raymond Humphries. The call from Raymond Humphries had come as quite a surprise. He'd claimed to have gotten her name and number from a client she'd represented during a home closing, and because she was familiar with real estate, he wanted her to oversee a special project. "I have to go. I'll see you when you get back."

Placing an arm around her waist, Jordan

pressed a kiss to the column of her neck. "Have fun with the girls."

"Oh, we plan to. Maybe we'll get some male strippers for our halftime entertainment."

Jordan gave her an incredulous look. "You wouldn't."

"Maybe yes, maybe no. It all depends how much we'll miss our guys."

"If you want a stripper, then I promise to strip for you when I get back."

Aziza sucked her teeth. "Yeah, right."

"I will."

Going on tiptoe, she kissed his jaw. "I'll see you when you get back. Safe trip."

"Thanks. Love you," he said glibly.

She smiled. "Love you back." Aziza walked away, feeling the heat of Jordan's gaze on her back. They'd ended telephone calls with the two words, but it wasn't the same as *I love you,* so she didn't make much of it.

She walked out of the courthouse and headed for the subway.

Aziza had searched on Google for Raymond Humphries and had been surprised to find more than twenty pages of information on the real estate mogul. She was intrigued but cautious. Whenever she contemplated taking on a new client, she always adopted a wait-and-see attitude. She'd

311

always eschewed ambulance-chancing lawyers who accepted any client for money.

She liked her clients, loved running her own practice and if she were truly honest with herself, she would admit that she was falling in love with Jordan Wainwright.

Aziza was escorted into Raymond Humphries's private office for RLH Realty. The exquisitely maintained three-story town house was in the Mount Morris Historic District and two blocks from Ivan and Nayo's brownstone and another five blocks from Kyle, Ivan and Duncan's offices.

Raymond smiled when Minerva closed the door. The photos of Aziza Fleming hadn't done her justice. She was stunningly beautiful in person. Her large eyes and lush mouth caught and held his rapt attention. It was easy to see why Jordan Wainwright was taken with her.

His smile was still in place when he extended his hand. "Thank you for agreeing to meet with me."

Aziza transferred her calfskin glove to her left hand and took his, surprised to find it as smooth as a baby's bottom. It was obvious the man hadn't done any hard labor in his life. "My pleasure, Mr. Humphries."

"Please, let me hang up your coat." Raymond made a mental note to get on Minerva about not taking the woman's coat. *She looks and smells nice.* The lady lawyer was batting a thousand. Physical appearance, fastidiousness and intelligence went a long way with him, and it was apparent Aziza Fleming had all three.

He hung her coat in a closet. "I've taken the liberty of ordering a light repast because it is technically the hours wherein lunch is still being served. Please, sit down." Raymond pulled out a chair from under the table in the alcove he used for small, intimate meetings.

Aziza sat, staring at what Raymond Humphries considered a light repast: mashed potatoes, meatloaf, baked chicken, collard greens, sweet potatoes and corn bread. She'd only had a cup of coffee for breakfast but had planned to stop and eat at a restaurant near Grand Central Station before catching a train for home.

"Everything looks so good."

Raymond smiled. "It is. There's a little eating place that's not much more than a hole in the wall that serves some of the best food Harlem has to offer. Are you from Harlem, Miss Fleming? It is miss, isn't it?"

She stared across the table at the man who owned so many parcels in Harlem that people had stopped counting at one hundred. He was short and slight, but there was something about him that made him appear a much larger man. His thinning hair was salt-and-pepper, and he'd been blessed with wonderful skin. It was so smooth it appeared poreless. The information she'd gleaned on him indicated he'd recently celebrated fifty years of marriage to the same woman — not an easy feat nowadays. He was the father of one and grandfather of two. A recent update said his son-in-law had decided on a political career, challenging a long-time incumbent for his state assembly seat.

"Yes. It is Miss Fleming. Answer one question for me, Mr. Humphries."

"What is it?"

"Why me and not some other lawyer? Why not one based here in Harlem?"

"That's two questions, Miss Fleming." Raymond chuckled as if it was a private joke. "I'll answer the second one first. I have a team of lawyers working for me, and none of them have offices or live in Harlem. Therefore, they have no vested interest in the community. They do what I tell them to do and for that I pay them very well. And, to answer your first question. Why you? Why not you, Miss Fleming? As I told you on the phone, you come highly recommended, and it's about time I come into the twenty-first century and hire a female attorney. And one that is African-American."

A shiver of remembrance raced up Aziza's spine. It was something similar to what Kenneth Moore had told her during her interview. She'd wanted to tell him he didn't have to concern himself with affirmative action because her law school transcript validated that she was more than qualified for the position.

"So, I'll be your token female?"

Raymond clasped his hands in a prayerful gesture. "No. I've lived long enough to come to hate that word — token black, token female, token whatever. You are a person, not some symbol for what someone wants to flaunt. I've made it a practice over the years not to put all my eggs in one basket, and this applies to my properties. I divide them up between the legal and accounting staff. This year you may handle the properties in the grid from 125th and Fifth to 125th and Frederick Douglass Boulevard. Then the following year it will be the parcels in Morningside Heights.

"People tend to think of Harlem as one homogenous community the same way they think of black folks. We may look similar,

315

but there are very distinct differences among us. Hamilton Heights is different from the St. Nicholas and Mount Morris Historic Districts. Not only does the architecture differ but the people who reside in these areas differ. I'm currently looking to pick up several parcels off 118th and St. Nicholas. The owner of the properties died eight years ago and his children, who are handling his estate, have been dragging their feet about selling it."

"It is occupied?" Aziza asked Raymond.

"No. That's what makes it so bizarre. They're paying taxes on unoccupied units. Initially, it was taken over by squatters and crackheads, but they did manage to pay someone to get them out and brick up the buildings."

"How many units are you talking about?"

"Forty."

"Are you looking to turn them into condos or rentals?"

"Condos. I think of renters as transients. Folks who own property tend to take care of it."

"What exactly do you want me to do, Mr. Humphries?"

"I want you to convince the current owners to sell the buildings to RLH Realty, and I'm willing to pay them fair market value."

"Do you have a time frame?"

"Say what?"

Aziza knew she'd shocked him with her query. "I'm asking because I'm going to send you a statement each month for billable hours. I can either work to tie it up quickly, or I can drag it out for a couple of years and make a small fortune."

A muscle twitched in Raymond's jaw when he clenched his teeth. Now he knew why Wainwright was attracted to the lady lawyer. They were two of a kind: brash and arrogant. "Let's start with sixty days with an option for another sixty days."

"That's doable." Aziza didn't want to neglect her other clients if Raymond Humphries decided to monopolize her services. "Where do they live?"

"Tampa."

"Tampa, as in Florida?"

Raymond nodded. "Just let Ms. Jackson know when you're available to travel to meet with them, and she will make all the arrangements. You'll fly first-class, be provided with ground transportation and will stay in the best hotels. All of your meals and incidentals will be billed directly to RLH Realty." Reaching for a pad stamped with the company's logo, he wrote down a figure and pushed the pad across the table. "I'm

317

willing to pay this for your billable hours. Does it meet with your approval?"

The expression on Aziza's face did not change when she stared at what Raymond had scrawled on the pad. He was offering her a fee comparable to what Wall Street and Park Avenue law firms charged their clients. She blinked.

"It's doable," she repeated, "but I'm unable to confirm whether I'll be able to accept your offer until next week. I'm involved with another case where I might be called as a witness."

Aziza didn't want to say that she was suing another attorney, and she didn't know whether Kenneth would cop a plea or hold out and go to trial. He had deep pockets and an entire law firm behind him. But she had Jordan Wainwright, and judging from what she'd witnessed earlier that morning, he could hold his own in any courtroom. He was so skillful that the D.A. had never been given the opportunity to cross the defendant.

Her man was definitely no joke!

Raymond successfully concealed his disappointment behind a too-bright smile. He'd expected Aziza Fleming to jump at his offer. But she hadn't said no, and to him, that was a yes. He always saw the glass as half full rather than half empty. He knew that Wyatt Wainwright had his sights on the two buildings, and he'd be damned if the Wainwright Developers Group would gobble another address in his backyard.

Aziza Fleming would become his secret weapon when he used her to take down her boyfriend's grandfather. "Please serve yourself, Miss Fleming. It's sinful to let all this food go to waste. Remember there are a lot of hungry people in this city."

Reaching for a plate, Aziza spooned a portion of greens, sweet potatoes and meat loaf onto the china plate. She speared a piece of meat loaf, chewing slowly. "You're right. This is delicious."

"I told you," Raymond said smugly. He fixed a plate for himself, and over the next forty minutes, he and the lady lawyer talked about national politics and the Super Bowl game. None of their New York teams had made it to the finals, but that didn't diminish the hype or the excitement of a day that sports fans considered an unofficial holiday.

CHAPTER 16

The telephone rang Sunday morning, and when Aziza glanced at the display she was surprised to see Wildflowers and Other Treasures on the caller ID. She picked up the receiver. "Hello."

"Hi, Zee, this is Simone Madison. I'm sorry about calling so early."

"That's all right, Simone. I've been up for hours. What's up?"

She'd gotten up early to make salads and marinate meats that would go in the oven before her guests arrived. Her schoolteacher girlfriends had sent her a text informing her they were spending the weekend in Atlantic City. They would've invited her to come with them, but she'd turned off her cell.

"Do you mind if I hang out with you guys?"

"Of course I don't mind. I thought you were going to watch the game with your husband."

"Please don't get me started. I dropped his behind off at the airport early this morning. He's flying out to L.A. for the game."

"But I thought he didn't have a ticket."

"He didn't until a former baseball teammate called and told him to be at the airport at six because they were taking a private jet to the west coast. Rafe thought I was driving too slowly, so he made me pull over and he got behind the wheel. A cop stopped him for doing ninety in a fifty-five zone, but when he showed his U.S. Marshal badge he let him go. When I called my sister she told me to hang out with her and Micah, but I'm not driving to Brooklyn. I'm certain Micah would've jetted off with the other guys if Tessa wasn't pregnant."

"Come on over, Simone. The more the merrier."

"What do you need?"

"Nothing really."

"I can't come empty-handed."

"Yes, you can. The others are expected to arrive around four, but if you want to come earlier you can."

"Maybe I will. I can always help you set up."

Aziza straightened a row of forks, knives and spoons on the embroidered tablecloth draped over a long folding table she'd set up on the back porch. Rather than serve her guests in the kitchen or formal dining room, she'd decided the enclosed area would provide a much more relaxing atmosphere.

Simone Whitfield-Madison, as promised, had come at two with a large wicker basket filled with freshly cut flowers. She'd watched transfixed as the floral designer put together a bouquet that would double as a centerpiece.

"The flowers really dress up the table, Simone." An all-white bouquet of tulips, gardenia, sweet pea, roses and calla lilies added a touch of elegance.

Folding her arms under her breasts, Simone angled her head. "They do look nice." A mop of reddish curls framing her bare face made her appear younger than thirty-four.

Aziza stepped back, surveying her handiwork. A buffet would replace her usual sitdown dinner. "I need to light some votives, start a fire in the fireplace and mix a pitcher of margaritas."

"I don't mind lighting the candles and building the fire."

"I didn't invite you here to work, so relax."

Simone blew out a breath. "I'm going to

admit something you may find a little strange. Compared to my sister and cousin Faith, I'm inept when it comes to working in the kitchen. Give me some soil and I'll build a monument."

"Who does the cooking in your house?"

"Rafe."

Aziza smiled. "Your husband is gorgeous."

"And your boyfriend is delicious," Simone countered. "How long have the two of you been together?"

"Three weeks."

"You're kidding me."

Aziza's smile faded, and she stared at the petite floral designer with a dusky-gold complexion and hazel eyes that reminded her of Jordan's. "No, I'm not kidding. Why do you seem so surprised?"

"I . . . It's just that I thought the two of you were together a lot longer. I don't think you're aware of how you look at each other."

"How do we look at each other?"

"With adoration. The man is in love with you."

"I doubt that." What Aziza wouldn't admit to Simone was that she was falling in love with Jordan.

"Why, Aziza. I don't know you and you don't know me, but after two marriages, I think I've learned a little something about men. I married my high school sweetheart, believing I knew all there was to know about him. I stayed with him because I wanted it to work, but when it didn't, I divorced him. I even tried giving him a second chance when I agreed to a temporary reconciliation. In the end, I knew I couldn't make a silk purse out of a sow's ear.

"Then along came Raphael Madison. I witnessed an attempted murder and Rafe was assigned to witness protection. He moved into my house, shadowing me 24/7. It took about two weeks until I realized I couldn't imagine my life without him. He'd become everything my ex-husband wasn't or couldn't be. And what made it so pitiful was that it'd taken sixteen years for me to come to that conclusion."

Aziza affected a sad smile. "That sounds like a rerun of my life." She told Simone about her relationship and eventual marriage to a man who didn't have her back. "Once you give an undeserving cretin so many years of your life it's a little hard to trust the next one to come along."

"Do you have to deal with a woman from Jordan's past?"

"No."

"Then, it's not fair to Jordan that he has to pay for the sins of your ex."

Simone's words played over and over in Aziza's head when she walked into the kitchen to check the dishes in the oven and prepare a margarita punch. The doorbell rang, and Aziza opened the door to see Tamara, Nayo and Ava on the porch laden with shopping bags. She shook her head, stepped back and welcomed them in.

"I told y'all not to bring anything."

Nayo looked at her cohorts. "Did you hear her say that?"

"Nah!" Tamara and Ava said in unison.

Tamara kicked off her running shoes. "Something smells good."

Ava walked in, slipping out of a pair of leather clogs, leaving them on a thick straw mat near the door. "Nice house."

Nayo handed Aziza a shopping bag with several bottles of wine. "I don't know about the rest of you, but I'm starved."

Tamara gave her a quizzical look. "Didn't you eat before we left the city?"

"Maybe she's pregnant," Ava drawled.

Three pairs of eyes were fixed on the petite photographer. "If you are, then you can't have anything alcoholic," Aziza said firmly.

Nayo's eyelids fluttered. "I think I am."

Tamara folded her hands at the waist. "Either you are or you aren't."

"I took a pregnancy test this morning and it came out positive."

"Mrs. Campbell," Tamara said softly, "if the test came out positive, then you *are* pregnant."

Ava hugged Nayo. "Congratulations! Does Ivan know?"

"No. I'll tell him when he comes back."

Nayo's possible pregnancy became the topic of conversation as Aziza and the four women gathered on the back porch to eat and drink until the coin toss that signaled the game had begun. Instead of the requisite chips, dips, Buffalo wings and guacamole, she'd served roast turkey, honey ham, potato salad, smothered cabbage and a tossed salad with vinaigrette. Simone received her share of teasing after she was forced to tell them about her husband's impromptu escape.

Ava gestured to Simone. "The only thing I'm going to say about Rafe is still water runs deep. He pretends all is right in River City, and when you're not looking, the brother bolts like a bat out of hell."

Everyone laughed, Simone included. After several glasses of chilled margaritas, the laughter increased and they ignored the flickering images on the screen to enjoy the camaraderie that was natural and easygoing.

The game ended with a winner, the commercials had become a part of history and the five women worked quickly and efficiently to put away food and load the dishwasher. Ava, who had appointed herself the designated driver, was sprawled over the love seat on the porch, declaring she was much too full to drive back to Manhattan.

Removing the fireplace screen, Aziza placed a piece of wood on the dying embers. "All of you are welcome to stay over."

Ava sat up and ran a hand over her short coiffed hair. "I was just joking."

"Well, I'm not," Aziza countered. "I have four bedrooms, so that eliminates doubling up. I'll give you each something to wear and grooming supplies. Just let me know what time you want to wake up in the morning and I'll get you up."

Simone stretched like a lithe cat. "I don't have to stay over. I don't live that far from here."

Aziza replaced the screen and hung the poker on a stand. "Ladies, I'm not chasing anyone out of my house. If you've had more than a couple of drinks, then you're not leaving. I'm not going to be responsible for supplying the alcohol in case you get into an accident. You will not sue me."

"Hear, hear," Tamara intoned. "Spoken

like a lawyer." She laughed along with the others. "I need a show of hands as to who is staying over." Four hands went up. "It's unanimous." Reaching for a glass of water she'd left on a side table, she held it aloft. "Here's to our first post–Super Bowl sleep-over."

The others hoisted imaginary glasses. "Hear! Hear!"

Aziza sat in the car parked in the driveway to her home, staring out the window. It was January 31, a day she would always remember, a day in which her life would change — and she prayed for the better. Jordan and the other men had flown back to New York the day after the Super Bowl, and instead of flying into JFK or LaGuardia, he'd flown into the smaller Westchester Regional airport.

He'd shocked her when she'd opened the door to find him standing on her porch. She'd welcomed him home, into her bed and into her body. Aziza had realized how much she'd missed Jordan, how much he'd become an integral part of her life.

Jordan accompanied her when she went to the bank and retrieved the envelope from the safe deposit box that could change the course of hers and Kenneth Moore's life —

forever. She'd spoken to a female police officer who handled rape cases, who'd asked if she could tape her statement. Jordan had given his approval and everything had poured out as she'd recounted the harassment she'd encountered as an employee of Moore, Bloch and Taylor.

Jordan had handed over the envelope containing the evidence needed to indict and hopefully convict Aziza's former boss. Aziza confirmed her fingerprints would not appear on the condom, because she'd looked in the envelope but never touched its contents. Kenneth's DNA and fingerprints were certain to literally and figuratively hang the man.

"Are you all right?"

Jordan's query pulled Aziza from her reverie. "I'm okay."

"If you're okay, then why won't you look at me?"

She turned her head as if she were a robot. "I'm looking at you, Jordan."

He ran the back of his right hand over her cheek. "Don't second-guess yourself, baby. You did what you had to do to stop a predator. The first time you tried to get Kenny, you went it alone. This time you're not alone. You have me, and together we're going to stop him from doing what he did to you to another woman or women."

Her eyelids fluttered wildly as twin emotions of relief and apprehension raced through her chest. She was relieved because she'd followed through and followed the law to beat Kenny at his own game. The apprehension came from knowing he would come back at her with everything in his legal arsenal to escape the humiliation that was certain to come once the story broke about his workplace behavior. There was no doubt his firm's reputation would also take a hit. Clients — female ones in particular — would seek out other firms for representation.

Aziza unbuckled her seat belt after they returned to her home and leaned into Jordan. "I know you're right, but a nagging voice in the back of my head keeps telling me that he's going to come after me like a wounded animal, that he's going to go for the kill before he dies."

"Kenny Moore is a rattlesnake who will bite himself before he bites anyone."

Breathing a kiss on Jordan's warm throat, she closed her eyes and prayed he was right. "How long do you think it's going to take from arrest to indictment?"

"I don't know, baby. They're going to arrest Kenny and charge him with multiple counts of sexual harassment. He'll be asked to give a DNA sample, and if he's smart, he will. There's no doubt he'll be granted bail. If there is a DNA match, then the real waiting begins. It could be six months, maybe even a year before we go to trial — that is, if he doesn't decide to accept a plea."

"I can't wait another year in limbo, Jordan."

"Don't say what you can't do, Zee. Remember, before you handed over that envelope you had no case because your taped conversations with your boss were inadmissible. Now, if you don't feel safe staying here alone, you can always move in with me."

She shook her head. "No. I can't do that."

"Why not?"

Aziza stared into the eyes that bored into her like sharp daggers. "I'm surprised you have to ask why not."

"Well, I am. Why not, Aziza?"

"I have a practice to run."

"A practice you can run out of my place."

She ignored him as if he hadn't spoken. "And I wasn't raised to shack up with men."

"I'm not men, but a man," he countered. "Would it make it more palatable to you if we got married? And instead of running your practice out of *our* home, we get you an office in a midtown building."

Aziza's eyes narrowed. "I'm not marrying you, Jordan."

Jordan felt as if she'd plunged a dagger into his heart. If she would've said she couldn't marry him it would've lessened the blow. But the declaration that she wasn't marrying him spoke volumes.

"You don't have to marry me, Aziza. I was just offering an alternative."

"A marriage proposal is hardly an alternative, Jordan. It is a lifelong commitment — something that's a legal *and* emotional contract between two people."

"Wrong, Zee. Look what happened between you and your ex. When you married him you'd believed you spend the rest of your life with him. How long were you married? One year? Two? I don't remember you telling me you made it to your third anniversary."

Tears pricked the backs of Aziza's eyelids. "I didn't disclose my personal life to you so you could throw it in my face. I told you why I divorced my husband. I'd been victimized by my boss, and there was no way in hell I was going to hang around to be victimized again by my husband."

"I am not your enemy, Aziza."

She sniffled. "I know."

"If you know, then why are you treating

me like one? I care for you, baby. I care a lot more than I'd planned to or want to. I spend four days away from you and the whole time I was like a junkie who needed a hit when I wanted to call just to hear your voice. I needed to reconnect with you."

"I told you not to call me."

A wry smile twisted his mouth. "And like a fool I didn't call you."

"I didn't want you checking up on me and I didn't want the guys to think you had to check in."

Jordan snorted. "Do you really think I care what other men think? If I want to call my girlfriend while we're in a strip club, then I'd do it."

"Did you go to a strip club?"

"I plead the Fifth."

"You guys went to Vegas, didn't you? And you probably went to a strip club!"

"What happens in Vegas, stays in Vegas. Hey, weren't you the one who talked about getting a male stripper for your halftime entertainment?"

"Don't try to shift the blame, Jordan Wainwright. I was just bluffing when I mentioned male strippers."

"Look, babe, it was nothing."

"Nothing! You let some half-naked heifer spreading her legs from east to west for a couple of dollars touch you."

Jordan swallowed the f-bomb. He'd slipped up. Ivan, Duncan, Chat and Raphael Madison, who'd caught up with them the day of the game, had sworn an oath they wouldn't tell their women about the side trip to Vegas.

"No one touched me. And I didn't touch anyone."

"Did you put money in her G-string?"

"No."

"Are you sure, Jordan?"

"I'm sure, baby. I threw it on the stage." He threw up his hands to ward off her swatting at him as if she were brushing away an annoying mosquito. "Stop it, baby." He couldn't stop laughing.

Aziza pushed out her lower lip. "It's not funny, Jordan."

He caught her wrists. "I know it's not. We did go to Vegas but only to gamble. Ivan and Rafe are married and Chat and Duncan are engaged to be married. Do you really think those guys would disrespect their women like that?"

"I don't know."

"Well, I know they wouldn't. I hear women complain about men being dogs, that they can't be faithful and they don't want to take care of their wives and/or children, but the men I spent the weekend with aren't those dogs. They love their wives and fiancées and they will take care of their children."

"Nayo's pregnant."

"How do you know?"

"She told us. You'll probably hear it from Ivan when you go into the office tomorrow."

"That's wonderful news because that's all he's been talking about — becoming a father."

"Well, it will happen before the end of the year."

"What do you have on your agenda today?" Jordan had deftly changed the topic of conversation. The talk about marriage and children bothered him. All the guys he'd hung out with over the past four days were older than him, and what had been missing in his life became more apparent when they talked about their wives. All had confessed to tiring of the serial dating before they met the woman with whom they would plan their future.

Jordan knew he had tired of it after Natasha had returned to culinary school. Although he'd known in advance that their relationship wasn't going anywhere, that it had an expiration date, he still hadn't wanted to see her go.

"Do you want to come in, or do you want

me to drive you to the train station?"

"Drive me to the station. I'll get off at one-two-five street and stop by the office."

Aziza laughed, the sound low and sultry. "You know you sound like someone straight out of Harlem. They usually say one-two-five for One Hundred Twenty-fifth Street."

Jordan wanted to tell Aziza how close she'd come to the truth. He knew if he could hope for any type of future with her — even if it didn't end in marriage — he had to tell her about the circumstances surrounding his birth. He'd come to know firsthand how a family secret had almost shattered his life and his relationship with his grandfather.

His relationship with Aziza had changed him. He had become more tolerant and accepting. He'd extended Wyatt the olive branch, but didn't know how long the fragile truce would last. At least for now they could occupy the same space and be civil to each other.

"What are you doing?" Aziza asked when Jordan backed out of the driveway.

"If we leave now, I should make the next train."

"Don't you want to get your luggage?"

"I'll get it some other time."

Jordan accelerated, and when he maneuvered into the parking lot at the Bronxville Metro-North station, the train was just pulling in. He unbuckled his seat belt and kissed Aziza in one continuous motion. "I love you."

He was there, then he was gone, she watching him sprint to catch the train. Aziza waited until the doors closed, then got out of the Murano, came around and sat down behind the wheel. Jordan's *I love you* was very different from *love you.*

Was he in love with her? Was that why he'd asked her to live with him? And had gone as far as to ask her to marry him?

Even if he wasn't in love with her, she knew for certain that she was in love with him.

CHAPTER 17

Jordan sat with Kyle in the senior partner's inner office. Both wore jeans, pullover sweaters and running shoes. They'd discussed and decided on casual Fridays based on the practice of not scheduling clients for that day. It was a day when case records were updated, telephone calls returned and billable hours reviewed.

Kyle had known from their tenure at TCB that Jordan was a skilled litigator. Any reservations he'd had as to whether Jordan would advocate as passionately for Harlem clients were completely shattered when he'd publicly revealed his grandfather as a slumlord. That had made him a local hero. The attempted rape charge against Robinson Fields, dismissed within half an hour of his cross-examination of Roslyn Chance, had garnered the attention of local newspapers in record time. Jordan Wainwright had become a favorite of *The Amsterdam News*.

The weekly had called him "*gangsta* sheriff of Harlem" and the sobriquet stuck. It was on a rare occasion he didn't walk down the streets of the neighborhood and not be called out affectionately as "*yo, gangsta.*"

"Are you certain you don't want to take my possession-with-intent-to-sell?" Kyle asked, successfully hiding a grin.

"Hell no, Chat." Jordan rested his feet on the leather chair's ottoman, crossing his legs at the ankles. "You know how I feel about drug cases."

Kyle smiled. "I thought because you just did a bang-up job getting Robinson Fields off you'd want another challenging case."

Jordan closed his eyes, reliving a time when he'd witnessed firsthand how narcotics had destroyed the life of a cousin. What had horrified him was that the boy who'd sold him the drugs managed to escape prosecution. He opened his eyes. "No drug cases, Chat."

Kyle heard something in his partner's voice that made him take notice. It was hard, unyielding. As senior partner, he could assign his subordinate any case he chose. What he didn't want to do was give Jordan a case where he wouldn't give one hundred percent. An attorney had to believe in his client in order to go the extra mile for him.

Jordan had believed Robinson Fields enough to play the controversial race card, which may or may not go over well with a judge, and it'd paid off.

"Okay. No drug cases."

Jordan smiled. "Thanks. Are you ready to give up your single status?"

Kyle nodded. "I was ready two weeks after I met Ava. The only advice I'm ever going to give you in the love department is not to wait until you're as old as I am to turn in your bachelor card. I'm thirty-nine and will be forty if and when I become a father for the first time. Trust me, Jordan, when I say it's not going to be a pretty sight to see me lying on my back looking up at the sky trying to catch my breath after going one-on-one on the court after a b-ball game with my sixteen-year-old son."

Lines fanned out around Jordan's eyes when he smiled. "I hear you."

Kyle sat up straight. "Do you really hear me? Or are you just saying you do to shut me up?"

Jordan sobered quickly. "I do hear you."

"I've dated more women than I can re-member, but when I met Ava something just clicked. It wasn't about how she looked but how we connected to each other. When Ivan told me he was marrying Nayo six weeks after meeting her for the first time, I knew exactly what he was talking about. It's when you meet that special woman something inside you goes off like you've tripped an alarm. It's saying 'don't be no fool, fool. Don't let this one go or you'll regret it for the rest of your life.' "

"It's like that?"

"Don't try to play it off, Jordan. I've seen you with enough ladies to know that Aziza is special, so special that you're representing her in a sexual harassment case when you're involved with your client."

Jordan's eyebrows lifted a fraction. "I agreed to handle the case before we got involved."

"It still looks bad, and when Moore finds out, your ethics will be questioned."

"I'm not as concerned about ethics as much as putting this pig away."

"That still can happen if you let me handle it. I know she's suing him for violation of her sexual and civil rights, so tell me if I'm wrong. Does her race also factor into this?" Jordan nodded. "Well, I'm going to enjoy ripping him a new one. Tell your girlfriend that I'm going to take over. I know Moore entered a not guilty plea at his arraignment, but from what you told me what was on those tapes he's as guilty as sin."

"He is," Jordan confirmed.

The news that the head of an influential Park Avenue law firm had been charged with sexual and racial harassment had become fodder for countless conversations among those in the field. And when Kyle had approached Jordan, he'd given him a detailed account of the lawsuit. What Jordan hadn't known until now was that his partner wasn't too happy with his involvement.

"When I come back from my honeymoon, I want to listen to the tapes. You've got to know I'm pissed with you, Jordan, because I had to find out like everyone else. Hell, man, I'm your friend and partner."

"This was personal."

"I'm going to say this once, and then it's moot. I haven't known you as long as I have Duncan and Ivan, but the only thing that's personal between us is what we do when we close the bedroom door. My problems are their problems, and vice versa. It's the same with you, Jordan. If you'd trusted me, you would've come to me —"

"I trust you, Chat," Jordan interrupted.

"Not enough, Wainwright. You get an attitude when I mention you not being a brother, but you are. You're as close to me as my biological brother and Ivan and Duncan. So, don't ever forget that I'll always have your back. That's the way we roll up here in Harlem — *brother.*"

A wry smile twisted Jordan's mouth. "There's no way I can forget it if you put it that way."

"I'm sorry I can't take you up on your offer to sail down to San Juan for the wedding. Ava has horrific motion sickness that she can't control even with the patch behind her ear."

"That's too bad because we plan to kick back and relax before you get there." Duncan, Nayo, Tamara and Ivan had accepted his offer to sail down to Puerto Rico for the destination wedding.

"I hope y'all don't party too hard and forget y'all have to stand up straight as my groomsmen." Micah Sanborn, who Kyle had mentored in law school, was to have been part of the wedding party but had opted out, so Jordan was recruited to take his place. Tessa Whitfield-Sanborn's obstetrician had recommended she not travel so late in her confinement. Tessa was now in her last trimester.

"Don't worry, Chat. No more tequila shots."

"I tried that nonsense once and I was sick for two weeks," Kyle admitted. "It was enough to swear me off the hard stuff for a long time."

"I hear you, brother," Jordan intoned.

"What's up with you and Aziza?" Kyle asked. "How serious are you about her?"

"More serious than she is about me."

"More serious than you were about that girl you were seeing in D.C.?"

Jordan nodded. "There's no comparison. Don't get me wrong. I really liked Kirsten, but when we finally decided to end it, I wasn't broken up over it. That's not to say I didn't have feelings for her, because I did. I'd asked her to move to New York and she said no. I never tried to put any pressure on her or tried to persuade her to change her mind with an offer of marriage, and I don't think she was expecting me to propose to her. But it's different with Zee."

"What's different?" Kyle asked when Jordan stared at the pattern on the rug.

"I don't know." His gaze shifted and he stared directly at Kyle. "You've heard people talking about meeting their soul mate. Well, I feel as if I've met mine. And because we're both lawyers that doesn't even factor into the equation."

"It helps that she's gorgeous. Duncan and Ivan were talking about what would've happened if they weren't committed and they'd met her first."

"Nothing would've happened, Chat. Because if they'd tried coming on to my woman they would find out how gangsta I can be."

"All they have to do is look to Wyatt Wainwright to know the apple doesn't fall that far from the tree. You're better educated and more urbane, thanks to your mother, but under the cultured speech and tailored wardrobe, you're Wyatt. That's probably why you don't get along as well as you should."

"That's where you're wrong, Chat. Wyatt is what you'd call OSG — an old-school gangster. By the time he was fifteen he was cutting school and picking up number slips for the biggest policymaker on the Lower East Side. By seventeen he was carrying a gun and using it when it became necessary to put the muscle on someone who owed money to a ruthless loan shark. What saved him from serving a life sentence in Sing Sing was marrying my grandmother. She got him to go to church and finish high school. What helped was that her family had money — a lot of money. My grandfather may have cleaned up on the outside, but he's gangster at heart. He still carries a handgun. It's registered, but he says he feels naked without it."

"Please don't tell me you have a licensed handgun," Kyle teased, smiling.

"No. I don't like guns. I'd take care of Duncan and Ivan the old-fashioned way. I'd invite them outside, then stomp a mud hole in their asses!"

"Damn, gangsta! Lighten up. I've seen you wreck a speed bag, but you have to remember it will be the Upper East Side versus Harlem, and that may not be much of a fair fight."

"I've got some Harlem in me," Jordan admitted.

"Working in Harlem doesn't count, partner."

Jordan sobered, wondering how much he should tell Kyle about himself. When he'd found out he'd been adopted, it had nearly destroyed him emotionally, but it was his love for his adoptive mother that had kept him grounded. Christiane had been forced to accept a situation not of her choosing.

Pushing off the chair, Jordan walked to the door of the outer office. Cherise Robinson stood at the file cabinet, putting away the stack on her desk. "Cherise, can you please hold all Kyle's calls?"

The legal secretary smiled at him over her shoulder. "Sure. Do you want me to have

Juliana hold yours, too?"

"Please. If anything you feel is important comes in, then transfer it over to Kieran."

Jordan becoming partner had permitted the firm to hire additional staff that included a full-time law clerk and researcher. He'd contacted his former secretary at Trilling, Carlyle and Browne, asking if she wanted to come uptown and work for him. It'd taken all of thirty seconds for Juliana to give him an answer. She lived less than ten blocks away from the office, so it had become a no-brainer for her.

He returned to Kyle's inner office, closed the door, sat down and told him what no one, other than a Wainwright and his birth mother's family, knew.

"I wouldn't have asked you to come if I didn't need you, son."

Jordan waved a hand at Wyatt. "Stop apologizing, Grandpa. What do you need?"

He'd come to the Fifth Avenue mansion rather than the Wainwright office building. Christiane was hosting a party later that evening to celebrate her father-in-law's seventy-ninth birthday. Wyatt, who eschewed birthday celebrations, was overruled when Christiane insisted that once someone reached their seventy-fifth birthday, every subsequent was very special. Folding his tall frame down to a cushioned chair in the solarium, Jordan crossed one leg over the other at the knee, the same gesture Wyatt had affected.

He had to admit his grandfather didn't look as if he were approaching eighty. The shock of black hair of his youth was now a snowy white; there were a few deep lines around a pair of brilliant topaz-blue eyes that hadn't faded with age, and Wyatt's waist was the same size it'd been at twenty-five. No matter how much or how little he ate, his weight had remained constant over the years, and he'd managed to look elegant whether in a tailored suit, or the shirt and slacks he now wore.

"Are you coming to the circus tonight?"

Jordan smiled. He knew Wyatt was referring to the party that would be held in the smaller of two ballrooms. "I wouldn't miss it."

Wyatt's bright blue eyes lingered on his grandson's face. He looked good — very good. In fact, he looked better each time he saw him. His lean face had filled out, and he appeared less hostile, more relaxed.

"Your mother told me about the young woman you took to the museum fund-raiser."

Jordan went still. "Did you ask me to come see you to talk about a woman?"

"No, I didn't. I'm just trying to make small talk."

"What do you want to know about her, Grandpa? That is, if you haven't already had her investigated."

A hint of a smile softened the lines around Wyatt's firm mouth. "That's where you're wrong, Jordan. I didn't have her investigated because whoever you sleep with is your business. Besides, I heard she's smart and quite beautiful."

"She is."

"Have you invited her to accompany you tonight?"

Jordan nodded. "Yes."

"Good. I'm looking forward to meeting her."

"Her name is Aziza Fleming."

"What I did hear is that her brother is on same team as Brandt."

"They're roomies whenever they play away games. Enough talk about my girlfriend. What's bothering you, Grandpa?"

"I'm still having a problem contacting the owners of the property at 118th and St. Nick. Official records show that the owner died some time ago, and his kids are handling his estate. Some want to sell and some don't. Noah managed to make contact with the oldest boy, who said another lawyer has been talking to him about purchasing the properties for her client. He wouldn't give me her name, but what I want is for you to talk to her and see if you can't work out a deal."

"What kind of a deal, Grandpa?"

"We're talking about four buildings. I'm willing to purchase two and let them have the other two. What's nice about these parcels is that there're only ten units in each building. Some apartments can be reconfigured for a duplex and others into large studio units. The possibilities are endless."

"So, you want me to contact the executors of the estate and try to work a deal?" Wyatt nodded. "How high are you willing to go?" Wyatt quoted a figure that made Jordan lift his eyebrows. "You must really want those parcels."

"I do."

"Do you know who else is trying to get them?"

The seconds ticked as the two men stared at each other. "RLH Realty."

Running a hand over his face, Jordan glared at his grandfather. "I've heard you say it enough, that 'if you stir up old shit it will stink.' Why after more than thirty years do you want to revive a feud with Raymond Humphries?"

Wyatt's eyes grew wide until Jordan could see the dark blue irises. "He doesn't own Harlem."

"And you proved that when you bought those buildings on 114th."

Wyatt leaned forward. "You work in Harlem, Jordan. Every day you see changes going on around you. If India was the British Empire's jewel in the crown, then Harlem is Manhattan's jewel in the crown. I'd be willing give up half of Wainwright Developers Group's parcels to own ten square blocks of prime Harlem real estate."

Jordan appeared deep in thought. "Do you think it's wise for me to get involved in the negotiations with Humphries's attorney?"

"Who would you suggest?" Wyatt asked.

"Noah."

"He's not ready. He's got the edge but not the experience to deal with Ray Humphries. And don't mention your father. If left up to him, he'd give away the farm."

A scowl distorted Jordan's pleasant features. "That's enough about my father." He'd always been protective of Edward Wainwright, who never was able to come into his own because of his tyrannical father and haughty wife.

"Edward doesn't need you to defend him, Jordan."

"And you should know better than to get in my face and put down my father. I respect him because he is who he is, and he makes no apologies for being a nice guy."

"Nice guys finish last."

"No, they don't, Grandfather."

Grandfather. The title was like the flashing red lights and ringing bells at a railroad crossing. It was time for Wyatt to stop, or he would shatter their fragile truce. "I'm sorry about what I said about your father."

Jordan knew how difficult it was for Wyatt to apologize to anyone, even if he didn't mean it. "Okay, I'll contract RLH for you and see if I can talk to their attorney. I'm not going to promise whether I can get you what you want, but I will try."

Wyatt ran two fingers down the sharp crease in his navy-blue slacks. "You managed to take care of that hooligan shaking down my tenants."

Jordan wanted to remind Wyatt that he, too, was still a hooligan, only now he masqueraded as a businessman. "Kyle Chatham took care of that for you."

"Maybe I'll get to meet him again and thank him myself."

"Maybe," Jordan drawled, rising to his

feet. "I have to go home and get dressed. I'll see you later."

He walked out of the solarium, taking a back staircase to avoid running into anyone — his mother in particular — or else he wouldn't make it home in time to be there for Aziza's arrival. Jordan had arranged for Sergio to pick her up from her home and drive her down to the city. He hadn't told her where they were going, just that it was a semiformal affair.

CHAPTER 18

The instant the formally dressed man greeted Jordan as "Master Jordan," Aziza knew she'd been invited to a social event at his parents' home. The memory of the museum fundraiser was still fresh in her mind. *You are not what I'd expected my son to date.* Christiane Wainwright hadn't approved of her son's girlfriend, but there wasn't anything she could do about it.

Aziza not only loved Jordan Wainwright, she was also in love with him. He'd suggested she marry him and her answer had been a resounding no. When or *if* he would ask her again, then her answer would be an unequivocal yes.

It was hard to believe she'd only met him six weeks ago, and in two days they would embark on a romantic journey on a yacht to a destination wedding. She didn't know why, but Aziza secretly wished it could be hers and Jordan's wedding.

They'd become a couple — in and out of bed. They understood postponed dates when working late because of an emergency with a client. They respected each other's attorney-client privilege when they discussed cases without divulging names. Time spent together was quality time whether watching their favorite films, cooking together or challenging each other over arcade games or pool.

Making love with each other had become a different experience each and every time they came together. Sometimes it would be slow, as if they'd wanted it to last forever, and other times it would be hard and fast, as if it would be the last time they would be together.

Jordan's hand tightened around Aziza's waist. "Darling, this is Walter. Walter, Aziza Fleming."

The butler bowed to Aziza as if she were royalty. "Welcome, Miss Fleming."

She inclined her head. "Thank you, Mr. Walter."

He compressed his lips into a thin, hard line. "It's just Walter."

Aziza didn't want to tell the straitlaced man that she'd been raised to address older people as Miss or Mister. "Walter," she said, acquiescing.

Thousands of lights from the massive chandelier were reflected on the gleaming marble floor in the entrance hall as elegantly dressed men and women greeted one another with handshakes and air kisses. Meanwhile, a gluttonous fire roaring behind a fireplace decorative screen offset the cold air coming into the mansion whenever the front door opened.

Jordan's arm dropped and he took Aziza's hand. "Come with me."

"Where are we going?" she whispered as they wove their way through the crowd, some who were waiting to board an elevator.

"I'm taking you to my apartment."

He led her up the staircase to the second floor, bumping into Noah as he walked to his suite. "Hey, brother. I want you to meet someone."

Noah Wainwright stared at Aziza for a long moment, then a slow, sensual smile crossed his handsome face. "That's what I'm talking about." He extended his hand. "No-wah."

Aziza laughed at the pronunciation of his name. Noah Wainwright was tall, blond and tanned with sparkling blue eyes. "My pleasure, Noah. Aziza Fleming."

He took her hand, kissing her fingers one

by one. "Do you have a sister or a cousin who looks like you? I'll even take a niece but only if she's legal," he added with a wolfish grin.

"That's enough, Noah," Jordan warned softly.

Noah dropped Aziza's hand as if it were a venomous reptile. "No foul, brother." He winked at his brother's date. "Save me a dance." He slapped Jordan on the shoulder and he whistled softly as he walked down the hallway to the staircase.

"You have to forgive Noah," Jordan said, leading Aziza into his suite. "He's always in party mode. It's going to take a while before he settles down."

"How old is he?"

"Twenty-three."

"At twenty-three he's supposed to be in party mode, Jordan. Weren't you hanging loose at that age?"

"No. I was in law school and quite serious."

Aziza followed Jordan into an exquisitely furnished living/dining room. The enormity of who she was dating hit her for the first time. Jordan Wainwright had grown up with things most people fantasized about: a mansion, butler and servants. It wasn't about living from paycheck to paycheck but about having everything at one's disposal.

She walked over to the tall windows, peering through the drapes at the lights along the avenue throughout Central Park. "How old were you before you had your own apartment?" she asked when she felt the heat from his body after he came up behind her.

"Ten."

"Why so young?"

"I was ten when Noah was born, so it was his turn to occupy what everyone referred to as the nursery. Actually, it is a large bedroom that's accessible through my parents' apartment. He and Rhett shared the room until Chanel came along."

"Everyone has his or her own apartment?"

Resting his hands on Aziza's shoulders, Jordan turned her to face him. He always liked when she wore heels. "Yes. This side of the house is restricted to the family. My grandfather has the entire first floor, my brother and I the second floor, my parents and Chanel have the third floor and the fourth is set aside for houseguests." He unbuttoned her coat, sliding it off her shoulders. The one-shoulder smoky-gray silk dress ending at her knees and matching stilettos were certain to garner a lot of attention. "You have two options tonight."

"What are they?"

His gaze was fixed on the soft magenta color on her lush mouth. "If you get tired you can come up here and rest."

She nodded, forcing a smile. There was no way she was going to sleep with Jordan under his parents' roof unless they were married. She didn't care what he'd done in the past with his other girlfriends, but that wasn't going to happen with her.

"I'll think about it."

Jordan lowered his head and kissed the hair she'd had her stylist pin up in a hairdo reminiscent of the one Michelle Obama had worn for her husband's inaugural ball. "I said rest, not sleep with me. I've never slept here with a woman."

Aziza smiled. He'd read her mind. "What about your brothers?"

"I plead the Fifth."

Reaching up, she straightened the dark gray silk tie. Tonight he'd worn an updated tuxedo, stark white shirt with a spread collar and a Windsor knotted tie. Instead of the dress patent leather slip-ons, he'd substituted a pair of imported Italian slip-ons. Her gaze swept over his cropped black hair and clean-shaven face. A shiver of awareness snaked its way throughout her body when she saw the glint of lust in his eyes. It'd been more than a week since they'd last made love, and she wanted him as much as he wanted her.

"That's better."

Extending his arm, Jordan waited for her to place her hand in the crook of his elbow, then escorted her out of the suite and down the hallway to a door that connected one wing of the mansion to the other.

The smaller of the two ballrooms, which could easily accommodate one hundred, was so brightly lit it could have been twelve noon; dozens of waitstaff moved silently, filling water goblets. Banquet-style tabletops dressed in white satin showcased the votives and vases filled with orange orchids placed atop mirrors; the chairs were draped in orange organza and tied with matching silk ribbon.

Jordan rested a hand over the one tucked into his elbow. "Come, baby. I want to introduce you to my grandfather."

Aziza knew what Jordan would look like in fifty years. The infamous Wyatt Wainwright was tall and straight, and his shockingly blue eyes looked through instead of at her. Tilting her chin, she narrowed her gaze. To say he was intimidating was putting it mildly, but after Kenneth Moore, no man would ever intimidate her again.

Wyatt's eyebrows flickered as he stared at the woman beside his grandson. "So, you're the one who has my grandson's heart. I hope you know how lucky you are." Those standing close enough to overhear Wyatt gasped.

"I beg to differ with you, Mr. Wainwright," Aziza said quietly.

"How's that?"

"I'd like to think Jordan *and* I are very lucky to have met each other." She extended a manicured hand. "Happy birthday."

Wyatt stared at the slender groomed hand, then took it in his much larger callused one. "You don't scare easily, do you?"

"No. In fact, there aren't too many things that frighten me."

Wyatt gave her a rare smile. "Good for you. Come with me. You can have her back, Jordan," he said when his grandson frowned at him. "I just want to talk to Aziza."

There wasn't much Jordan could do but stare at Aziza as Wyatt led her across the ballroom and out the door. If it had been any woman but Aziza, he knew she would've either shrunk or run away from his grandfather.

"Is that your girlfriend with Grandpa?"

He turned to find Rhett with Amelia. If he'd invited her to Christmas dinner with his family and his grandfather's birthday party, then it was apparent he was serious about her. "Yes."

Rhett pounded his shoulder. "Nice going, big brother. She's smokin' hot!"

"Rhett!" Amelia's face turned beet red.

Jordan grasped his brother's arm, pulling him close. "Don't ever disrespect your girlfriend like that again," he whispered in his ear. Staring over Rhett's head, he smiled at Amelia. "You look lovely tonight, Amelia."

A blush replaced mortification. "Thank you, Jordan."

"You're welcome, Amelia."

Jordan's mouth was smiling, but his eyes weren't. His mother had called him on every social faux pas he'd ever made, yet Noah and Rhett broke all the rules of social protocol with impunity. He made a mental note to talk to his brothers about their treatment of women because he didn't want either of them to wind up like Kenneth Moore when they uttered inappropriate sexual innuendos. Brothers notwithstanding, he wouldn't make a move to defend them.

Jordan approached his father, who stood with a group of men, pantomiming a golf swing. Edward Wainwright had officially retired as president of the real estate conglomerate but was available as a consultant. He was currently training Noah to eventually take over as president and CEO.

Edward looked up, excused himself and gave Jordan a rough embrace. "I'm glad you could make it."

He knew his father was referring to the past two years when he hadn't attended Wyatt's birthday celebrations. "I promised Grandpa I would."

Edward scanned the crowd. "Where is your grandfather?"

Jordan noticed there was less gold and more silver in Edward's hair. However, at fifty-five, he still was a very attractive man. "He's giving Aziza the third degree, and she's probably giving him the business."

"You really like this girl, don't you?"

"No, Dad, I don't like her. I'm in love with her."

Edward smothered a groan. "Why am I looking at a rerun of my life, Jordan?"

"That's where you're wrong, Dad. I would never permit anyone to tell me who I can fall in love with or marry."

"But I was already engaged to Christiane —"

"I understand that," Jordan interrupted. "But you could've ended the engagement if you'd fallen in love with another woman."

Edward's expression changed, becoming a mask of stone. "We've debated this ad nauseam, and I'm through with it, Jordan. The only thing I'm going to say to you is live your life however you want. You're thirty-three, an attorney and independently wealthy. When I was faced with a similar decision, I was twenty-two, a recent college grad and completely dependent upon my father for financial support. Sure, I could've moved out and gotten a job, but without work experience there would've been no way I could've earned enough to rent a decent apartment and take care of a wife and child. I still had another three years before I would come into my trust.

"I was faced with the decision as to whether I was willing to give up a lifestyle I'd known all my life to live in a walk-up where I'd have to step over garbage and winos before I'd get to my apartment. Am I an elitist? Yes. But I'm also a realist, Jordan. I know who I am and what I want and don't want."

"What do you want for me?" Jordan asked his father.

Edward accepted a glass of champagne from a passing waiter, handed the flute to Jordan, then took one for himself. "I want you to be happy."

"I am happy."

Edward smiled — a sad smile that made him look as if he'd wanted to cry. "Are you complete, son?"

It took Jordan a full minute before he realized what his father was asking. He and his father hadn't had the requisite father-son talks like the boys with whom he'd attended school. Edward Wainwright had always been too involved with trying to please *his* father and get his approval to pay much attention to his firstborn.

The one time Jordan had sought out his father was after he'd discovered the girl he'd been sleeping with was also sleeping with one of his fraternity brothers. Edward's advice had been, *"if she doesn't complete you, then she's not worth the angst."* It was years later, after he'd discovered the circumstances behind his birth, that Jordan had realized why Edward Wainwright appeared indifferent to Christiane Johnston Wainwright's constant fault-finding. She did not complete him. Jordan's biological mother did.

"No, Dad, and I won't be complete until Zee becomes a part of my future."

Edward put the flute to his mouth, eyes narrowing as he peered over the rim. "Here comes your future right now. And she

365

doesn't look the worse for wear after dealing with your grandfather."

Jordan had to agree with his father. Aziza and Wyatt were smiling and holding hands. Not waiting for his grandfather to bring her back to him, he walked across the ballroom to reclaim the woman who completed him.

Dancing with music from a live band followed a seven-course dinner and numerous toasts to Wyatt Wainwright. Aziza pressed closer to Jordan as he led her over the dance floor. "Why do you continue to keep me off balance whenever you want me to interact with your family?"

"What are you talking about?"

"You invite me to go with you to a social event, but you never let me know your family will be in attendance. It's like you spring me on them and wait for their reaction."

"No, I don't, Zee."

"Yes, you do, Jordan. You said we were going to a birthday celebration, yet you didn't tell me the celebrant was your grandfather."

"By the way, what did you and my grandfather talk about?"

"What's said between Wyatt and Aziza stays between Wyatt and Aziza."

"Oh! It's like that, baby."

"Yes. Now don't try to change the subject. Why didn't you tell them I was coming with you?"

"Because I never tell them who I'm bringing, that's why."

Jordan had proven he was his own man living his life by his leave. He spun her around and around in an intricate dance step. "Where did you learn to dance?"

"I had dancing classes and what some call lessons in deportment at that froufrou school that combined social protocol with academics."

"You must have been a very good student."

Jordan pulled back and stared down at the woman who made him feel things he'd never felt before, the woman for whom he would give up all the material trappings if only she agreed to become his wife.

He'd dated Kirsten for two years, yet the call or pull of happily-ever-after had never been evident. He'd asked her to move to New York because he'd tired of an I-95 relationship. His male pride had been off the charts because Jordan had been certain the legislative aide would jump at his offer. It had taken several weeks of self-examination for him to realize he hadn't offered her stability, permanence. It was "come to New York and shack up with me" without a declaration of love or a proposal of marriage. But it was different with Aziza. He loved her and had asked her to marry him, but she'd refused because she wasn't willing to risk loving and losing again.

"I was," he admitted. "I've always been a good student, but there is one subject where I've been getting a failing grade."

Aziza stared at the length of lashes shadowing his luminous eyes. "What subject is that?"

"Love. I'm terrible when it comes to love, baby."

"Why do you believe that?"

Jordan focused on the diamond hoop in her ear. "I find a woman I didn't know I was looking for, fall in love with her at first sight, then when I tell her I want to marry her she doesn't even think about it and says, 'I'm not marrying you, Jordan,' " he mimicked in falsetto.

Aziza pressed her face to the side of his neck. "Maybe you should ask that woman again."

Jordan missed a step but recovered quickly. "What did you say?"

"You heard what I said, Jordan Wyatt Wainwright."

"Damn, girl. Did you have to use my

government name?"

"Yes, because when I exchange vows with my groom I'll have to say your legally recognized government name to make it official."

"I'm not into playing head games, Aziza. You should know that by now."

"If I know nothing else about you, Jordan, I know that."

"Good. Now, we'll talk about this some other time."

Aziza didn't know why, but she felt like crying in the middle of the dance floor in front of nearly a hundred people. The chandeliers were dimmed and hundreds of flickering votives had created a romantic, fairy-tale-like setting that was perfect for love and seduction. She wanted Jordan to propose marriage when she hadn't told him she was in love with him. What did she expect?

The tempo changed, the music becoming more upbeat with an infectious Latin rhythm. Jordan pulled Aziza flush to his length. "Are you ready to show me your Latin ballroom moves, Señorita Fleming?"

Aziza was never given the chance to protest when he spun her around and around, her hips swaying sensuously to the sexy beat. Other couples joined them, and without warning, she found herself in the arms of another man who had to be a professional dancer. There was one partner, then another. It was obvious when Christiane had planned the party she'd hired professional dancers to make certain the guests would end up dancing. The music played on nonstop, the quartet of vocalists singing everything from Sade, the Rolling Stones, Whitney Houston, Bon Jovi, Alicia Keys, Usher and the Black Eyed Peas. There was something for everyone.

The celebrating continued past midnight, beyond the time when the guest of honor had retired for bed. It was three in the morning when the waitstaff began removing tablecloths, stacking silver, china and crystal and removing the gauzy fabric from the cushioned chairs.

Jordan and Aziza walked into his maisonette at four, undressed, shared a shower and fell into bed together. All talk about love and marriage were forgotten until another time.

Aziza stood at the rail of the sleek yacht; she'd closed her eyes and turned her face to take advantage of the warmth from the rising sun. She, along with Jordan, Duncan, Tamara, Ivan and Nayo were sailing to

Puerto Rico for Kyle Chatham and Ava Warrick's wedding. They had boarded the ship in Hoboken, New Jersey, two days ago and were expected to reach their destination midafternoon.

Sailing to the Caribbean had become the perfect remedy to what had become an unusually cold and snowy Northeast winter. When it snowed, accumulations averaged between two and three inches — not enough to completely cripple cities or hamper the delivery of essential services, but enough to become a nuisance.

Her initial apprehension about filing charges against Kenneth Moore for sexual harassment had been abated when Jordan suggested she not attend the arraignment. The judge had ordered Kenneth to give a sample of his DNA and his bail was set at two million, which he promptly posted and left the court in a chauffeur-driven limo. His arrest wasn't front-page news, but Jordan had reported the topic was on everyone's lips when he'd joined a group of former classmates for a lunch at the Harvard Club.

RLH Realty had become her latest client after she'd contacted Raymond Humphries to let him know she would negotiate the sale of the buildings off 118th and St. Nicholas Avenue. A subsequent meeting with Raymond, CFO Robert Andrews and the head of the company's legal division was more than enlightening for Aziza. She was asked and required to sign a confidentiality agreement. The blustery attorney told her in the more than thirty years he'd worked for RLH Realty, he'd never taken his work home or discussed what had gone on at the office with his wife. When he'd mentioned *pillow talk,* Aziza told him she understood loud and clear what he wanted from her.

Before the meeting had concluded, she'd signed the confidentiality agreement and been given a file containing the information on the properties and a retainer. After spending hours on the phone and two trips to Tampa to meet with the children of the late owner, Aziza was able to discern that, among the four surviving offspring, two were in favor of selling and the remaining two wanted to renovate the buildings, turning them into condos. A clause in their late father's will stipulated all sale of properties would require a unanimous, not a majority decision.

"What are you doing up here?"

Additional warmth and a mint-scented breath swept over her. "I'm watching the sun rise."

Jordan's arms went around Aziza's waist, pulling her back against his body. "We can watch it rise through the stateroom's portal."

She smiled. "I could be enticed to return to the stateroom, but what are you offering?"

"A hug and a couple of kisses for a start."

"Oo-oo. That sounds like fun. What else?"

"I'll have to show you."

Turning in his loose embrace, Aziza stared up at the man who'd stolen her heart, while refusing to give it back. He'd showered but hadn't shaved. Whenever she saw the stubble she was reminded of romance novel covers with images of a sexy pirate sweeping her up and carrying her to his cabin as a willing captive.

He'd pulled on a pair of white drawstring linen lounging pants that showcased his toned upper body when he'd left his chest bare. Sailing down to Puerto Rico for the wedding had become even more significant. It had become a peace offering. When she'd flown to Tampa, she hadn't told him where she was going, and Jordan had blown up her cell with voice mail and text messages. She'd accused him of clocking her every move, and he countered it was concern, not clocking or stalking. Before her second trip to Florida, she'd told him she was leaving the state on business, without giving him any details as to where or why. He'd given her a long, penetrating stare, but hadn't pursued it, recognizing the need for attorney-client privilege.

She knew what Jordan wanted because she wanted the same. There was something very romantic about making love while at sea. "What are you waiting for? Show me."

Jordan Wainwright became her pirate when he picked her up, carried her across the smooth polished deck and down a flight of stairs to the staterooms. An efficient professional crew was on hand to take care of the needs of the passengers on the sixty-foot sailing vessel. She buried her face between his neck and shoulder when she spied a crew member's approach.

"Good morning, Mr. Wainwright."

"Beautiful morning, Mr. Reilly."

The *Mary Catherine,* named for his late grandmother and the love of Wyatt's life, was usually stored at a shipyard along the Chesapeake during the winter months. But this winter Jordan planned to use the family yacht to fulfill his promise to take Aziza to several islands in the Caribbean. Inviting Ivan and Duncan and their partners along added a partylike atmosphere whenever the three couples sat down to dinner that was followed by either a spirited card game or dancing under the stars. He pushed open the door leading to their stateroom with all the amenities of a four-star hotel.

They'd planned to spend four days in Puerto Rico before returning to the mainland, and Jordan intended to take advantage of every day, hour, minute and second he would spend with Aziza. He'd found it ironic they'd spent more time together within the first two weeks of their meeting than they did now. It wasn't his caseload that had increased, but hers.

Whoever the new client she'd taken on was, he or she had kept her busy with trips that took her out of the state. Other times when she'd stayed behind the closed door to her office talking at length on the phone. Jordan had felt he was losing Aziza, but his fears were belied their first night aboard the ship. She'd come to him with a passion that had snatched the breath from his lungs, leaving him lightheaded and gasping.

It was times like that in which he'd come to believe that she loved him as much as he loved her. He'd lost track of the number of times he'd confessed to loving her, and he'd stopped waiting for her to respond in kind. Maybe she'd heard the declaration too many times from her ex-husband, and now hearing it from another man meant nothing. Perhaps she was numbed when it came to love. She'd asked him to propose marriage again and he hadn't. Not until she confessed to loving him. As much as he wanted her as his wife, Jordan refused to marry a woman who didn't love him.

However, it wasn't the same when it came to passion. He had found Aziza to be the most passionate woman he'd ever known — in and out of bed. It was the only time they were completely in sync with each other. There were no cases, clients, courtrooms or ex-husbands or girlfriends.

Jordan placed Aziza on the unmade bed, his gaze fusing with hers when he untied the drawstring at his waist. The lounging pants fell down round his hips and knees, he stepping out of them.

Smiling, Aziza wrapped her arms around his hips, as she moved closer to the edge of the bed. The scent of soap lingered on his body as she buried her face between his thighs, placing soft kisses on the inverted tangle of pubic hair cradling his semi-erect sex.

"No!" Jordan bellowed when he realized her intent. Her mouth closed around his penis like a heat-seeking missile, suckling him until he doubted whether his knees would support his body.

Aziza took as much of the hardened flesh into her mouth without gagging, her tongue moving around the blood-engorged flesh until she established a rhythm that had Jordan close to ejaculating. Applying the slightest pressure with her thumb, she stopped him time and time again all the while he moaned, groaned and bellowed as if he were being tortured.

Jordan knew if he didn't stop Aziza he would spill his seed in her mouth — the last place he wanted to do so when his intent was to be inside her. Resting his hands on her shoulders, he applied pressure to the nerves above her collarbone, and she released him. What happened next defied description and common sense.

He had Aziza on her back, and pulled down her shorts and panties in one motion. He pushed into her with the velocity of someone possessed. Splaying a hand under her hips, he lifted her higher as he began to move in a slow, measured rhythm, pulling back as far as he could go without pulling out before he repeated the pushing in and out of her hot, wet flesh.

It was as if they were making love for the first time. The scent of their lovemaking had become an aphrodisiac as potent as the most addictive narcotic. It pulled him, sucking him under like a powerful undertow where he was drowning in the scented embrace of the woman in whose arms he wanted to breathe his last breath.

He managed to pull the T-shirt up and over her head until her ripe breasts were bared for his hungry eyes. He suckled them the way she'd suckled him, eliciting a keening from Aziza that made the hair on the nape of his neck stand up in response. She was on fire. He was on fire. In the split second between sanity and insanity he surrendered everything he was and had when he released his passion inside her.

"I love you. I love you," Aziza repeated over and over like a litany.

"Marry me, baby. Please, marry me," Jordan whispered in her ear, his heart pumping painfully in his chest.

Raising his head, he looked at Aziza. He'd promised himself that he wouldn't ask her to marry him again until she admitted to loving him. Had he imagined she'd said it, or had she really said she loved him?

"Say it again."

Aziza half opened her eyes to look up at Jordan. A smile had softened her mouth. His face was flush, his eyes a deep moss green, and his chest rose and fell as if he'd run a grueling race. "You picked the wrong time to make love to me without a condom, darling."

"Does that bother you, darling?"

"Not so much."

"Why not, baby?"

Her eyes opened. "I think it would be nice having a child in my life."

"A child?"

Her smile grew wider. "Okay. Your child, Jordan. And I know I would love our baby as much as I love you."

"Do you love me?"

Her smile faded. "Of course I love you. You did hear me say it, didn't you?"

"And you did hear me ask you to marry me."

"Ask me again, Jordan."

"Aziza, will you do me the honor of becoming my wife and the mother of our children?"

A beat passed. The tears Aziza had wanted to shed the night of Wyatt Wainwright's birthday celebration flooded her eyes and rolled down her cheeks like fat raindrops. When she'd walked into Brandt Wainwright's penthouse, she never would've imagined the man who would change her and her life would be there waiting for her.

It was because of Jordan she was given a second chance at love and had learned to trust a man again.

"Yes, Jordan. I will marry you, become your wife and the mother of our children."

They lay joined until Jordan finally rolled off Aziza. He undressed her completely, pulled her close and they slept the sleep of sated lovers. When they woke again, the sun was high in the sky and the outline of the island of Puerto Rico had come into view.

CHAPTER 19

Jordan and Aziza, along with the two other couples, checked into the Hotel Casablanca after disembarking and piling into cars that took them from the pier to the sizzling new boutique hotel in the heart of Old San Juan.

Signature Bridals' wedding planner had arranged to take over the thirty-five guest rooms in the Moroccan-inspired hotel for the Warrick-Chatham nuptials. The hotel was erected on one of the hottest streets in Old San Juan with a string of trendy restaurants and a thumping, pumping, blue-light club called Basiliko. Kyle and Ava were expected to arrive later that afternoon, and a rehearsal dinner was scheduled on the hotel's rooftop where guests could soak in the five stone hot tubs that took the place of a pool.

Immediately after Aziza and Jordan checked into their room — that had pottery vessel sinks, an antique armoire, gilt mirrors and ornate bedding — they went shopping, looking for an engagement ring.

She felt as if she'd stepped back in time when walking the cobblestone streets of a part of the island that had its fifteenth-century flavor. They managed to find a small shop without hordes of tourists, and an hour after walking in, she left the shop wearing a platinum-and-yellow diamond engagement ring on her left hand. The price of the ring was mind-boggling, but Jordan hadn't hesitated when he handed the man his Black Card. They'd left the shop, stopping at a restaurant for a light repast, then returned to their room to make love for the second time that day without using protection.

Jordan rolled off Aziza and reached for her hand. He knew he had to reveal the circumstances surrounding his birth because he didn't want to begin their lives together keeping secrets.

A ceiling fan stirring the warm air swept over their naked bodies. "Baby, I have something to tell you."

Aziza smiled but didn't open her eyes. "Are you going to tell me you're married with a bunch of babies hidden away somewhere?"

"It's not that simple."

Her eyes opened, and she turned to stare at his profile. He could have been made out of stone. "What is it, Jordan?"

He took a deep breath. "Did you ever read Philip Roth's *Human Stain*?"

A slight frown furrowed her forehead. "Wasn't that a movie with Anthony Hopkins and Nicole Kidman?"

"Yes. Did you see it?"

"No. What does it have to do with you?"

"If you saw the film, then you'd know what I'm about to say. The protagonist of the book is Coleman Silk and he's passing."

"Passing? Are you saying you're passing for white?"

Jordan tightened his hold on Aziza's fingers when she attempted to pull away. "Please, baby, let me explain."

"Okay. I won't interrupt."

"Thank you. In the book Coleman Silk didn't dispute he wasn't white when a military recruiter put him down as white. Coleman knew the truth. I didn't know my birth mother was black, though, until I overheard my father arguing with my grandfather.

"I had to wait thirty years to find out that the woman I thought was my mother hadn't given birth to me. My father was still a college student when he met and fell in love

383

with a young black woman who was an editorial assistant for a literary magazine. Neither of their parents knew they were seeing each other, but when she discovered herself pregnant, the shit hit the fan. My dad was engaged to Christiane and was expected to marry her within weeks of his graduation.

"Meanwhile, my grandfathers got together and concocted a scheme. Edward Wainwright would marry Christiane Johnston and she would take to her bed with the excuse that she was at risk of losing her baby. I have to assume they used movie props to make her appear pregnant, and when my mother, who was living with an aunt in Connecticut, went into labor, she was taken to a private hospital where she delivered me. My father, Christiane and Wyatt were on hand when the birth records were filled out. They walked out of the hospital with a baby boy they'd named Jordan Wyatt Wainwright, and my birth mother returned home to pick up the pieces of her life."

"What if you had been born looking like your birth mother?"

Jordan smiled. "They had a story for that, too. They would've said I was the adopted son of Edward's friend who'd died in an accident. Somehow Wyatt would've finagled some legal document with a bogus guardianship clause. Although I was born with blond hair, it darkened as I grew older. But then Wyatt had black hair, so we're only a few dark-haired Wainwrights in a family where most are blond. And looking like Wyatt sealed my fate that I was a Wainwright through and through."

"Didn't they think of the possibility that if you'd fathered a child it could've come out looking more black than white?"

Jordan grunted. "I suppose they would've had an answer for that, too."

"How did you react when you found out that you were biracial?"

"Being biracial didn't bother me because I've never let a woman's race factor into why I wanted to see her. It was the subterfuge that bothered me. What if I'd met and fallen in love with my half sister? Can you imagine how that would've messed with my head?"

"Do you have a half sister?"

He nodded. "I have two of them. They're in their mid-twenties."

"Do they know about you?" Aziza asked.

"I don't know, baby."

"Have you ever met your birth mother?"

"No, and I don't want to. She's married

and I don't know whether her husband knows about the child she was forced to give up within minutes of his birth. I was told she never saw me, because they'd given her drugs where she'd drifted in and out of consciousness. She knows who I am, although I doubt she knows that I know who she is."

"Do your brothers and sister know you don't have the same biological mother?"

"I had to tell them, Zee. Ironically, it didn't make a difference to any of them. We have the same father, so they still viewed me as the older brother. Noah told Dad he'd been irresponsible, not that he'd slept with a black girl, but because he hadn't protected her from an unplanned pregnancy. Rhett got on him for cheating on Mother, but that ended. Chanel said she thought it was cool to have a mixed-race brother.

"The only victim in all of this was Christiane. She was forced to raise another woman's child, and she punished her husband by not sleeping with him nine years. Once she got pregnant with Noah, she and my dad lived together as husband and wife for the first time in a decade. I love her, Zee, because she's the only mother I've ever known. I love her as much as she loves me.

I never understood when she used to say I was a child of her heart and not her body. Next to you, she is the most important person in my life. Without her I don't think I would've become who I am."

Turning on her side, Aziza snuggled closer to her fiancé. "Who else knows the Wainwright family secret?"

"Kyle Chatham. I told him two weeks ago. He knows everything except the name of my birth mother. That's something I swore never to reveal. I had to tell you because, after all, you're going to become a Wainwright and you should be privy to all the sordid family secrets. Speaking of weddings, when do you want to get married? And, I'm going to tell you now that my mother is going to want some big Hollywood red-carpet business."

"I'll be certain to include her in the plans."

"What if we get married at the house? There's certainly enough room for a large gathering."

"That's something to consider. It would alleviate trying to find a catering hall — wait, when do you want to marry?"

"If we don't stop having unprotected sex, then next month. Duncan and Tamara are getting married in June, so let's shoot for July."

"A summer wedding is always nice. And if the weather holds, we could always take photographs in the park."

Letting go of her hand, Jordan turned to face Aziza. He kissed the end of her nose. "Now, you see why I fell in love with you. You're so smart."

Aziza looked at Jordan through a fringe of lashes. "We can't make love anymore without protection. I don't want to walk down the aisle sporting a belly."

"When do you want to start trying for a baby?"

Her smile was dazzling. "Our wedding night."

Throwing back his head, Jordan laughed loudly. "That's the same thing Kyle said when I asked him if he and Ava were planning a family."

"What about a honeymoon, Jordan?"

"How about Fiji?"

Screaming, she jumped on him, planting kisses over his face until the teasing stopped when they found themselves aroused again. Somehow they managed to temper their passions long enough to shower and dress for the evening's festivities.

They had time to make love again. In fact, they had the rest of their lives.

The hotel rooftop had become a tropical oasis as exotic flowers, planters with palms and dozens of flickering candles competed with the brightness of stars in the nighttime sky. Ava, wearing a simple silk slip-dress gown that floated around her sandaled feet, held hands with Kyle as she repeated her vows. The groom wore a pair of linen slacks and matching Asian-inspired shirt. He had foregone shoes in lieu of a pair of woven sandals. Everyone in the wedding party wore white: sundresses, shirts, slacks and the requisite sandals. Ava had insisted on comfort and simplicity.

Aziza hadn't worn her ring, leaving it in the hotel room safe. She didn't want the news of her engagement to Jordan to take any attention away from the bride and groom. Tonight she planned to eat and dance until she dropped from exhaustion.

She stared at Jordan, who'd stood in for Micah, wondering if he was role-playing for what would become his own wedding within another six months. After the exchange of rings there was thunderous applause, and then it was over. Ava and Kyle were husband and wife.

Hip-hop and jazz fusion blared as the newlyweds greeted each guest personally. Waiters came around with mojitos, margaritas, piña coladas and daiquiris to offset spicy hors d'oeuvres of empanadas, shrimp and avocado salad with a cocktail sauce, guacamole, spiced olives, miniature slices of sausage, flat bread, *bacalaitos* — salt cod fritters — and *alcapurria* — yucca fritters stuffed with beef, pork or seafood.

Aziza didn't believe she could ingest another morsel until they sat down to a dinner of rice with pigeon peas, fried sweet and green bananas, paella, black beans, white rice, potato salad, roast chicken, shrimp in a garlic sauce and *pernil* — roast pork shoulder.

Everyone ate, drank and danced, while a DJ played nonstop music. And for the second time in a month Aziza found her hips moving to the infectious African-Latin rhythms. The skirt of her colorful halter dress flared out around her long legs when Jordan spun her around and around until she begged him to stop. When the selection ended, she collapsed into his arms, and Duncan offered her a glass of water.

"Thanks," she gasped, accepting the glass from the man with the almost too beautiful face. Breathing heavily and leaning against

Jordan, she took furtive sips of water until her heart resumed a normal rhythm.

"How are you holding up, baby?" Jordan whispered in her ear.

"I'm good. I love dancing, but I'm not used to being up on my feet nonstop for half an hour."

"Let me know when you want to turn in."

Aziza glanced at the timepiece on Jordan's wrist. It was after two in the morning. Kyle and Ava had retreated to their suite hours ago. "Let's go."

Instead of returning to the mainland by boat, Jordan made arrangements to fly into New York. His driver was waiting for them when they left the terminal at JFK. Tanned, at least five pounds heavier and wearing a ring that hadn't been on her finger when she'd left the States, Aziza settled back against her fiancé and closed her eyes. She hadn't realized she'd fallen asleep until Jordan shook her.

"Wake up, baby. We're here."

She sat up straighter, looking around her. "Where are we?"

"We're at my parents' house."

"I thought you were taking me home."

Cradling the back of her head, Jordan pressed a kiss to her forehead. "I'll take you home after we tell my folks the good news."

"Okay."

Aziza wanted to tell Jordan she was exhausted and all she wanted was to go home and fall into bed and sleep. She needed to be completely rested and alert when she met with the executors of the estate of the man who owned the properties Raymond Humphries wanted. She'd convinced the four siblings to come to New York to talk to Raymond about his plans for the parcels.

Sergio opened the rear door, and Aziza placed her gloved hand on his as he assisted her from the car. The temperatures were hovering around freezing, but it felt much colder after spending five nights and four days in the Caribbean.

Jordan got out, his arm going around Aziza's waist when he led her up the stairs to the gray stone building. He unlocked the front door, pushed it opened and walked into the entrance hall. The chandeliers were dimmed and a fire crackled in the fireplace, adding comforting warmth to the cavernous space. It was late Sunday afternoon and he knew his family would still be in the dining room.

He slipped out of his jacket, then helped Aziza out of her coat, leaving them both on a chair. "Come with me."

Jordan punched the button for the elevator, pulling his fiancée into the car when the doors opened. He barely had time to brush a kiss over her lips when the car stopped at the second floor.

"Master Jordan. I didn't expect to see you."

He smiled at the butler. "How are you, Walter?"

"I'm well, sir." He nodded to Aziza. "Miss Aziza."

She returned his nod, smiling. "Mr. . . . I'm sorry. How have you been, Walter?"

"Wonderful, Miss. Truly wonderful."

"I think he has a crush on you," Jordan whispered once they were out of earshot.

Aziza wasn't given the opportunity to form a comeback when she found herself in a dining room staring at Wainwrights staring at her and Jordan. Wyatt, Edward, Noah and Rhett all stood up. She knew she looked nothing like she had the night of Wyatt's party. She wasn't wearing makeup, her hair was pulled into a ponytail, and her jeans, boots and peasant blouse were far from haute couture.

Christiane rested a hand over her heart. "Oh, my goodness! Did I forget you were coming?"

Jordan approached his mother, kissing her

cheek. "No. We just came from Puerto Rico. Zee and I came by because we want to tell you something."

"Jordan and his girlfriend are having a baby!" Chanel shouted.

Christiane blushed to the roots of her pale hair. "Chanel Wainwright! You apologize to Aziza right now."

"But, Mother —"

"Now, Chanel."

The teenager dropped her head. "I'm sorry, Aziza."

Aziza met Christiane's eyes, wondering if the older woman's thoughts echoed her daughter's query. "Apology accepted."

Edward gestured to a chair. "Sit down, son. You, too, Aziza."

Wyatt stepped away from his seat at the head of the table. "Aziza, please take my seat."

She hesitated, then came around the table when he beckoned her closer. A collective gasp went up when he kissed her cheek. "Thank you, Wyatt."

He leaned over her head. "Don't you mean Grandpa?"

Her left hand covered his on her shoulder, the overhead light reflecting off the diamonds on her fingers. "Okay, Grandpa."

Chanel screamed, the piercing sound

almost ear-shattering. "Aziza and Jordan are getting married!"

Suddenly Aziza had Wainwrights coming at her from all sides. Wyatt kissed her cheek, Edward gave her a hug, and Rhett and Noah picked her up and gave her noisy kisses.

When she managed to catch her breath, she walked into Christiane's outstretched arms. "Welcome to the family."

Aziza hugged the woman who was to become her mother-in-law. "Thank you for raising a remarkable son. If I can love him half as much as you do, then my life with him will be as close to perfect as it can be."

Christiane found herself fighting tears. "Thank you, sweetheart." She'd been wrong. Jordan *had* chosen well.

Chanel jumped up and down. "I'm going to get a sister!"

Aziza hugged and kissed the teenager. "Me, too. I also have three brothers and no sister. We can make dates for a full day of beauty that includes facials, massages and of course a mani-pedi."

"Do you like shopping?" Chanel whispered like a coconspirator.

"I love shopping. Especially for shoes."

When Christiane called for two more place settings, Jordan lifted his shoulders in supplication. He knew Aziza wanted to go home, but he also wanted to share the joy that she had agreed to become his wife with his family. The family that would also become her family.

It was after nine when Aziza settled into bed, picked up the telephone receiver and called family members. She began with her parents, then her brothers on the west coast. Each call lasted less than five minutes, she promising to call again and give them more particulars once she committed to a date and venue.

Turning off the lamp on the bedside table, she moaned softly. The slight cramping in her lower belly was a distinct indicator that her menses was coming. She and Jordan had dodged a bullet.

"No more unprotected sex," she whispered in the silent room.

After her meeting, she would call her gynecologist and schedule an appointment to get some birth control. She couldn't believe she was planning to marry a man she'd only known six weeks. A silent voice told her some people had to do it twice in order to get it right.

It was apparent she was one of those people.

■ ■ ■ ■

Aziza was shown into the conference room where she would confer with the siblings who appeared willing to agree to a compromise. "Everyone is running late, so if you'd like some coffee I'll get it for you, Miss Fleming."

She smiled at Raymond Humphries's assistant. "No, thank you, Ms. Jackson. I'm good."

Placing her leather case on the conference table, Aziza took out the file on the four parcels that had become more of a nuisance than she'd originally thought. Firstly, whenever she spoke to someone about the property she had to use a fictitious name, which hadn't set right with her. Why all the secrecy and subterfuge? She'd spoken to someone from a holding company who'd seemed equally secretive, identifying himself as Mr. Scott. There had been something about Mr. Scott's voice that was vaguely familiar, but after searching her memory she couldn't identify where she'd heard it before.

Maybe all the questions would be answered today, and once she closed this deal for RLH Realty she planned to walk away and not look back. Although Raymond

Humphries was more than generous, she didn't like the feeling that she was being sucked into something unethical if not illegal.

Jordan slipped on his topcoat. His appointment at RLH Realty had been pushed up to eleven. "Juliana, I should be back in a couple of hours," he told his personal secretary as he walked past her desk.

With Kyle away on his two-week honeymoon, the responsibility of running the firm had fallen on him. That meant coming in even earlier and leaving later. He took the stairs to the first floor, nodding to those sitting in the reception area waiting to be seen by Duncan or Ivan.

RLH was within walking distance, so turning up the collar to his coat, Jordan set off in that direction. Winter still hadn't relaxed its cruel grip on New York. It was either snow or sleet or frigid if the sun did decide to make an appearance. He nodded to a man who hung out in the doorway of a building from sunup to sundown.

"What's up, Mr. Burns?"

"Nothin' much, gangsta. How you doin'?"

"It's all good, Mr. Burns."

Slipping his hands in his pockets, Jordan ducked his head into the wind and kept walking. Aziza had asked if he liked Harlem, and he'd said he loved it. The residents were real and basically honest. If they liked you, then they really liked you. He'd walked the streets day and night without fear of anyone trying to mug him. Maybe they recognized him and maybe they didn't, but he still felt safe.

He'd lost sensation in his face by the time he rang the bell to the townhouse containing the offices of RLH Realty. He identified himself when a voice came through the intercom asking who he was. Using his shoulder, he pushed open the door, stepping into a lobby with welcoming heat. A young woman with neatly braided hair sat behind a Plexiglas partition.

"Mr. Wainwright, you can take the elevator to the third floor. Someone will direct you from there."

He stepped into the elevator, pushing the button for the third floor. The short ride was enough for him to regain some feeling in his face. He had come with a blank check. He hadn't just come to talk.

The doors opened and a fastidiously dressed middle-aged woman smiled at him. "Mr. Wainwright. I'm Ms. Jackson. Please follow me."

Jordan followed her down a carpeted

hallway, noticing the richness of the tasteful furnishings in the town house. This was the first time he'd come to the offices of his grandfather's rival. The rivalry between the two men had gone on way before he was born and continued to this day.

But Jordan was willing to rise above the pettiness to conduct business. For him it was only business, never personal. There had been only one exception: when he'd offered to represent Aziza in her harassment suit. Kyle was right. He should've trusted him enough to come to him and have him file the suit. Kyle Chatham was one of the best trial attorneys in the city, and if anyone could break Kenneth Moore, Chat would.

Ms. Jackson stepped aside and Jordan walked into the conference room. He hadn't taken more than three steps when he stopped. Sitting at the table with Raymond Humphries, Robert Andrews and the four executors of the estate was his fiancée.

Aziza felt a pain in her chest as if she were having a heart attack. How could Jordan be the lawyer for the holding company when she hadn't spoken to him? Rising slowly, she shook her head.

"I'm sorry, but I must recuse myself."

Raymond also stood up. "What the hell are you talking about?"

Aziza rounded on Raymond Humphries. "I have to remove myself from this participation to avoid a conflict of interest. Opposing counsel happens to be my fiancé."

"I don't care if he's your daddy. I've paid you to handle this and you will."

Jordan had heard and seen enough. "Will everyone please leave so Mr. Humphries, Miss Fleming and I can come to some agreement?"

Robert Andrews nodded to the siblings who'd come from Florida to hopefully settle an issue that was a long time coming. "We all can wait in the lounge."

Waiting until the door closed behind Raymond's son-in-law, Jordan stalked to the older man, backing him into a corner. "What kind of game do you think you're playing? You had to know my grandfather wanted those parcels, but why bring my fiancée into your sick twisted game?"

"I didn't know she was your fiancée. Now, I want you to back the hell up outta my face before —"

"Before what, Raymond? You'll have me arrested? I don't think so, because then everyone will know your business. I suggest you let it go."

Raymond pulled back his shoulders. "I'm not going to let it go as long as Wyatt

401

continues to buy property in Harlem."

A flush darkened Jordan's face under his deep tan. "You don't own Harlem, despite what you think! It was here before you and it'll be here after you're dead and buried. Give it a rest!" He'd enunciated each word. "We can do this nice, or it can get very nasty."

"You would love nasty, wouldn't you? You're just like Wyatt!"

Jordan took several backward steps, allowing Raymond to move out of the corner. "That's where you're wrong. If I was Wyatt I would've blown your brains out." He ignored Aziza's gasp. "What happened between your daughter and my father is history — ancient history. You and Wyatt took care of that, so I'm warning you for the last time to let it go."

Raymond, trying to regain a modicum of bravado, crossed his arms over his chest. "What do *you* want?"

Resting his hands at his waist, Jordan pushed back his topcoat and suit jacket. "Instead of bidding on all four parcels, I'm willing to take two and give you the other two."

"You give me? I don't think so, Wainwright. You have nothing to give."

"I have Wyatt Wainwright's approval to offer the family waiting for us to resume this meeting and an obscene amount of money to keep you from getting the parcels. But because I'm not Wyatt, I'm willing to split them with you. Two for you and two for me."

Raymond bared his teeth. "You bastard!"

A deep frown settled between Jordan's eyes. "Do me a favor. Watch your mouth." He shifted his attention to Aziza, his expression softening. "I'd like you to stay, but because you've already recused yourself, you will just be an observer. *My* maternal grandfather is going to have those good people come back in and we're going to negotiate the sale of the four parcels at 118th and St. Nicholas Avenue. There will be two for RLH and two for Wainwright Developers Group. And the nonsense that has been going on for more than thirty years will end today. Does that meet with your approval, Mr. Humphries?"

"And if it doesn't?" Raymond refused to believe he'd been bested, that his scheme had backfired.

A beat passed. "Maybe it's time I introduce myself to my half sisters."

"You wouldn't!"

"I would," Jordan threatened. "What's it going to be? Half, or I'll put your business

403

in the street. Remember, I have nothing to lose."

Raymond's shoulders slumped, indicating defeat. "Okay. Half it is."

Two hours later Jordan and Aziza walked out of the building housing RLH Realty. "I'm sorry you had to get involved in that."

Aziza shook her head. "I still don't understand why Raymond hates your grandfather. It can't be about who can gobble up more property like a Monopoly game."

"Raymond is still angry that my father got his daughter pregnant."

"But Wyatt saved his daughter's reputation when they arranged the private adoption."

"That's true. But Raymond never forgave my father for seducing his virginal daughter when he was engaged to another woman."

Aziza reached for Jordan's hand. "Not only were you able to secure the properties, but you also declared a truce and formed a partnership between RLH and Wainwright Developers Group."

"That wasn't my initial intent but I supposed it all worked out in the end."

"What do you think your grandfather will say?"

Jordan gave Aziza a quick glance. "Which one?"

She laughed. "You know which one I'm talking about."

"I think Wyatt will forgive me when I had to make a deal with his enemy to get those buildings."

"What do you think about inviting Raymond to our wedding?"

"I don't know, but it is something to think about." He stopped, lowered his head and kissed her. "Did I tell you that I love you today?"

"Yo gangsta! Why you disrespectin' that woman like that? Get a room," a deep voice boomed.

Jordan turned and raised his fist in a salute. He loved Harlem, its people and the woman who'd promised to share her future with him.

The employees of Thorndike Press hope you have enjoyed this Large Print book. All our Thorndike, Wheeler, and Kennebec Large Print titles are designed for easy reading, and all our books are made to last. Other Thorndike Press Large Print books are available at your library, through selected bookstores, or directly from us.

For information about titles, please call:
(800) 223-1244

or visit our Web site at:
http://gale.cengage.com/thorndike

To share your comments, please write:
Publisher
Thorndike Press
295 Kennedy Memorial Drive
Waterville, ME 04901